Raven's Lament

By

Frank Talaber

ISBN: 978-1-77145-399-8

Books We Love, Ltd.
Calgary, Alberta
Canada

Dedication

To Ashley, thanks for listening to the leaves fall. To Rory, very proud of you, and I will beat you one of these days in backgammon. To my mother, Judy, who raised seven kids on her own. Don't know how you did it, but you put your love, heart and soul into us, I thank you for that. Especially to my wife Jenny, whom I love very much, thanks for loving me, putting up with me, moving to Canada and just being there. I love you all.

And to Jacquie, thanks for the twenty-one days of muse-induced madness. Otherwise this book would have never been possible without you helping to edit it on the other side of Canada.

People came to be here then,
and they have been here since,
the ones who will continue being born here.
They were listening to myths back then,
and they are thinking of them still.
The land and the myths have grown together this
way from then until now.
Now almost all those myths are disappearing.
Shlawtxan, native shaman 1928

Prologue

Muffled, incessant scratching rents the air. The abandoned village of Ninstints lies hidden in the fog.

In the security of the cedars, a totem stands apart from the rest. Face gaunt, eye sockets empty. A man on the verge of dying.

Raven's razor-edged beak gleams menacingly, his talons wrapped around the human's mid-section. The human's hands clamp Raven's throat. Trapped in eternity's grasp, myth and mortal struggle endlessly, locked in boughs of wood.

A caw echoes, a flutter of large black wings breaks the darkness.

The human turns and flees. *There has to be a way out.*

Sobs tremble from within the wood.

There is a wind that blows through these islands that blows nowhere else. It blows in from the East in the fall bearing the sghaay haw (spirit-beings) and leaves in the spring. It gives this land its richness, its culture, its trees, its vitality. Most of all, the spirit wind gives our people the strength to return to the land, its old ways and to change with the new. It gave us the spirit-beings, Raven, Foam Woman and all that followed. Through the vision quests and the winter dances we find our sghaay haw and reconnect to the spirits. It is this wind that sings our song, our birthright. The Windsongs of the Haida gives us our soul. Charlie Stillwaters, Haida Skaga

Chapter One

Thick sap oozed from the Golden Spruce, congealing like blood. The death chant of Gordon Chatwick's axe shuddered through the tall tree. Amidst this forest of varying shades of green, the Golden Spruce was unique. Its needles of gold were viewed as a hybrid to the scientists, a precious jewel to the natives. The oral stories spoke of a prince trapped within it.

The axe bit one last time, cutting past the cambium membrane. Gordon paused to swipe at the sweat burning his eyes. The chainsaw had sweated the hard part; now he wielded the axe. There was only an hour of darkness left before the chance any tourists would arrive and discover what he'd done. But before that, the winds would pick up and send the ancient Golden Spruce crashing to the earth. His opposition to the continued raping of the planet's resources would soon be complete.

Overhead, the tree groaned under its own weight, protesting its demise. Sap flowed down its gouged sides, sticking to Gordon's boot as he moved.

Damn, this goop is everywhere. Never seen a tree bleed this much. Then again, I've never cut a Golden Spruce. Good. This will get their attention.

Gordon pinned the note he'd scribbled to the base of the trunk. The handle of the axe stuck to his fingers as he gathered his knapsack. Every step was hampered by the gummy sap sucking at his feet.

I got this stuff all over me. Better burn my clothes back at camp. I wonder if the public will let this damage go unnoticed.

The Golden Spruce cried in agony. Splintering cracks echoed as the wind increased.

Gordon swallowed hard, the iron taste of fear clinging to his mouth. A former logger, he'd cut down many trees in his day, but this was more like murdering a living being. "Oh God, I've killed something beautiful." He rushed to its aid, trying to support the groaning trunk. Muscles strained, tears streaked the sweat on his cheeks. "What have I done?"

With his hands covered in warm sap, and the winds picking up, it was too late for remorse. "I'm so sorry." He retreated to the bank of the Yakoun River, where his kayak waited to whisk him to the ocean waters of Masset Inlet.

* * *

Brook Grant stared at the 'Dear John' letter Georgina left last month. Her empty closet and dresser answered any questions he might have

7

had about a possible reconciliation. To distract himself, he flipped through the pages of his journal again, trying to retrace his footsteps at Ninstints. The totems had intrigued him then, filled him with an ache for what was lost. How could the vibrancy of the Haida and their artistry be reduced to yellowed photographs consigned to musty books?

Reading his entries brought the realization he'd lost that feeling of living on the edge, like walking between worlds. Georgina's departure left him feeling empty. Adrift, with no compass to guide him.

She was supposed to be his one true love. Soulmates. But somewhere, between the illusion of commitment and his belief in the relationship, he let it all slip away, including the romance. Just like the Haida at Sghaan Gway, where now only enigmatic gods etched into cedar remained; she was gone.

Where had he gone wrong? Seeking the answers, he'd come across the memoirs of his trip to the Charlottes. *How could you let her go? How did you not see this coming? Did you care?* Evocative memories, yet none bringing him any solace.

He'd written, '*There are nights on the West Coast, particularly on the mist-shrouded isles of the Queen Charlottes, when the fog rolls in so thick it mutes the background thunder of the surf. Nights when, if you look closely enough,*

8

wavering shapes emerge in the full moon's shimmering light. A breath of cold wind brushes against your face and you shiver, believing as the Haida do, that you've been caressed by the spirits. Soon you begin to understand why they say everything has a soul and that we are anchored to this realm and to our physical bodies only by tenuous threads of waangaay, of spirit.

The Haida call this place Xhaaydla Gwaayaay, the Islands on the Boundary between Worlds.

Brook set the journal down on his nightstand and shut off the light. He lay, eyes wide, his mind whirling.

The Islands on the Boundary between Worlds. Ninstints, the totems, their connection to earth and home. Returning to roots. Somehow that was important. Tonight his dreams would be full of ghosts, insistent, summoning voices, the round eyes, calling him.

Calling, but to what?

A line from a familiar song played in his head: only time can mend a broken heart. Then how do you fill a gaping hole in your soul?

The three Watchmen squinting out from under top hats of outlandish ferns, bearing coats of moss and lichens, staring with empty eyes and mute tongues. Eternally watching. The totems towered in his memory, silent faces full of voices speaking to a quiet place inside him where he was unbroken. The place he needed to return to.

As sleep finally came, Brook remembered the peace of that Ninstints morning.

* * *

In the vanishing darkness, the sap from the Golden Spruce congealed into two body-shaped pools. Solidifying and expanding, filling with more substance than the sap alone could account for. The fresh aroma of spruce spread thickly across the glade, mingling with other smells that didn't belong. Putrid, nauseating odors of decayed meat.

Shapes began to emerge in the muck, one taking the form of a young male warrior. The other was leaner, more avian with long black feathers fluttering in the dawn breeze.

As if the spruce sensed its demise, more sap gushed from its wounds, flowing like a watery vein into the two still figures, imbuing them with substance.

Both cocooned forms jerked and kicked at the same time, struggling with the effort of leaving another reality and entering a former one. The feathered figure had been tricked into being trapped in the tree. It had to be the first to emerge. There was no other way.

The young male fought against the insanity haunting his mind. He'd spent many lifetimes trapped in dimensions not meant for humans.

A final cannon-ball crack shattered the morning as the wind gusted and the Golden Spruce was disconnected, for the first time in its life, from the earth. The umbilical cord severed, freeing the two trapped within.

The male's lips parted, freed for the first time in nearly a hundred and fifty years, he cried out.

* * *

Some say Raven walks among us still.

Brook stared at the words on his computer screen, the same words he'd written in his journal eight years ago. Words uttered by Tom Wilson, the Haida Watchman he'd met at Ninstints.

The endless drone of office fax machines, ringing telephones and chattering people faded into the background. Brook stared at the line in the article he was proofreading. Raven. Raven-colored hair.

It was almost three months since Georgina left, and still Raven and the totems invaded his dreams. Which was okay, since it helped take his mind off her. Three months and still the emptiness tasted bitter like seawater on his tongue. He'd even chucked his job with the *Toronto Star* and accepted a temporary position with the *New York Times*, hoping that being away from TO and any connection to Georgina would be a good thing, like chasing wasabe with chili sauce. But, damn it, nothing seemed to ease the pain.

Brook shook his head and refocused on the article on the screen. Haida Gwaii. About the only thing he could put any real emotion into lately. The Haida were suddenly a big news item, even in New York. Recently, they'd come to the American Museum of Natural History and asked for the bones of their ancestors back. Bones stolen from their graves in the late 1800s when the Haida were dying from smallpox, TB, and other white-man afflictions. The Americans were astounded at the audacity of the Haida, not to mention concerned about the ramifications for museum collections across the country. With the treaty negotiations relating to Haida Gwaii going sour as well, he was compiling a major news article, along with some lighter tourist pieces. He'd missed so much the first time he went there. Brook hoped this article could shake the images out of his head, only all that shaking seemed to stir up more ghosts to steal at his dreams.

Some say Raven walks among us still.

Brook ended the article with the same words he'd started it. One thing he knew for sure: Raven and the totems were definitely walking through his head.

Maybe the images were calling him to Ninstints again?

12

* * *

As Prince Kiidkayaas cried out, a black wing tore free from the ooze. With a horrible sucking sound, Raven stood up on his two spindly legs. The prince continued to wail as Raven shook himself free of the gooey sap. Raven had landed himself into many predicaments, but being trapped inside a tree wasn't something he ever wanted to do again. He hopped over to where the prince was now fighting to escape from the cloying webs.

"Caw," he crowed. "So, you thought you could defeat me, silly boy." He leaned forward and deftly tore into the prince's body. A gush of blood spurted skyward as he yanked the beating heart free and flung it into the boughs of a cedar tree. Needles, still falling from the Golden Spruce, fluttered downward, covering the heart, which spewed a fine spray of crimson droplets before lying still. The prince's lifeblood mixed with the sap oozing into the folds of the cedar.

Raven watched the body convulse. Satisfied the prince was dead, he sauntered over to where he had flung the heart. He would devour it and the soul of its owner, ensuring not only his victory, but also gaining the spirit and attributes of such a brave warrior. Alas, the scattering of needles carpeted the heart. Too impatient to search, Raven cawed to himself. He didn't have time for this. What he needed was a decent meal.

13

"No matter," he thought. "I've won, after all this time. I've won and defeated you, brave prince."

He snickered as he strutted back to his adversary's messy remains. Robbed of their soul, they were quickly returning to the puddle of sap that had temporarily infused them with life.

Raven searched for the reason he'd originally become trapped in the Golden Spruce with Kiidkayaas. Squinting in the dim light he was unable to spy what he sought. His immortal stone ... where was it? Did the prince realize how close he had come to winning? Raven shuddered. He'd almost lost to one of the people that he, himself, had created. What irony, he crowed.

Frustrated again, he straightened and sniffed the air. Late summer, the winter spirit winds would arrive soon. Only something was different. The scent of metal ore stung Raven's nostrils as he strutted around the base of the conifer, an odd smell in the middle of the forest. The Golden Spruce had been felled by human means. How grand the tree had grown since he and the prince had been trapped in it. How many cycles of life had passed? He glanced around, noticing the crush of moccasin prints in the soft earth. The tracks of whoever downed the tree?

He sniffed again; something unnatural. First, before he told any others, he had to find the one that had freed him. A trail of crumpled vegetation led to the heavily wooded banks of the Yakoun River. The first rays of sunlight, brilliant in their hues of vibrant pinks and reds, tried to penetrate the mists. A slender canoe, carrying a lone figure, bobbed where the craft exited the freshwaters and entered the brackish currents of Masset Inlet. Raven's immortal stone could wait; he had more pressing business to attend to.

Time to reward the human for freeing me, he thought, closing his eyes. His sleek body shimmered, shades of white and brown bubbling to the surface as Raven shifted into a bald eagle. With a hunting cry he lifted skyward, reveling in the sheer strength of his wings before focusing on the odd-looking canoe below.

Raven dove toward the upturned face of the human, meeting his gaze, before the outstretched talons found their mark. Blood cascaded up the human's throat as he went limp. Raven lifted both man and canoe skyward, claws ripping the canoe's skirt away from the dangling body. The vessel tumbled to the sea. He made a large turn over the inlet and shook the figure once. His talons accurately penetrated vital organs, and another rain of red peppered the blue-gray surface far below. Certain the human was dead, Raven released him. As the body fell, he noticed for the first time the male was extremely pale skinned, not the darker hue of the Haida.

Lungs pierced, the corpse sank quickly. He was theirs now, in the realm of the *Kushtakas*, the sea otter people.

Weariness seared his wings as Raven headed towards the Golden Spruce. He glided most of the way; each stroke from those enormous wings a huge effort. Tired, why was he so tired? With a thump he settled on the branch of a cedar by the river's edge. He closed his eyes and struggled to shift to his true self. Slowly, the feathers of the eagle flushed to black and the majestic white plumage on his head shimmered and darkened. Razor-sharp talons and mighty wings shrunk until he was Raven again. He yawned, weariness sucking at his consciousness.

Raven's eyelids fluttered as he fought to stay awake. He'd been in limbo for so long, perhaps that was what made him weak. Weak and hungry, but then again, he was always hungry. An unending appetite was his curse to bear.

Sleep first, he thought, ignoring his growling stomach. He'd have to find food before returning to the Golden Spruce to retrieve his immortal stone. The light would be stronger then and it would be easier to find.

He steadied himself on the cedar limb and sniffed the air again. Something was definitely different, not right, though he still didn't know what it was. Surely things couldn't have changed that much since he'd last walked this land?

He wasn't used to tiring so easily. The shape changing took too much energy. Shifting would have been as easy as picking *ghals* from the beach before.

* * *

Freed from his body Prince Kiidkayaas floated in wisps of mist and light above the carnage. This was his soul essence? Was he dead?

His heart had landed with an unpalatable splat in the bough of a great cedar. Golden spruce needles rained down, covering the heart like a warm blanket, hiding it from Raven's gluttonous hunger. If Raven devoured his heart before his soul could be released, he'd be part of Raven now. Kiidkayaas sent a mental 'thank you' to the great tree spirit.

The prince stared at the scene below. What happened? The corporeal body wasn't real flesh and blood, but composed of matter from the spirit of the spruce tree. Someone, or something, must have released him and Raven from their imprisonment. Groggy, he remembered the long journey, the trials, the matching of wits, how Raven had originally tried to trick him, in order to get back his immortal stone. The stone — where was it? A fleeting image of it covered in golden needles flashed into his mind. It was safe, for now.

Weary of fighting, Kiidkayaas stared skyward. He wanted only to go to the land of his ancestors. His people … what had become of his people? He'd been unable to save his village and that could only mean one thing. He continued to gaze upward, troubled. Where were his people? If he were truly dead, he would soon find out in the afterlife. He tried to lift himself from the clearing. Tenuous threads of spirit reached up from the cedar, anchoring themselves to his spirit.

First one, then another … the threads wound around his soul. It was indeed too late. Prince Kiidkayaas swirled earthward, dragged into the confines of the great cedar.

A figure shimmered into view. Pure white, it stared at the remains and at the shattered cedar, gliimpsing black Raven asleep on a branch overhead.

Clacking its beak, the bird lifted itself on white shimmering wings, looking for food.

* * *

"Well, hello, Tom Wilson." Someone spoke beyond the partition that marked the edges of Brook's office.

Tom Wilson. Images of a native elder sprang to mind, long braid white against the blue of his denim jacket. What would a Haida Watchman be doing in downtown Manhattan?

Brook looked up, hoping to see the Watchman he'd met at Ninstints eight years ago,

18

but instead a white man in a suit, bearing a briefcase, met his gaze.

He sank back into his chair, yawning. If the dreams of Georgina weren't haunting him every night, native images swirling in his sleep were. Why were the images of Ninstints so strong? Why wouldn't they let him go? Evocative eyes; silence in the mouths carved from the cedar, yet full of words; plaguing him with unanswered questions.

Grabbing his coffee, he called up the Associated Press website and keyed in his password to check the latest news stories. About halfway through, a headline snagged his attention: *Environmentalist fells rare tree on Queen Charlottes.*

The swig of coffee nearly choked him. Haida tongues chattered in his brain. Totems leered at him from the edge of his vision, pulling his attention away from the screen and filling his head. His heart pounded in rhythm to native drums.

Golden Spruce axed at dawn. Environmentalist takes the blame.

Brook scrolled through the breaking news story, scanning until he came to the section reporting the note the environmentalist pinned to the tree.

My actions are to express my abhorrence of the crimes that so-called experts are perpetrating on our environment. Wholesale logging, mass destruction of our forests cannot continue. How can those who travel to this tree ignore the genocide going on all over our planet? We, the people, must first express our outrage, and then take action to support our beliefs. Today, I am making a stand against the unholy clearcutting that is tearing our ecosystems apart and destroying the life dependent on them.

I apologize to the Haida for my actions.

Gordon Chatwick

Concerned citizen and Greenpeace member

So much for the tree huggers, Brook thought. But was this a Greenpeace sanctioned environmental protest, or something more? Was it somehow connected to the treaty negotiations for Haida land claims settlements? A bit of a leap, perhaps, but he was intrigued enough to read further.

Shortly after the incident, an abandoned kayak was found between Port Clements and Masset. Owner's identification sought. Stains on kayak, possibly blood. Results of investigations awaited.

His breath caught in his throat. At this point the two events weren't being officially linked, but his reporter's intuition said different. Brook brought up the RCMP website and navigated to the press release section, where he found one from the Queen Charlotte City division.

Investigation ongoing. Chatwick unlocated. Believed to be camped in area. It then reiterated some basic information. RCMP press releases tended to stick to facts and not possibilities.

Brook's hand shook as he set down his coffee cup. Too much caffeine? More like too much racing through his head. *Facts, let's deal with facts.* Tree chopped down, environmentalist's note, possible bloody kayak, but no body found. He could turn up the home address of Gordon Chatwick. Was he native or white? An experienced kayaker? Brook knew from experience, the currents of Masset Sound could be pretty brutal and the weather unpredictable. However, there was always the possibility Chatwick might have run into foul play. Suicide seemed unlikely.

Would the Haida do Chatwick in? There was no real mention of them, or their reaction, in any of the stuff Brook had found so far. Would they get involved? That wouldn't exactly help the treaty negotiations. Or maybe they set the whole thing up in the first place? Make it look like a white guy did it and use that to weight the treaty talks in their favor. No, that seemed way too far off base. True, the Haida were once feared warriors and were proving themselves to be fairly aggressive in dealing with territorial and heritage issues. Still, that didn't mean they'd go so far as to do away with a guy just because

21

he'd cut down some tree. They were generally law-abiding people.

The prince, it is whispered, is trapped in a Golden Spruce tree up north.

The words tumbled into Brook's head, out of nowhere. The words of the Watchman at Ninstints, eight years ago.

A strange sadness filtered through Brook. Could it be the same tree?

If it was, then it wouldn't be just any old conifer. It would hold great religious significance to the Haida. But would they kill Chatwick just to avenge the dead prince?

The totem. The human and the Raven locked in eternal combat. Adrenaline flooded Brook's veins. Intuition screamed at him. A story lurked here, but what? He sure as hell wanted to head up to the Charlottes to find out. Aside from the BC treaty negotiations and the repatriation issues, aboriginals and native militancy were hot news these days. Together with the articles he was already working on, it could make a great basis for an exposé. All he had to do now was convince his editor of that.

Too many questions and no answers. "Ach, ya, unt vhat makes you tink, big news story, ja," Brook muttered to himself in a poor German accent. He suppressed a thrill. Too many things were coming together. His journal, the dreams of the totems, uttering ancient tongues that as hard as he tried, he couldn't decipher. Yet a part of him understood that somehow, he needed to be there again. There was no such thing as coincidence. Everything, he knew, entered his life for a reason. Only he'd no time for figuring it out right now.

Time for action. He missed that fire, the zeal of sifting through information and finding the kernel of truth. It was why he'd become a reporter. He needed to tackle this story head on.

He hit print and glanced at his watch. Plenty of time to catch a flight out of JFK to Vancouver. Meanwhile, he could throw a few things into a backpack and do some nosing around. Brook rose from his desk and headed towards his editor's office. Stan could be a downright bastard and had given him a blast about how his work sucked recently. But at least the guy admired tenacity, the balls not to take no for an answer and to continue probing. And when it came to digging up a story, Brook Grant was born with a pen in one hand, shovel in the other.

Besides, he needed to get away from the non-stop action of the city that never slept. There was something to be said for just being in his kayak at Haida Gwaii. Maybe he could begin to forget about Toronto, Georgina, and their life together. Somehow, he had to convince Stan to let him investigate this story about the dead environmentalist.

He shrugged as he punched the elevator button. Let's see, the Haida were scheduled to head for Chicago to ask for more of their ancestral bones. And what about the angle of stirring up the Haida population in Alaska ... until now they'd been pretty quiet. He dredged his brain for every conceivable angle. Maybe the story wouldn't amount to much, but then again ... what if there was a dead prince trapped in the tree, and like a mummy he came to life, and murdered Chatwick? Brook laughed at his own craziness. He hadn't laughed aloud in months, and it felt good.

"Who dares, wins," he muttered as the elevator arrived at Stan's floor. Well, he hadn't been daring lately. And he hadn't been winning either.

Chapter Two

Chelen Davidshaw held the damp cloth to her Grandmother Rosemary's forehead. Rosemary lay in bed, drenched in sweat; she'd been deathly ill the last few days and Chelen feared she wouldn't make it through the night. She'd called for her Uncle Charlie, a shaman, but he'd yet to arrive at her cabin just north of Skidegate. Rosemary had little use for Western medicine, as did most of the elders on Haida Gwaii, preferring to stick to traditional remedies. Chelen was certain whatever afflicted her grandmother was something only a *skaga* could deal with, and if he couldn't, then he'd be needed to help Rosemary on her journey to the afterworld.

Wood smoke from the cast-iron stove filtered into every corner of the ancient cabin. The pungent scent was one of the things Chelen loved about her grandmother's home. Fragrances of crackling logs, burning sap and cooking food, had comforted her as she'd grown up within these wooden walls hung with cedar mats, animal furs, and drying herbs. Aromas mingling together to become Rosemary's unique perfume. Chelen rose to wring out the hand towel. The softness of a deerskin wall hanging brought tears to her eyes; she was instantly a child again. If only that were possible. Memories were all that kept her company as she maintained her vigil over Rosemary.

Chelen's mother died when she was only seven. She'd drunk herself into oblivion, and Rosemary had elected to raise the young girl. Chelen had never known her father; Bethany never even told her who he was and Chelen presumed she was the product of an embarrassing one-night-stand. Eight years ago, when Rosemary became frailer and Chelen had turned twenty-one, she returned the favor and looked after her grandmother.

A knock shattered the stillness. The floorboards creaked beneath her bare feet as she went to answer the summons, stirring memories of the times when she'd try to sneak out as a teen.

Like the rattle of old bones the heavy door groaned open.

"Charlie, it is good to see you. Come in,"

"Sorry. I would have been here earlier, but there was a very important meeting of the Band Council. They had called an emergency session and wanted me there." Her uncle's usual smile was missing.

"What happened?" For the Council to convene, it must be something dire.

"Someone took an axe to the Golden Spruce."

"What! Who would dare?"

"We don't know, but the RCMP found a note pinned to the stump by some guy named Gordon Chatwick. I've been asked by the Council to visit the site and investigate. See what I can find out."

"White guy, I'll bet."

"That would be my guess. I was going to leave right away, but it was more important to stop by and see Rosemary."

The news of the Golden Spruce stunned her for a moment, pulling her from her anxiety. "Yes. I fear the *sghaana giidas* have her in their hands."

"Me, too." Charlie Stillwaters walked over to the frail woman he called Mother. His hair, like Rosemary's, had long since turned to white fire, but his was tied into braids underneath his pin-adorned Toronto Blue Jays baseball cap. A gift from a relative, since Charlie himself had never left the islands. Haida Gwaii was not only his home, but his connection to the spirits. A connection he never cared to break. Still, he loved to watch baseball on TV and the Blue Jays were his favorite team. "I heard the screech of *sttaw,* the owl, just as I got out of my truck. A very bad sign. I fear it whispers her name." He touched Rosemary's forehead and closed his eyes. "Many spirits are gathered here this evening. Not good," was all he said, speaking the words carefully, with his usual deliberation.

Chelen abandoned the lemongrass tea she had been about to brew, even though the clarity of thought it bestowed would definitely be welcome on a night like this. "What do you mean, not good?"

"I mean — "

"*Sghaana giidas, waagusa naay sghaana giidas!*" Rosemary cried out.

"What's she saying?" She held the old lady's hand. Cold and weightless. The body seemed well on its way to becoming a husk that had once held her grandmother's spirit. She was the only mother she'd ever known. Chelen choked back the tears.

Charlie leaned closer as Rosemary's voice became even fainter. "She said, 'Spirit beings, there I see the spirit beings.'" And then, "*Giistuuiidjin*? Where are you?" he murmured in Rosemary's ear.

"*Hlghahl, ttl gam geexa dii.*"

"'Dark, it is dark,' she said. 'They don't see me.'" Charlie strained to hear her. "She grows very weak, Chelen. Death's rattle plays in her throat. I fear her soul has begun its journey."

Be brave, be a warrior princess, her grandmother would tell her. But the teardrops spilled over and splattered the sheets, grief drowning her grandmother's fading speech.

"*I'nk xhuuya, lla gaarundyaas, laagang lla skin dalaang sta qqadiigai. Ttl gaarundyaas an dii xaagai xudj xiagang guuda'laa naay hlk'yaan."*

Chelen wrinkled her brow. She'd picked up the words "raven" and "wolf". "Raven? What does that mean?"

"I think she's hallucinating," Charlie said. "She says she sees Raven. He walks past her and awakens the others. Wolf and Grizzly Bear spirits follow behind, on their way to the forest."

"Ttl gaarundyass sqaati guutgi hinaan sgoannsin stlaay."

Charlie's eyes widened at the old woman's last sentence. He squinted and whispered to Rosemary, *"Sgoannsin stlaay."*

"Dalaang aagusa sghaana giidas, ttl tl'l aagusa kkiaaoga dii."

Rosemary's final words were barely a gasp as her head rolled to one side. Eyelids flickered, a long sigh escaped her lips, and the body grew still. Numb, Chelen stared as Charlie looked up to watch the spirit rise. She knew Charlie could see Rosemary's soul mingling with others in the room, floating in the rafters.

"I'm sorry. The spirits have taken her to meet the Creator. Goodbye, Mother."

Chelen gently stroked her grandmother's hair. Tears rained onto the worn Hudson's Bay blanket atop the sheets. Memories of everything Rosemary had done for her flooded her. "Goodbye, *Jaatahl Qqaygaanga*, Myth Woman. Thank you for being here and in my life when I needed you the most, when my mother was unable. I'll never forget you."

The cabin's silence was disturbed only by the crackle of the fireplace, and the creak of displaced ghosts as the sundering of spirit threads filled the darkness. Myth Woman's journey to the other realms had begun. Finally Chelen spoke. "Tell me, what did she say?"

"I don't understand. She said Raven walks with us again, and he awakens Bear and Wolf. She said, as they walked past where she was concealed in the underbrush, she noticed their footprints in the soft dirt. She saw three of them, but they only left one set of footprints."

"What does that mean, Charlie? That Grandmother would see Raven waking up the ancient spirit beings and them walking together, leaving only one set of prints."

Charlie Stillwaters shook his head. "*Huuk*. Bad omen. Not good. Not good at all."

* * *

"I'd forgotten how gorgeous the view is from here."

Brook spoke to an elderly man standing beside him on the upper deck of the BC Ferry, sailing from Prince Rupert to Skidegate Landing, Haida Gwaii. The native fellow just smiled back. He'd probably seen the same sight a hundred times, Brook thought. Crisp ocean air, so different from New York and Toronto. He'd forgotten the feel of fresh, clean wind whistling through his hair, stirring memories of times when things were simple. He smiled. It was good to be alone and alive.

When they'd set sail the day had been clear, but as they approached, the coastline of Haida Gwaii was shrouded in billowy white. It being late summer, whales weren't crossing the strait by the thousands, but he did catch sight of the odd straggler marked by a spray of water not too far off. Near the halfway point of the journey, the shrill cry of a sea lion startled Brook. The creature poked its head up out of the water as if to say, "Hey, which way to Alaska," before diving back under. He marveled at the avian acrobatic stunts of the Shearwaters skimming alongside the boat on their saber-edged wings. Daring the waters to reach up and clutch them in a watery grasp.

The mists parted as the ferry approached Graham Island, revealing snow-capped peaks to the south and the occasional glimpse of the coast to the north. The islands had the cleanest beaches he'd ever seen, and the emptiest. Although, a beachcomber could often find interesting objects like glass fishing balls, chunks of whalebone, teak and bamboo, along with bits of plastic and other flotsam. Lining the beaches he could swear he saw the looming, intricately etched totems of abandoned native villages. Illusions caused by the washed-up logs, although he did spy the whiteness marking the first landfall of Rose Spit.

Magical Rose Spit, where Raven opened the clamshell that released the Haida to this world. One of the places he wanted to visit this time around, to walk out to that point of land and its rocky beach where huge agates and crystals were reportedly found. As the ferry neared the end of its journey he glimpsed the brightly painted totems in front of the Haida Gwaii Museum at Qay'llnagaay, tucked into a tiny bay in Skidegate.

Brook took a deep breath of the salt air. Now he knew why he'd wanted to come here. It was like leaving the civilized world and journeying into another land, another time. The literal translation of Haida Gwaii was "Islands on the Boundary between Worlds". Definitely a place of wonder, which was exactly what Gwaii Haanas meant. Being here was like being separated from the rest of the world.

Craving a coffee, Brook headed inside the glass-enclosed portion of the upper deck. A glance at his watch told him they were over an hour from reaching the Skidegate Landing. The ferry began to pitch slightly; the shallowness of the narrow Hecate Strait made for rough sailings, especially during winter storms.

He returned to the seats with his coffee, spotting the native man who'd been standing next to him outside at the railing. "May I sit here?"

"Go ahead." He smiled back at Brook.

It was as good a place as any to start asking questions. In his experience there was no better way to get to know the truth behind local events than to talk to the locals.

"Is Haida Gwaii home, or are you just visiting?"

The native looked at him, an enigmatic expression on his face. "Home."

As he half-expected, the fellow didn't respond with a question. If Brook wanted his companion to open up he'd have to volunteer some information of his own.

"I'm just visiting, myself. Brook Grant's the name. I was here a few years ago. Went down to Ninstints. I mean, Sghaan Gway." He made a show of trying to pronounce the name correctly, but failed on purpose.

His companion chuckled and offered his hand. "I'm Henry Richardson, and it's Sghaan Gway."

"Skun-gwy. Sorry, your language is so difficult."

They shook hands.

"Only for the whites." Henry softened his words with a grin.

"Yeah, I guess English would've been the same for you when you were growing up."

Brook sensed he'd already started to break through the natural Haida reserve.

"I only learned Haida five years ago, through the Band," Henry continued. "Very few speak it. As a youngster, I used to speak my language, but they only taught English in the residential schools." There was a faint note of bitterness in his tone.

"Coming here is like an adventure for me," he told Henry. "I've always felt something special for the cedar tree. Once, when I was five or six, I went to Victoria on a family holiday. We visited one of the gardens. Butchart, I think. Somehow I got separated from my parents, and I remember walking down a row of saplings and at the end was a really sorry-looking tree. Its roots were wrapped up in a burlap ball, and the branches were hanging low with its needles drooping. The longer I stared at the tree, the greater the urge I had to water it. I really felt sorry for that cedar. So I found a nearby hose and dragged it over, stuck the end in the top of the burlap bag and let the water run until it started pouring out the bottom."

Brook stopped. It was one of his earliest memories, and one he'd forgotten about until now. He never could figure out why he'd wanted to water that tree. Funnier still was the fact that it was he who was coughing out his life story to a complete stranger, and not the other way around.

"My parents, of course, had nearly given me up for lost, and gave me supreme heck for playing with the water. I didn't care. Even at that early age I knew the tree needed my help. A man who worked there said it was a cedar of some sort."

Henry smiled and nodded. "That was the moment in time when you became human."

"Human? How do you mean?"

"It is said by our elders that until the age of five or six we are not much different than the creatures around us. Then the *sghaana giidas*, spirit beings, come along and enter us, sometimes to stay with us forever, and begin our journey to becoming human."

"Would these spirits be like angels?"

"The spirit beings are our guides, our helpers and protectors, and, some tribes believe, our consciousness."

"More like your soul, then?"

"Yes. Later in life, around adolescence, we go on vision quests or winter dances, and begin to understand who these spirits are that are within us. We also believe that we do not die, that our ancestors are born again into the next generation." He stopped and stared at Brook. "If we don't recognize and honor them, then they can get angry or leave. The soul, we believe, is very light, like a feather, and can become dislodged from its owner easily."

"Is that why some people become bad? Do they have evil spirits within them?"

"The *sghaana giidas* can, and do, influence you. If you are connected to your spirit powers, you can even influence others, good or not."

Brook found the Haida beliefs and mythology intriguing. "How did you pronounce these spirits again?"

"*Sghaana giidas.*"

"S-gana gi-das."

"It's not often I'm teaching a white man to speak Haida!" Henry's mouth betrayed his amusement, and not looking directly at Brook, he repeated more slowly, shaking his head, "*Sghaana giidas.*"

"*Sghaana giidas.*"

"Good. When you began to tell me the story about the cedar I could feel a strong presence around you. You're one of the few white guys that I sense has a spirit helper or guide."

Brook blinked. He felt like Luke Skywalker with Obi-Wan Kenobi saying, 'The force is strong in this one'. "A spirit helper? Ah, you probably say that to all the tourists, but it's funny you should mention it. At times, I feel as if someone's watching over me. You must know the Haida legends?"

"Yes. We call them oral stories."

"Sorry. What do you know, then, about Raven?" Uttering those words sent a shiver through Brook. Carved images swam in his mind, Raven and the prince locked in eternal combat.

"Let me see. Raven is the one that created us. In the beginning the great flood covered the earth for a long time. Finally, the waters started to recede and Raven flew to Rose Spit to feast. As he was walking along the beach, he spied a huge clamshell. Raven pried the clamshell open and much to his surprise, a number of naked, pink-skinned beings emerged. None bore radiant feathers or strong beaks like him. They had circular heads, and instead of wings, they had limbs like sticks. So were the first Haida released to this World. And Raven, you know, was many things: creator, protector, transformer, and trickster. He was always cajoling others to get food, since he was cursed with an unending appetite."

Brook sipped at his coffee. "Raven doesn't sound like anyone I'd want to mess with. He had some pretty heavy powers. And you mentioned him being a transformer. What's that?"

"A transformer can change his shape, become anything, animal, or even human."

"Perhaps you're actually Raven that I'm talking to," Brook joked.

"Unlikely. I'd not have sat here this long without convincing you to buy me a meal or several." Henry laughed. "Although, I am getting a bit hungry."

Brook chuckled. The fellow seemed easy enough to chat with. "I'm afraid they've already shut down the kitchen. Say, have you heard of the Golden Spruce?"

Henry's smile fell away. "Someone cut it down a couple of days ago."

For the first time, Brook detected anger in the man. "I'm sorry, I didn't know," he lied.

"The Golden Spruce is important to us. Our oral stories tell of a prince named Kiidkayaas," Henry explained. "He came from the southern tribes, and had survived a terrible snowstorm with his grandfather. Everyone else in his village died in the storm, and the two were looking for a new home. As they walked, Kiidkayaas' grandfather told the boy not to turn around and look back. Soul loss is an ever-present danger to natives. The longing for a place or person left behind, grieving over a loved one, the death of a spouse, or the return of a warrior from battle, are all things that can cause soul loss. Kiidkayaas did not heed his grandfather's warnings and turned to stare longingly at his former village. As he did, his feet became stiff and roots grew from his legs, transforming him into a tree. The needles of that tree turned golden, forming perpetual tears for the sadness of the prince."

"So, I'd imagine cutting down that tree would be construed as an outrage by the Haida."

He waited patiently for Henry's reply. Six golden spruce trees had been discovered on the Queen Charlottes so far. A genetic defect gave the trees too little of the pigment that protected them from excessive light and resulted in the yellowish color in their needles.

"To us, they cut down a real person," Henry finally replied.

"And killing a living prince would mean what?" He hung on Henry's next words, but he already knew what the answer would be.

"We would have to have our revenge."

Brook was uneasy with the turn the conversation had taken. He needed to change the topic before he killed his rapport with Henry.

"On my last visit to Vancouver, I saw the magnificent Raven sculpture at the Museum of Anthropology. Carved by Bill Reid, I believe. He was Haida too, wasn't he?"

Henry sat up straighter. "Bill was half Haida, yes."

"Sorry to hear about his death. He was an amazing artist. These *sghaana giidas*, do you think they guided him in his visions when he worked on those projects?"

One project Brook had in mind was the canoe built in part by Reid. Loo Taas, the Wave Eater, was one of the few vessels in existence that came close to those ancient wondrous vessels.

"Unfortunately, I never met Bill," Henry said. "But I know his resting place is by the old village of Ttaanuu, the birthplace of his mother. A shaman I know figured he had several *sghaana giidas* with him."

"Several? Is it possible to have more than one? Wouldn't that be like having more than one soul?"

"No, to answer your last question first, and yes, it is possible. In order to become a shaman you must control several *sghaana giidas*. In the past shamans were our religious or spiritual leaders, in addition to being our doctors. But there aren't many around anymore, at least not many real ones. I've bumped into a few people at shows and stuff along the coast. They call themselves shamans, but they're not the real thing."

"Yeah," muttered Brook, "I met some colas like that."

"Huh?"

"Sorry, a cultural thing from the States." He had visions of a serene white-haired, bearded old man sitting cross-legged on a mountaintop, wearing a headdress and robe and saying, "Now grasshopper, today's lesson."

"I can tell you don't believe." Henry stared hard at him. "Yet something tells me you'll stumble across one here on this visit and need his services."

What the devil would I ever need a medicine man for?

"We are approaching the terminal. You may begin boarding your vehicles," the intercom blared.

"Say, before I forget to ask, do you know of any good guides or kayak rental places? I want to explore the coast and it would be cool to go with someone who knows a bit about the islands."

Henry stood up and stretched. "Go to the Haida Gwaii Museum and ask for Chelen Davidshaw. She is a guide and a very good one. Chelen knows the history of our people and this land well. She does kayak tours all over, including Sghaan Gway. She could show you around."

"Thank you."

Henry turned and left Brook staring over the choppy seas, occasional whitecaps breaking the unending blue. Mists still cloaked the horizon, allowing scraps of green and brown coastline to peek through. The Queen Charlottes. The last time he'd been here, Brook had heard another version of Henry's story, told to him by a Haida Watchman named Tom Wilson and centering around a roughly hewn totem at Ninstints.

He'd met Tom in front of the totems on the shore at Ninstints. A native elder with his hair in a single braid, starkly white against the blue denim of his jacket. They were standing by the

Raven totem and Brook gazed up at the human and Raven caught in immortal combat. He'd asked Tom about it, fascinated by the intensity of the unfinished carving.

"It was the last totem carved here. It tells the story of Prince Kiidkayaas and Raven. The artist was probably one of the final inhabitants, before the people of Sghaan Gway succumbed to smallpox in 1862," Tom told him. Then the Watchman recounted the how the Ironmen, the King George Men, brought smallpox to the village. Prince Kiidkayaas went in search of the shaman of another village who could cure the disease, but instead he was met by Raven in disguise. To save his people the prince attempted to steal the immortal stone that kept Raven from aging. That is the image on the totem, the prince with his hands around Raven's throat and Raven with his talons in the prince's guts.

What intrigued him the most was he didn't know how the tale ended. How Prince Kiidkayaas become trapped in the Golden Spruce near Port Clements, far to the north of Ninstints.

Brook walked towards the off-ramp, deep in thought. Now he was more fascinated than ever by the legend behind the Ninstints totem. His newspaper reporter intuition was humming as he'd talked to Henry. There was a lot more here than the official reports alluded to — the situation with the Golden Spruce just didn't smell right. A little more digging seemed in order.

* * *

Raven stirred from his slumber at the sound of angry buzzing. Similar to bees on a rampage when *xuuadjii*, grizzly bear, had broken into their hive and stolen their honey, only much shriller.

He flew down to where the Golden Spruce lay toppled over. The body of the prince had already vanished into the undergrowth, leaving a sticky residue. The needles of the spruce had shriveled up and many were littering the ground with a faded golden carpet. He remembered falling into an exhausted sleep after he'd transformed himself into Bald Eagle and thanked the pale-skinned one for freeing him. Odd. Never had a transformation left him so drained. Perhaps his long, imposed exile had left him very weak. Weak and famished. Raven clicked his beak together. He was always famished.

He searched for the immortal stone in all that remained of Prince Kiidkayaas, flinging leaves and debris aside. What had the wily prince done with it? A sniff revealed that others had been and gone while he slept.

Looking up, Raven saw the multitude of new tracks. Tracks that hadn't been there before he'd taken his nap. How long had he slept? One of the humans who left the footprints, perhaps, had stolen his immortal stone.

The shrill noise broke his concentration. He stopped and sniffed the air again. The irritation in the background made it hard for him to concentrate, but something was definitely out of place. He had noted it before, when he'd first escaped from the Golden Spruce, but at the time he'd been occupied with ensuring his victory over Prince Kiidkayaas.

It was the silence. A great emptiness sucked free of all spirits. The trees were around him and he could hear the insects. But where were the voices of the s*ixhasttdaalgaanga*, small birds? Or the animals, like *ttsing*, the beaver, and *taan*, the black bear. Voices that were part of the forest, like the fish were part of the sea.

Just the annoying growling persisted, and that too was only sound, no spirit voice to accompany it. Raven lifted upward. Maybe the buzzing had something to do with this uneasy void. He would look into the noise, and perhaps it would lead to food.

Clearing the security of the trees, he stopped beating his wings and fell earthward, his heart in his throat. He caught himself at the last possible moment, digging his talons into the bark of the topmost perch on a mighty cedar. The sly Trickster stared in horror at the vision before him. How long had he slept since the prince had first trapped him in the Golden Spruce tree, and how long had he slept since he'd delivered the pale man in the strange-looking canoe to the sea spirits?

Devastation. Total devastation lay everywhere.

The Golden Spruce stood in a small green reserve of forest, beyond which lay nothing but stumps where giants once towered. An alien, more acrid stench, like a volcano's sulfuric breath, came drifting with the hornet buzz from somewhere on the other side of the denuded hills.

Death, in its many voices, whispered its cold-hearted message on a heavy wind of desolation.

Everything Raven held sacred was gone. Heart pounding madly, he flew down to one of the stumps. He closed his eyes and prayed to *Sruhlru Jaad*, Foam Woman, and to *Watghadagaang*, the spirit of the wood-maker, and he prayed to himself, the Creator. This couldn't be real.

The slopes before him formed an unending sea of red soil bleeding down to the ocean. The few remaining trees cried over it. Raven choked, as he sometimes did when picking through offered food at abundant feasts. Not even Raven could have conceived something this devious, this cruel.

He looked around him again. Where did *sdlgu*, the land otter go? Or *jiijaat*, brother hawk, or *kkaat*, the gentle deer? None of them could live here now nothing remained to support them.

Raven sailed down from his perch and walked around the circumference of a stump, circling the sharp edge. The acrid signature of metal remained attached to the bark. Metal and fetid volcanoes' breath clung to the remains like barnacles to a rock.

Endless droning turned his head again. Raven spread his wings and flew in search of the source of this annoyance. Deafening echoes intensified until the very air vibrated. Over the last hill he found the cause and settled close to the men and beasts cutting away at the trees. A cedar crashed to the ground, shaking the earth. Several men gathered around it like wolves at the collapse of a stricken elk. In their hands, the containers of the angry hornets rose in unity in insatiable hunger, hewing the wood with swirling, sharp razor teeth like those of *kkung*, the killer whale.

Yes, much had changed since Raven last walked the world.

But not only did he feel the terror of what he was seeing, he also shared the exhilaration, the power behind those little hornet boxes. Stripped of its limbs, the trunk lay bare. The sweet scent of wounded cedar dissipated as the workers quickly moved on to the next tree. In minutes, they did with those savage hornet boxes what braves would have taken days to accomplish.

Raven stared at the pale flesh under the sweat and grime. None bore the dusky hues of the people he had released from the clamshell. These looked more like the ones that came on the mighty winged boats. The Boston Men and the King George Men, ones who had come to trade with the Haida, just when Raven became trapped in the Golden Spruce. Raven hated what he saw. Tears streaked his face. He would go to the nearest villages and find food. Food and answers.

* * *

Ethereal gusts howled past, reminiscent of eagles' chants. A hawk's cry died on the stillness. The warrior-born closed his eyes, allowing his mind to quiet in its panic.

He no longer bore the body of a prince, like in his former imprisonment. Raven didn't exist here, but there was life. There were others, many others in this peaceful darkness. Memories of a former life, of his way of existence, cowered, shrinking away in this sea of dark firmament.

What he was or was becoming the prince didn't know, except that he knew he wasn't dead. No body but a spirit that still reeked of dignity, of fearlessness, and of pride.

Was this the mother earth that nourished him? So hard to focus. He closed off senses that held no use here, yet there were new ones instead. Was this evolution?

He simply quit being and just was.

His soul stole at the solitude, allowing prevailing winds to peel him through unending canyons of ebony. Floating, bobbing along; a seed of aura borne away on harsh breezes.

This way, that, the whisper of worlds adrift in interstellar currents, pulling at him. Evoking sadness, tearing, until, like bones baked to dust under a sun's brutal gaze, he finally crumbled. Fingers of draft tore at each sundered section and stole them away. Scattered, flung into the sea of dark nothingness. Somewhere a tear floated.

A dream, gone.

Whisked away.

All that remained of what once was, washed into the ether.

Chapter Three

The soil you see is not ordinary soil — it is
the dust of the blood, the flesh, and bones
of our ancestors. You will have to dig down
through the surface before you can find
nature's earth, as the upper portion is crow.
The land, as it is, is my blood and my dead;
It is consecrated.
She-his (late 19th century) Crow

The ferry shuddered as its engines brought it to a halt at the terminal outside Skidegate. Eerie shivers ran through Brook as he viewed the imposing coastline extending north towards Rose Spit. The last time he'd stood on deck waiting to disembark, he'd been eager to explore the islands. But this time, he gripped the rail.

"You okay?" Henry Richardson asked. "Look pale, even for a white guy."

"Yeah, too much coffee, I think," Brook lied. He felt claustrophobic, like he'd entered another land, another time, and Canada was a dim memory. The present washing away, as if his whole life was nothing but an illusion. Talking to Henry had stirred the images of his last visit, and now they merged with visions of Georgina, her face joining the crowd in his head. Fading, finally. His childhood; his dad yelling; beating him; those memories remained the longest. Could a child love and hate his parents at the same time? Hate was a strong word.

"Fuck," he muttered under his breath. Wasn't the sensation of coming home after a lengthy absence supposed to be a happy one?

He stood beside the docks for the longest time, staring back at the boat as the vehicles unloaded. Wanting to get back on and leave, like so many times when he'd come home and stood outside the front door to his parents' house, fortifying himself for the onslaught that was his father. Some part of his guts warned him to get away. Forget this crazy trip and get back on the ferry, before his life changed forever.

Brook stared a moment longer and shouldered his backpack. He had a story to check out, and perhaps that was part of the uneasiness. Henry's talk of spirits and shamans came from a world of naiveté, fairy tales designed to keep the innocent fearful and blind. Yet at the same time, the oral stories were every bit as powerful as the myths of Homer and the other roots of Western culture. Yes, the real world, the one he knew so well, was slipping away.

He shuffled the position of his sixty-pound pack and set off to find a hotel. In the morning he'd fix himself up with a rental car, check out the museum and see if he could contact Chelen Davidshaw. If she wasn't available then he'd seek someone else.

Behind him, he heard the last of the vehicles driving ashore. As he walked along he couldn't fight the comfortable, kick-your-legs-back-grab-a-coffee-and-relax feeling. The folks out here definitely lived that way. It was something the natives like the Spanish, who came to this coast long before the English, called mañana. He smiled. Homecoming. Maybe that was why he'd wanted to come back here. It was all so real again, his past repeating itself, as if he'd been given a second chance.

Still, his heart hammered hard. He wanted to run and dive across the widening waters separating him from his former existence. Timbers, too tall, closed around him, isolating him. A haunting semblance of ... home? Not the home of his childhood; this was the home he'd always sought. Safe, natural and whole.

He breathed deep, trying to settle his nerves. Being a journalist, he'd traveled to many places, but rarely had the feeling of being home. Only here. Cut loose from his life in New York and Toronto.

As he gazed up at the houses built into the hills that descended towards the ocean, a truck pulled up beside him. "Hey, want a ride?"

Henry Richardson, the fellow from the ferry. Brook smiled. "Sure, why not? Know any good hotels?"

"No, just the one my brother owns." Henry grinned back at him.

"Is it good? Or are you recommending the place just because your brother owns it?" Brook joked.

Henry paused. "Well, I'd never suggest something if I didn't like it myself, even if my brother didn't own it. And besides, the other hotel is closed for renovations."

Brook shook his head and laughed as he unslung the backpack and tossed it into the bed of the brand new GMC truck. Henry obviously had money. "Sounds as good as any. Is it far?"

"Queen Charlotte City. The Sea Raven Motel. But I'm heading that way, so I'll drive you."

"Thanks."

"Anytime. There's no shortage of sights to see around here."

"One of the reasons I came back. Didn't catch it all the first time." He missed the open friendliness of the First Nations peoples. It was hard to shrug off that eastern coldness and sophistication he wore so well. This trip would be a chance to pull his life back together, a sort of retreat. After four years Georgina had been looking for a stronger commitment. Brook kept away from the subject every time it came up. So here he was. Mr. Carefree and footloose and alone. All bloody alone.

He looked back, catching a glimpse of the ferry shrinking back into the mists of Hecate Strait. An uncomfortable as hell feeling plagued him. He should trust his journalistic intuition and leave in the morning.

Just then a black truck containing two burly natives drove by, a logo of the three Watchmen on the door. "Interesting."

"The Watchmen," Henry explained proudly. "The Haida Nation organized them to keep an eye on the old villages during the tourist season."

Brook didn't like the feel of the black truck as it disappeared down the street. Observers, the Watchmen were intimidating, yet reassuring at the same time. He'd read reports that some of the government officials were afraid to make any moves because the Haida were always one step ahead of them. Perhaps that was a good thing, though, since it was important to watch over the living as well as the dead.

In any case, it was already too late to back out. Whatever was to happen here, he was now a part of it. Destiny had her hand on him.

"Any relatives own good cafés?" he asked with a grin.

"Several." Henry chuckled. "A few I'd even eat at."

* * *

Chelen sat very still, waiting for the wind to shift, watching the unsuspecting deer about twenty meters in front of her. The magnificent seven-point buck would be a worthy addition to her collection. She inched closer, but the bush was too thick for a clear shot.

It was early evening, fringes of fog drifting among the cedars draped with moss. Spirit fingers, her grandmother would call them. She sighed. Rosemary's funeral was in two days.

"First learn the ways of your ancestors then learn the white man ways," she'd say. "You'll need to know both in order to survive and prosper in this world. Not like in my time, when our ways were enough." But Chelen knew that prosper meant something different to her grandmother.

Breeze caressed her cheek as she crept through the forest. Rosemary taught her of her lineage, of her knowledge of plants, how to survive in the wilderness, even how to track, hunt and skin game. So much Rosemary had shown her, so much that died with her. She told her one day the woods knew everything, were brother to the native, sister to their souls and people to their hearts. Chelen hoped this trip into the midst of the tree people would give her a sign of what her future held. She felt sure the woods would give her an answer. They always did.

What to expect, now the most important person in her life, her guardian and true mother, was with the spirits. Yes, the tree spirits, the *Dida Cwaa Nang Qaaruns*, were always there; they were the essence of the cedars. The *sghaay haw*, the spirit winds, hadn't arrived yet. The forests were silent now, not like the winter when everything whispered with the voice of the spirit winds. Chelen wished they were here now. She could use a friend.

But it wasn't every day she had a chance to capture an animal like *kkaat*, brother deer. She needed to stop wool-gathering and concentrate.

The buck lifted its head. A long ear flickered. She stopped inching forward. Her finger sweated on the trigger.

Tears streamed down her face. Rosemary felt so near, but just out of reach. The deer had returned to its grazing. Chelen continued edging forward until she was some five meters away, yet she still wasn't quite close enough for a good sight line. But she was upwind, so the deer wouldn't suspect she was there, at least not until it would be too late. The metal in her hands was cold as she pressed the trigger. Less than three meters away. She waited, recalling an old saying she'd heard from her grandmother:

No people is broken, until the hearts of its women are on the ground.

Only then are they broken. Only then will they die.

Again the deer raised its head. Chelen took aim, less than two meters away. At this distance, even if it bolted, its fate was sealed. She slid closer, making as little noise as possible. Holding her finger over the hair trigger, she reached out and let the fingers of her other hand thread their way through the leaves that separated her from her quarry. Metal glinted in the green-hued forest light.

One hand touched the back of the deer; the other pressed the trigger and the deer jerked. More at her touch than at the camera's shutters as they snapped again and again.

In a heartbeat, the buck leapt, disappearing into the forest. Chelen laughed. "Let's see white hunters do that."

She laughed until she cried. Her grandmother taught her well in the ways of the hunt, although nowadays she only hunted with a camera. Rosemary taught her the woman things too, to weave baskets and hats from cured cedar bark. How to gather, dry, and smoke berries and fish. All these things Chelen remembered as she walked until she came to the foot of a large tree. There, she put her backpack on the ground and pulled out a short fold-up shovel. Tears splattered the ground as she began to dig.

"So much to let go of," she muttered, being careful not to damage any roots. Her sadness splashed into the shallow pit she was creating and Chelen sobbed for a long time, spewing her grief into the earth.

"Done." She straightened and spaded the loose dirt into the depression. She learned the tradition from her grandmother. When braves grieved, they would go into the forest, dig a hole, and after spilling their sorrow into the opening, they buried it. The tree would absorb the energy via its roots and transfer it to the air. Harming none, becoming part of the universe again.

"You must be conscious in everything you think, do, and say," Rosemary would tell her. "Everything consists of energy. Energy that cannot be taken back once it is put out there. So never speak words of anger, and let the woods, not others in your life, soak up your bad feelings."

Chelen let out a sigh. Just as she was about to return the shovel to her pack, a flutter of wings disturbed her solace. A furtive bird? Whatever it was flew just out of sight, but by the sound of the wing strokes she knew it was large. A flash of white stole through the branches.

"White? There's nothing in this forest that should be white with wings," she said aloud to the spirits. "Geese don't travel in the forest. Only owls and other hunters. Perhaps a snowy owl that has migrated south."

Another flutter. She grabbed her camera and backpack. This deserved a picture. Snowy owls normally only came in the winter; if indeed it was an owl. The birds were not good omens among her people. But they did possess the spirits of the recently departed and often were seen near people as they were dying. Charlie heard one just before Rosemary passed away. Maybe this was a sign from her grandmother. Maybe Rosemary had already returned with a message for her.

For a good hour, Chelen threaded her way through the trees, never getting any closer to the elusive bird. It didn't fly away, but stayed just out of range, hopping from branch to branch, teasing her like a raven would, only ravens weren't white. Finally, she realized she was only getting deeper into the forest and grew tired of the cat-and-mouse hunt. By now she was certain it was no owl. It didn't move like an owl, which were usually nocturnal.

"Two can play this game," she whispered. Squatting, she pulled out remnants of her lunch: trail mix, carrots, breadcrumbs from a half-eaten sandwich, and nibbled at the food then yawned loudly. She set a wrapper from a granola bar to reflect the rays peeking into the clearing, sunlight glinting off the silver foil. "Okay, white bird, let's see if you're curious as well as sneaky."

She rested against an adjacent gnarly pine that had probably been old when her grandmother's grandmother was young. With her camera beside her, she flicked on the automatic focus and held the trigger halfway down. Another yawn, and Chelen closed her eyes. Nothing happened for the longest time and then as she was getting drowsy, a flurry of wings. Her heart thumped.

The kiss of air displaced under outstretched feathers caressed her face. A rustle of plastic. Whatever the bird was, it was trying to peck into the bag containing her trail mix. Without opening her eyes, she lifted the camera and pressed the trigger the rest of the way. The click of the shutter shattered the air as she opened her eyes. A caw of indignation came from the beak of the raven caught in her trap. A white raven.

Chelen gasped as it flew off, her bag of trail mix speared on its beak. "Oh, my." This must be the sign she asked for.

Charlie said Rosemary had seen a raven, walking with wolf and bear through the forest. But they left only one set of footprints.

Now this. A chill, unusual in the summer air, lifted the delicate hairs on her neck. The woods, a friend before, grew still and foreboding. She was alone. Alone as a rare white raven must be.

Chelen rose and grabbed her backpack. She had to see Charlie. He'd know what it meant.

* * *

Brook lay in the in bed at the Sea Raven Motel and let his thoughts wander. He missed Georgina snuggled up against him and hated being alone. Her parting words still hurt: "You're just not enough for me, Brook. I want more out of life."

You're not good enough. How many times had he heard that phrase from his father? He still hated the man. No matter what he did, Brook could never measure up to the standards his dad had set for him.

Sleep eluded him and he sat up. Threads of memories ran through him. Something Henry said about the prince and the Golden Spruce tree didn't sit right. He grabbed his journal and flipped through the pages.

There it was: the end of the Watchman's tale of Raven and the Haida prince. Raven shifted to human form and Kiidkayaas withdrew a large lapis lazuli stone from the creature's throat. He used his prize as ransom to force Raven to take him to find someone to save his people from the terrible illness. Raven took him on his back and flew away. The prince's companion left behind returned to the village and told of the battle. They waited for the prince's return, but he never came. An artist carved a totem with the image of Raven and Kiidkayaas locked in mortal combat. The smallpox killed everyone in the village.

He scanned Tom's answer about what had happened to the pair. "That is a story for another day. The prince, it is whispered, is trapped in a Golden Spruce tree up north. Some elders say Raven walks among us still."

Raven walks among us still.

Moonlight shone on the open pages. Brook closed the journal and rolled over in bed. That's what was wrong with Henry's version of the oral story of Prince Kiidkayaas. No mention of Raven.

Had Raven kept the bargain he'd made with the prince? How had the prince become trapped in the Golden Spruce tree? Had Raven tricked him after all? Too many questions. His gut told him the oral story was tied into the downing of the Golden Spruce. Myth or fairy tale, it was important. Perhaps a visit to the museum tomorrow might offer some clues.

As sleep began to pull at his consciousness, outside the hotel window another raven called. A shiver coursed through him. Was it a sign or sheer coincidence? For a moment, as the memory of Tom's words echoed, Brook nearly believed.

"Mythical crap," he muttered. The phrase danced in his mind as he slept. *Raven walks among us still.*

* * *

Weariness leeched at Raven's wings, pulling him down to the damp earth. Ttsaa'ahl, Qaysun, Ttanuu, Sqiina, Yaku — the villages all empty. Only deserted beaches and encroaching forest to greet him. He settled at Sghaan Gway, where a few moldering totems remained. This is where it began so many years ago.

61

Every settlement he'd visited on Haida Gwaii was abandoned, covered in smothering blankets of lichen, moss, and graceful trees. Little else remained. Only a few bleached poles survived, like stark whalebones, reminders of the richness of Raven's people. Today, the carvings stared with muted tongues, like the Watchmen that crowned them.

Raven walked among the few remaining totems as silent summer breezes stole through the rocks, haunting this beach. He caught sight of stumps jutting up where totems once stood. He bent over, sniffed at the remnants.

He knew the smell. It lingered and clogged the air at the Golden Spruce, and kept the spirit beings away.

An older aroma pervaded the air. The scent of the disease that ravaged Sghaan Gway, the smell of old death lingered at all of the other villages.

His eyes narrowed at the sight of a footprint in the soil. These marks were like the ones made by the pale-skinned ones with the hornet buzzers. They had felled the totems like the trees.

Raven closed his eyes. An idea began to form in his mind. He'd fly to the villages on the northern islands and try to discover what happened to his people. First, he had to retrieve his immortal stone. He was aging, and fast.

Without the stone the past would exact its revenge with deliberate swiftness.

Once he found his stone he'd decide what to do about these newcomers. Perhaps what he needed was another clamshell.

* * *

Brook pulled the rented Chevy Blazer into the graveled parking lot of the Haida Gwaii Museum. He'd need the four by four if he went up to Rose Spit. So far the morning had been largely uneventful and yesterday's foreboding had begun to wear off. He locked the truck and walked towards the museum. Later, he planned to inquire at the Watchmen's office about the procedure for visiting Sghaan Gway and the other protected areas within Gwaii Haanas. But first he wanted to find the canoe, Loo Taas, and this Chelen Davidshaw. Probably some old battleax, he thought with a chuckle.

Inside the museum's main building, the first thing to snag his attention was the ancient totem raised within the high central gallery. Originally, it had been erected in front of the now-abandoned Ttanuu village. He spent several moments marveling at the ancient faces carved by hands long turned to dust. He dropped his gaze and noticed an older native woman studying him. She was a little overweight and wore a museum staff tag. Definitely a Chelen, if he'd ever seen one.

As he approached she glanced sideways at him, her nametag obscured in the rise of her rather large breasts. Her appearance was rugged, nearly masculine with short cropped hair and the angular roundness of some native females. "Can I help you?"

"Yes, I was looking for Chelen Davidshaw." He extended his hand.

"No, I'm afraid you've got the wrong person. You'll find Chelen in the canoe shed. That's a smaller wooden building down towards the end of the driveway."

"Oh. Sorry." He turned and retraced his steps. Six towering totems leered down at him, their etched figures bright in red, black, and sky blue. Traditional Haida colors. He thought he could make out Raven, Bear, Wolf, Beaver, and Killer Whale, dancing up and down the poles, stacked atop each other. He imagined they were guarding the canoe shed.

As he strode inside all twenty-odd meters of Loo Taas' magnificence caught his attention. The name meant Wave Eater, and crowning the ebony hull were Raven, Wolf, and Killer Whale, along with Bill Reid's family crest, painted blood red into the curvature that jutted up. He imagined Reid and his companions as they paddled Loo Taas over two hundred kilometers across Hecate Strait into Skidegate Inlet. The first canoe of its kind to be built in nearly a hundred years.

He gazed at the long prow projecting so strikingly upwards. The war canoe was meant to inspire and strike fear into the hearts of the enemies of the Haida.

Intent on Loo Taas, Brook barely noticed the native girl leaning over the gunwales of the vessel. She appeared to be a cleaner of some sort, wiping down the exhibits. He focused more closely on her and her image shimmered. Brook blinked at the vision of a native girl climbing from a beached canoe, dressed in the finest furs with tufts of eagle feathers adorning her ears. His libido stirred awake. What the hell was all that about, déjà vu, or some sort of erotic male fantasy? At the sound of his footsteps, she glanced up. "Hi, welcome to Haida Gwaii and our museum."

"Ah, yeah, thanks. This is obviously Loo Taas?" He forced the words out, tearing his eyes away from her Mona Lisa features and the beckoning curves of her body. He was suddenly unsure what to say as everything washed into the background.

"Yes, it is. You must know a little about the Haida culture."

"Well, not much. I came here about eight years ago. Kayaked to Ninstints and saw the totems there. That's why I … ah … decided to come back."

"That's great. Well, I hope you enjoy your stay, then."

"I'm sure I will." Trying to take a step away from her was like crawling out of a warm bed on a cold morning. He let out a deep breath. He'd met a lot of beautiful women in his work, so it wasn't her beauty that was seductive. He was good at getting people to open up and trust him, only he didn't need to do that here. It was already there, shining in her face. The odd sensation of intimacy, as if he recognized her in some weird way.

Brook swallowed hard. Now he understood, at least in part, the source of his apprehension yesterday. Destiny's hand heavy on his shoulder. "Fuck, this is nuts," he muttered.

"I'm sorry?"

"I, ah, nothing. Hey, I don't suppose you could tell me where to find Chelen Davidshaw?"

A frown crossed her brow. "Oh, I get it." She delved into a pocket and pulled out a nametag. "I'm always forgetting to pin this thing on. Hate wearing them, you know."

"Ah, I guess I should apologize, Chelen." He gave her his best sheepish grin.

"Why?" She looked up, wearing an expression that fell somewhere between amused and irritated. Perhaps her mood depended on his response. But that was the problem, he didn't know quite how to react. "Apologize? For what?" She tossed gleaming raven-colored hair over her shoulder.

Quit staring before she thinks you're some kind of freak, he scolded himself. "I'm sorry, I mistook you for the cleaning lady. When in actuality, I was directed here by someone who said you were one of the best guides on the islands."

She grinned. "That'd be Amanda, I bet!"

"Actually no, it was some guy I met on the ferry. But I did just run into an older lady in the museum, and ... well you see, I pictured someone a little more ... mature and certainly not anywhere near as ... " He swore she was trying not to giggle over his discomfort. He stopped excusing himself and blurted it out. "You're enjoying this, aren't you?"

"What?"

"Watching me squirm."

"I guess I was. No one's ever confused me with Amanda before."

"Ah, yeah, I'm sorry. No offense meant. You're definitely way prettier than her." He stuck out his hand, trying not to stare at the swell of her breasts under her blouse. "Brook Grant, formerly of Toronto."

The strength in her handshake confirmed she'd done her share of hard work. But it was the naturalness of feeling those fingers sliding along his that felt so familiar, waking desires he thought buried with his last failed relationship. Like he'd touched her before.

"I'm honored, I guess." She blushed slightly.

"So, you're an accomplished guide, I've been told." He tried to compose himself, her touch haunting.

"Well, let's just say that between working here as a curator, and guiding, that's pretty well my life."

"I do need a guide for two ventures while I'm here. I want to kayak around South Moresby and visit Sghaan Gway again. I'd also like to plan a trip to the Golden Spruce."

"I'm heading over to the Golden Spruce tomorrow with my uncle. But I hate to disappoint you. Someone just cut the tree down. There won't be much to see and I really didn't want anyone along who is —"

"What? White?"

"Well, it's a sacred site and considering what happened, I don't think it would be proper to have someone ... non-native ... intruding on that."

He caught the flare of passion in her eyes, and he could respect where she was coming from. But he wouldn't be the first white man to visit the Golden Spruce. "But you do allow tourists there on a regular basis. And hey, if something comes up while we're there, I'll understand and keep my distance. The tree is an important part of your oral history."

"I don't know." She gave him a long, probing stare while he gave her his best innocent-as-sheep-grazing look. "Okay, I'll check with my Uncle Charlie and if he's good with it, you're in."

"Thanks. You've got a deal."

"We'll meet here at seven tomorrow morning and bring a backpack as this could be an all-day event."

"Sounds okay. But what about the kayak trip? I'd love to hire you to guide me around Gwaii Haanas to Sghaan Gway."

"Well, I've something very important to do after tomorrow, but we'll talk further about the kayaking later. Do you want to know how much I charge or anything else?"

"No, whatever rate you set would be fine with me. For now, do you know any good places to eat around here?"

"Yeah, try the Skidegate Coffee and Deli shop up the road. Best sandwiches and taco salad around." She turned to direct him and as she did, he caught a scent of wood smoke, more seductive than any expensive cologne. He'd always loved the smell of an open fire. A pair of pewter earrings, in the graceful lines of the native carvings, caught the light when she tilted her head.

He wanted to reach up and touch them. "Nice earrings. Do they represent anything?"

She blushed a little. "These represent *teeaateea*, the song sparrow."

"Cool. See you tomorrow, then." The possibility of a week or so alone with Chelen in the middle of nowhere lifted his spirits.

* * *

As Chelen was going over the registry at the museum's front desk, Amanda walked over to her.

"I think you'd best be careful with that one, young lady."

She looked up. "Which one?"

"The handsome and smooth-talking fellow looking for you earlier."

"That, he is." She reached up and touched one of her earrings. "I mean about the smooth-talking thing."

"Yeah, right."

"I guess he is good looking, for a white guy."

"Nice buns, too. For a white guy."

"Oh, you're bad."

They both laughed.

"They're not all like Doug, you know," Amanda said gently, before she left to greet an elderly couple entering the building. Chelen rubbed the spot on her finger where his engagement ring had sat, Amanda's parting words ringing in her head.

"We'll see about that."

* * *

Brook climbed into the Blazer and threw his head back. "What the hell just happened back there?"

He grabbed his laptop and typed feverishly. He could never understand the concept of love at first sight. Or the kind of love classic literature seemed so full of; soul-mates and life bonding. How could anything like that possibly exist in this digital age? *Chivalry and romance died in the last century*, he'd written once. Well, maybe it had. But, maybe the notion of eternal soulmates really did exist.

He stared at the words he'd just typed onto his laptop.

Levels of awareness come at unexpected times. Sometimes, in the unexpectedness, everything we value as precious washes away and the present takes on a whole new meaning, grounding you from the trappings of your mind, pulling you away from the everyday things. I've come here looking for answers and have found only more questions. Why here, so far removed from the heart of civilization as I know it? But that's part of it, isn't it? To pull yourself from daily routine and place yourself on the edge of the unknown to contemplate ... that's where the learning comes from. It happened last time I came here and it's happening again, in totally unforeseen ways. I'm excited, yet scared. The remoteness allowing hinges rusted with civility to be flung open to portals of sensibility.

Brook was about to press save on his computer and hesitated adding,

It was like the first time I saw her, was the second time I loved her.

He pressed save, closed the journal entry and shut the lid to his computer. Shakespearean passions, that's what she'd awoken. Damning emotions that drove men mad and women to swoon.

Jesus, if she did that to him in a smile, ten minutes and a handshake, what would a week produce?

Chapter Four

Leaving the museum, Brook drove back to Queen Charlotte City and pulled into the parking lot of the RCMP detachment. He had questions to ask, and hopefully this was the logical place to visit if the pieces of the puzzle were to sort themselves out.

"Hi, I'm Brook Grant," he said to the cop on the desk. "I'm here on holidays and heard about the situation with the Golden Spruce. I was planning on visiting it. Is it safe to do so?" His best just-a-dumb-tourist smile lit his face.

The burly fellow looked him straight in the eye. His badge read Constable Miles Courtney. "What do you want to know, and what concern is it of yours?"

"I guess I just wanted to know if it was safe to go up there, and if the site is still open to the public?"

"Yes." The constable offered nothing more.

Brook pulled out his wallet and showed his press card. He had to go right to the punch, since pulling the dumb-tourist stunt was clearly getting him nowhere. "And I'd also like to know if anything has been released regarding the fellow who cut the tree down. Press business."

Miles stared back, not even glancing at the card. Most cops would buckle a little at this point and release whatever information was available. Obstructing the press was a serious issue, but obviously he wasn't like most policemen. Nor was he like most natives; he was Haida. He and his ancestors had never conceded an inch of their lands to the white man. Constable Courtney's demeanor made it clear he had little use for outsiders and less for reporters. They stood facing each other across the desk.

Miles didn't seem interested in blinking first. Bored of testing Brook he turned. When he returned from the back of the office he held a sheet of paper in his hand. "This was just released." He put the document on the desk, so Brook had to reach across to pick it up.

He perused it quickly. Speed-reading was something he'd learned long ago. "Great, but there's no mention of the bastard who axed the tree that Prince Kiidkayaas was trapped in. I was told the RCMP had sent samples to see if the blood found on the kayak belonging to Gordon Chatwick was indeed his."

"What are you talking about?" Miles narrowed his eyes, giving Brook his full attention.

"You can't go cutting down a sacred tree with a live prince inside. It's sacrilegious, like killing a real person."

Miles' expression changed subtly. His stance became slightly threatening as he crossed his arms in front of him.

"That'd be mighty foolish, all right. You staying in town?"

"Yeah, at the Sea Raven Motel. Mixing a little business with pleasure. I plan to kayak down to Sghaan Gway." Sucking up, when the occasion merited it, was a required element of good journalism. He'd made sure he pronounced Sghaan Gway properly. Right now, he was thankful he'd bumped into Henry Richardson on the ferry.

"The blood type on the kayak was O positive. The same as Chatwick's. No DNA test results yet. We have no leads regarding his whereabouts, at this point. We do know he was supposed to meet friends at Masset and never showed up. We can only assume that he lost control of his kayak and drowned. When the tides are turning, the waters in the inlet are very dangerous."

"Was it the wrong time for kayaking?"

"Couldn't tell you. Why don't you ask Mr. Chatwick?"

Brook pondered for a moment. He could pursue the matter. But more than likely, Mr. Stoneface had already shared more than he wanted to. No sense antagonizing the local authorities.

"Thanks. Can I keep this?"

"It's a photocopy."

Brook folded the piece of paper and tucked it into his pocket. "A pleasure chatting with you, Constable Courtney. You've been very helpful. A very helpful prick," he muttered under his breath as he walked out of earshot.

Miles was no dummy and Brook's alarm bells were going off. Either he'd overplayed his hand or Miles had detected his bullshit. If he was lucky, he wouldn't run into the constable again, because he'd just made his first enemy on the islands.

Still, something in the press release confirmed his gut feeling. Stan was right: a good journalist could smell it and this had "news" plastered all over it. Big-time, front-page news.

* * *

Chelen lay in her bed, unable to fall asleep. She thought of the way it once was with Doug beside her in this very bed. The last time she'd heard his truck idling down the driveway she'd been sleeping, the sheets still scented with the heady aroma of their lovemaking. The note she found after she got up, taped to the bathroom mirror.

Sorry Chelen,

I can only say I can't do this. I guess the realization that we are so different really hit me this week. I know we haven't been getting along. I apologize. But I have to return to Edmonton.

There's a job waiting for me on the rigs. The money is very good, I can't refuse it.

Sorry.

I can't live like this. And no matter what I do I'll hurt you. This seemed like the least painful way to split. Goodbye, and thanks for the incredible memories.

Doug

Obviously, he'd planned it well in advance, cleared everything out, except a few pictures and clothes. She burned them, along with anything to remind her of him, even the note. The hurt wouldn't go away.

She didn't want to become jaded. It wasn't who she was, a warrior, a Haida. Don't trust any white man, her grandmother had warned. She hadn't listened. Nothing Rosemary had said could prepare her for the ways of the heart. Some things had to be experienced.

She missed him, especially just before bedtime, on nights when moonbeams hung from the cedar branches and the air was sweet with the fragrance of damp moss.

Being connected to the land meant being connected to her body and soul. The moment she saw Brook a haunting familiarity came over her. Like meeting an old friend.

This was different from what she had with Doug. This was an ache for a lost bond that went beyond fantasy and lust.

She shook her head. A white raven, Rosemary's death, and now this. Life was an unending circle of change. Did she have the strength or the will to try again?

Her thoughts returned to the white raven. Its appearance meant something. But what?

She closed her eyes and dreamed of making love.

When Chelen woke in the morning, her body was covered in sweat. She rose and showered, letting the water cascade over her, cold and numbing. Just like her dream.

When she'd looked up into the face of her lover, it wasn't Doug with his blond hair and blue eyes. The dream had turned into a bizarre nightmare. Brook, who she knew nothing about, entered her fantasies. Him, and a six-foot raven, black, and not white.

Raven?

Chelen stood with her hands on the wall, head down, water pouring through her jet-black hair, replaying the dream in her mind. A black raven and a white man. Did they represent opposites of the same thing? Why both and why now? Everything was changing, and nothing was as it once was. Tears mixed with the water dripping from her hair. A black raven tore at her soul while a white man plucked at her heartstrings.

Chapter Five

As Brook pulled into the parking lot of the Haida Gwaii Museum he spotted two people climbing out of a battered red Ford truck with a canoe attached to the roof. He was looking forward to the trip to the Golden Spruce. It was one of those mornings where mist hung over everything and if it wasn't for the smell of salt water in the air you'd never realize you were anywhere near the ocean. In the foreground the Watchmen stood on their poles, cylindrical hats poking through the veil of cloud. It wouldn't take much to get attached to the place and want to stay.

"Good morning, Brook. I'm glad you're on time. This here's my uncle, Charlie Stillwaters. Charlie's a shaman."

Henry had been right about the fact he'd meet a shaman. Brook stared longer than he should have, but Charlie didn't look anything like a shaman. Not that he knew what a shaman looked like, but the image before him didn't quite fit the mental picture. The man must be in his sixties, wearing a well-worn Toronto Blue Jays baseball cap studded with pins. His blue jeans and lumberjack-style shirt had seen better days. He leaned on a wooden cane that was intricately carved; its handle, a swimming orca with onyx-inlaid eyes. Twin gray braids hung over his shoulders. Around his waist was an ancient leather pouch that stood out because of its simplicity.

Chelen was dressed for the occasion, her worn hiking pants and Gore-Tex jacket confirming she'd done this more than once. Maybe spending time with her wasn't a good idea, but at least today he'd be prepared for the effect she had on him. That was what scared him, the rush of intense emotion that flooded him yesterday. But he had to investigate the Golden Spruce, and without some sort of native escort he most likely wouldn't be allowed anywhere near it.

He needed to keep the outing strictly on a professional basis. "Hi, Chelen. Nice to meet you, Charlie. That's an interesting pouch you carry. Looks old. Could I see it?" He extended his hand in greeting and was surprised by the steely strength in the old man's grip.

Charlie smiled back with genuine friendliness while his eyes did a lazy appraisal of him. Brook imagined the man seeing things others couldn't. Auras and spirits, penetrating into his soul, seeing things only a shaman could see.

"Chelen said you'd be joining us, and no, you can't handle the pouch. It was given to me by one of our last medicine men, handed down from another shaman before him. If anyone with no shamanic training looked in this pouch, what they saw would cause them to go insane."

He spoke with such certainty Brook almost believed him. "You're an official shaman. I'm a little stunned. I've never met a ... ah ... one before." He'd almost said "witch doctor". He didn't want to make Chelen regret letting him come along.

"Official? Thanks, I ..." Charlie searched through his pockets. "Can't seem to find my union card at the moment. I'm in Local One, Member Three."

Brook tried not to chuckle. He didn't know if the man was intentionally insulting him, or merely being funny, or both.

"It's okay, Brook. You can laugh. Charlie's one of the craziest guys around. My relatives think he's got a few sticks not in the fire. As for me, I love him dearly." She nudged her uncle with her shoulder.

"Sorry, I meant no offense. But I was never introduced to a shaman before, and you sure don't look like the type."

"Crazy white man, been reading too many westerns. Well, you've met a shaman now. I don't grow my hair down to the ground, and I do bathe with soap, occasionally. Although I usually stick to Dove, don't want to wreck my delicate complexion with harsh chemicals." He smirked.

Judging by the state of his clothes, he doubted Charlie used shampoo or laundry soap in the last ten years.

"Nor do I slather myself in seal oil and dance around naked."

"Thank goodness," Chelen put in.

"My loving niece." Charlie shook his head at her. "Every family has black wolves and she's ours, and oh, I didn't bring any of my trading cards, but I do autographs and pictures for free. Levitations are ten bucks and miracles, well, that rate depends on how miraculous a feat I have to perform. Now, let's get a move on. The spirits are restless."

Brook liked the man already; they shared a similar sense of humor. Although Charlie seemed a bit more cracked than most. "As long as you promise not to purposely blur any of my photos, I'll promise not to bring any bad spirits along."

The shaman squinted at him. "No bad spirits, but I do sense a presence hanging around you. If I didn't know better, I'd say it was a native spirit. Interesting."

"Hey, I was just joking, but it's funny you should say that. I bumped into a native fellow on the ferry ride over here and he said the same thing, after I told him about an experience I had as a child."

"Uncle Henry." They both laughed, and he somehow got the feeling he'd been set up.

Chelen opened the passenger door of Charlie's venerable Ford truck. "Come on. We'll talk as we drive, or we'll never get there." She slid in next to Charlie as Brook unslung his backpack, took his camera out and hung it around his neck. He put the backpack on the floor before he climbed into the truck beside Chelen.

They drove along the two-lane highway leading to the summer village of Tlell on the eastern coast of Graham Island. The road hugged the coast, glimpses of ocean emerging between the trees. Later they'd head inland to the Golden Spruce, near the village of Port Clements. He'd never seen this section of Haida Gwaii, and much of their drive took in unending swaths of towering firs, Sitka spruce and cedars.

Trees … why had he always had a thing about trees? As they traveled, he told Charlie and Chelen of his incident with the cedar tree when he was young. "Funny thing is, I'd forgotten all about it until I was talking to your Uncle Henry. It happened such a long time ago."

"Well," Chelen said, "we believe that everything has a spirit, and we believe in supernatural beings. For instance, every fall the spirit winds come from the east bearing the *sghaana giidas*. These winds stay all winter."

"But how do you know the winds are here?"

"If you're connected to the land and are in unspoiled areas, because the *sghaana giidas* won't dwell in desecrated places, you can hear them. They whisper like a song as they travel through the forests."

"And you've heard them?" Windsongs? Brook didn't buy any of it. He'd never heard anything like a whispering wind in his life.

"Yes, I have. We would gather — still do — in the longhouses to begin the winter ceremonials in honor of the spirit winds."

"Winter ceremonials? You mean like a big party? What's that called?"

"Potlatching. No, this is different. It's a celebration called a vision quest. At a certain age, usually adolescence, we connect to the spirit beings we've had with us since birth. Then we sing and dance to increase our connection with the *sghaana giidas*, and bring the spirits inside us."

"You've lost me a little here. This connection thing is like a journey?"

Charlie interrupted, "Maybe I can enlighten our unbeliever. The highly technical term we use for those who receive a vision and became spirit dancers is 'What I got,' while those who saw no vision we call 'He ain't got nothing.' You might want to try connecting with your spirits one of these days. They can do much more than guide you."

"My spirits?"

"That presence I sense hanging around you. I've been reaching out and there's definitely something there, but I can't quite place it."

Brook remained silent for a moment. He'd always thought he had a guardian angel of some sort and even though he sensed that Charlie was speaking his own truth, he had difficulty believing the elder. His journalist's skepticism kept kicking in. Keep your mind open, he thought. "I'm curious ... what do you mean by reaching out?"

Chelen explained. "He sends his spirit out there to find out things."

"But is it wise to do that while driving along at eighty clicks an hour?"

Charlie let out a chuckle. "Relax. Section two of the shaman handbook, paragraph one, under 'Abilities', reads that shaman must be able to send spirits out while working and operating motorized equipment or vehicles."

Brook stared at Charlie and Chelen in disbelief for a moment before they all burst into laughter.

* * *

Chelen wasn't surprised when a few kilometers later, just past Lawn Hill, Charlie signaled to pull over.

"Hey, where are we going?" Brook asked.

"Oh, Charlie likes to stop at St. Mary's and fill up his containers with the spring water." She couldn't help being amused by the white man's surprise at the carved figure before them. Instead of the usual totems bearing Haida images was a sculpture of the Madonna Mary.

"Any particular reason why someone made this?"

"Just one of the locals practicing his talent for artwork."

He unslung his camera. "Cool. Is it okay to take pictures?"

"Yes, this is a public place. But thanks for asking." Smiling, she waited until he wandered off snapping photos. "Charlie, can I ask your opinion about something?" She didn't want Brook to overhear her explaining how she'd come across the white raven in the woods.

Her uncle paused before answering. "I've never heard of anyone meeting a white Raven, although an albino bird is a distinct possibility. But don't forget that Raven was white when he was first created and only after he got himself into trouble did he turn black. As for what this means, my guess would be renewal, and changes. A reversal to earlier times and values, or past lifetimes. Maybe a sign to take a second look at something with fresh eyes." He glanced over at Brook, who was approaching them. "If you get what I mean."

"Uncle Charlie! What are you suggesting?"

He winked at her. "If you could see the energies dancing between the two of you, like I can, you'd understand."

Brook came to stand beside them. "You drink from this spring?" He peered at the small pool where scores of mosquitoes hovered.

Charlie bent over, cupped his hands and took a long sip of the water. "Been drinking it for years, although in hot summer months it does tend to peter out, like now. Builds spirit and puts hair on your chest, I say."

"Spirit, right. Probably be having a very intimate conversation with the Tidy Bowl man by the end of the day. But hey, I'll trust ya." He was about to take a gulp when he caught her studying him.

"You know, I should warn you," she said. "The legends say that whoever drinks from these waters will return to these shores."

"Well, that would be okay, if one believes in legends." He took a sip. "Wow, this is actually pretty good, as pure as any spring water I've tasted. Has anyone ever thought of bottling the stuff and selling it? Probably make a fortune."

"That's whites for ya, one minute a disbeliever and the next trying to make a buck," Charlie snickered as they set off back towards the truck.

"Ignore Charlie. He doesn't have a very high opinion of white man's ways sometimes."

"Oh, that's okay. Sometimes I don't either. Especially after seeing some of the clear-cuts. Looks like the loggers left more trees on the ground than they actually took."

"They did." Charlie snorted.

"I've read reports that say some lumber companies took only the prime number one logs, leaving the rest to rot," Chelen added, trying to get her mind off the St. Mary's legend Brook so easily dismissed. He had the typical white man bias against spiritual beliefs. Unless, of course, she wanted him to return? To stay?

Get involved with another white guy? That would be the dumbest mistake she could ever make. But judging by the way he looked at her, Charlie was right: tension was building between them. Chelen closed her eyes and shuddered. She couldn't deny the ache. However much she fought to deny it, she wanted him.

* * *

"And you're saying the Band Council asked Charlie to check out what happened here? Why?" Brook asked as they came in sight of the Golden Spruce. He'd forgotten the serenity that pervaded the old-growth forests. Life unchanged for a thousand years.

They clambered into the small canoe he and Chelen lugged from the truck to the edge of the Yakoun River and pushed off towards the opposite bank. There he spotted the shattered golden branches drooping into the water.

"Because Charlie understands things we'll never comprehend," was all Chelen said as they disembarked, taking care to step around the splinters.

What an impact the tree must have made as it hit the forest floor. What reverse logic could possess someone to destroy something so irreplaceable as a statement supporting environmental protection? He hung back as Chelen and Charlie approached the horizontal tree, bowed their heads before it and made offerings of sacred tobacco.

Brook stared at the age rings radiating from the tree's center. How could a prince hide in there? The Golden Spruce looked solid enough, not like some of the big cedars that rotted from the inside out. Eyes moist, Chelen motioned for him to approach. "I imagine you probably have a hard time grasping how important the Golden Spruce tree was to the Haida," she said as she unslung her pack and arched her back.

"A little." He turned his gaze from the subtle thrust of her breasts and found Charlie staring at him. The elder, who'd walked most of the way leaning heavily into his orca-headed cane, sauntered over and smacked him lightly with it. "No mixing business with pleasure, now." He chuckled, low enough so that Chelen wouldn't hear him.

"Hey, I was just —"

"Filling your eyeballs with my niece."

"No, I was just taking in the environment," Brook replied, trying to cover his embarrassment.

"Ogling. It's called ogling where I come from. Now move aside and let me do my stuff, disbeliever." He walked around the stump a couple of times and stopped, bent over and touched the earth, closing his eyes.

Brook returned his attention to Chelen. "What's he doing? What happened here was some quasi-environmentalist came along and chopped down the tree before he managed to get drowned in Masset Inlet."

"Maybe to you, and the RCMP. But these other things and ways you know nothing of … they are what Charlie needs to check out."

"Does he believe Prince Kiidkayaas, who as far as I know has never actually been proven to exist, was really trapped in this, ah ... what's the word?"

"Transformer tree." She gave him a strange look. "So you've heard the oral legend about the Golden Spruce?"

"Heard it from Henry, the guy I met on the ferry. But I first learned of it from the Watchman at Ninstints, eight years ago. Do you believe Kiidkayaas was killed when the tree was cut down? I mean, really believe?"

"Perhaps. Charlie can trace the prince's spirit and find out what happened to him. Either he's been released from his imprisonment or he's been killed. If he's truly dead, then he'll be hanging about in the land of the souls."

"The land of what?"

"The realm people go to when they first die. There they wait for the canoe to ferry them across the river to other dimensions."

This whole situation was becoming too absurd. Who was he to judge what others believed to be the truth? Perception was reality. Did it really matter if the Haida perceived that some ancient prince had been released shortly after Gordon Chatwick cut down the Golden Spruce?

But the truth was that someone or something had killed Brook's guts were suggesting someone or something killed Chatwick shortly after he cut down the tree. *Okay, I need to stay open to possibilities even though this goes against everything I believe.*

Charlie stood up, running his hands over an area littered with glimmering needles. Then the shaman rose and moved back a little, his guise of humor and witty sarcasm gone.

On his haunches again, Charlie jerked his hand away from the ground, as if something stabbed it.

"Are you okay?" Chelen called.

He rubbed his palms together. "I think so. My hands went numb for a second. Something strange definitely happened recently. Needs a bit of meditation to figure out exactly what."

"I'm not trying to be a smartass, but what makes you think something funny went on here?" Brook bent over and touched the spot

Charlie reacted to and felt nothing. Maybe Charlie really was some kind of psychic.

"It's hard to explain. At this point, I'm not sure myself, but the energy is pretty strong." The shaman folded his legs and settled on the moss. Next he pulled several objects from his pouch and arranged them in front of him.

"What the heck's he up to?" Brook asked Chelen as Charlie pulled out his lighter and lit a small bundle of grayish-looking grass. Charlie let the aromatic smoke swirl upward and then swept his hands through it, directing it over his body.

Chelen grinned. "Well, I'm sure Charlie would say, 'just flicking my bic'. He's cleansing himself before he goes into a trance."

"O-oh. Why'd he be doing that?"

"I think he's trying to get a feel of the energy around here. It might give him an idea of what happened."

"A feel for what?"

"The energy around this area. Everything is energy-based. You, me, this tree, the earth ... we're all connected. A shaman trains himself to pick up energy emanations, and travel to other dimensions."

"Really?" Brook was more than a little confused. "Are you saying he can astral travel and talk to ghosts and stuff? Like some sort of esoteric detective?"

"No, it goes deeper than that. See, a shaman has control of one or several animal spirits, which he can communicate with. He often sends them to other dimensions to check things out on his behalf. He can go to these dimensions, but can't achieve all that his helpers can. Charlie's animal spirits can help him determine what happened here."

"You're pulling one on me, aren't you? This isn't anything like the Doctor Doolittle books where he talks to the animals, is it?"

"Nothing fictional about it. These beliefs are real. I'll try to explain this without sounding too textbookish, but I can give you the scientific version first, if you like?"

Hopefully an in-depth explanation would help with any articles on the Golden Spruce. "Sure. And don't get me wrong. I'm very interested, but having a hard time believing, you know? I mean, I've never been exposed to a shaman or anything to do with … ah … native spirits and woo-woo stuff, so this is a little too out there for me."

"Thanks for the honesty. I figured you'd brush poor old Charlie off as a complete flake. That was one reason I didn't want you to come along, at first. Charlie's quite serious about his work."

"I can tell."

"Which makes it harder for him when there's a skeptic in the crowd."

"Kinda like the bad karma thing."

"Exactly. Actually it was Charlie who consented to you joining us, once I told him what you'd said about keeping your distance if anything came up. And you seemed genuinely respectful and curious about the islands and our culture. Ever since Charlie became a shaman, I've been pretty interested in that subject myself. Studied it, even. Believe it or not, there's an explanation for what he's doing, based on Western scientific doctrine."

"Ah, now you're talking. Tell me more."

"Okay. Got a pen?"

"Matter of fact I do." He pulled out his ever-present writing pad and pen from his pocket. Normally he'd use his mini-Ipad, but had left it back on charge in his room.

"Where do I start? Okay, it goes something like this. A shaman moves between realms of consciousness like we open doors and enter other rooms. In the other realms, he can talk to and deal with things we have no conception of. What Charlie's doing now is entering a state of double consciousness, where awareness of the personal self is restricted while it coexists with the dreamlike consciousness. Basically, he has to dissociate from his corporeal body to enter the other realms. There. Did I bore you?"

"Not at all. Thanks for enlightening me. Gives me some understanding of what Charlie's trying to accomplish here. But where'd you go to school to learn that?"

"UBC."

"With your education you believe all this stuff about spirits and out-of-body-experiences?"

"Yes, of course. Now come, let's eat something and I'll try to explain a bit further. I think Charlie will be a while and it'll be best if our conversation isn't disturbing him."

At her mention of eating, Brook's stomach growled. His scant breakfast had consisted of toast and coffee. They grabbed their packs and went to the base of a cedar tree some distance from Charlie.

"Ah, exactly how long is he going to be?" Brook nodded toward the old man sitting motionless with his eyes closed.

"Depending on what he finds, he could be a few minutes, could be all night."

"You mean to tell me he'd sit here all night?"

"He has before. Once he's into his trance, you can't interrupt him. It would be dangerous, to him and to you."

"To me?"

"Yes. Because of the animal spirits all shamans control. Some will be assisting him, and others guarding him, while he's out there trying to find what he needs."

"Oh, right."

"So, if you really are a non-believer, go ahead and disturb him." With that, she ripped part of her sandwich up and flung it into the woods.

What the hell? He gave her a quizzical look.

"I learned that from my grandmother, Rosemary. You always give back part of your food, to pay respect to the earth and the plants and animals that died to provide you with their energy."

"Your grandmother told you that?"

"Yes. Before my mother died, the tribe allowed my grandmother to raise me, as my mother wasn't capable."

"Sounds to me like they gave you away."

"No. They knew she was an alcoholic, and in that state, she couldn't be a good parent to me. We do many things differently. I can explain later, when we're kayaking. That's if you're interested?"

"Sure. I'm always curious about other cultures." Because he was a journalist, but he didn't want to reveal that to Chelen just yet.

"My grandmother hid me when the Indian Agents would show up looking for children to put into the residential schools. She saw what that did to my mother, heard her horror stories. Rosemary didn't want to make the same mistake with me, and later she put me into a regular public school. I'm glad she looked after me. It gave me the ability to see both perspectives."

"Yeah, but spirit beings? The oral stories are as fascinating as ancient Greek mythology, but isn't that all they are?"

"That depends, I'd say. Isn't it a matter of viewpoint? Try this, for example." She held her hands together with her fingers forming a square in front of her face. "Look through this frame and what do you see?"

A beautiful woman, he wanted to say. "Hmmm ... I see the world."

"Well, sure. But your view of the world comes from a thin filter of perceptions based on judgments and experiences that formed your truths. These truths were established early in your life. No one in this world will look at life like you do, Brook."

"Yes, but everyone's taught the same general things. To some degree, we all think the same."

"Tell me again what you see around us." She waved her hand to indicate the surrounding woods.

"Cedar trees, spruce trees, bushes ... In the distance the fallen Golden Spruce tree. I see Charlie sitting there."

"Why do you think it was cut down?"

"As some sort of protest against the logging industry. I guess for its uniqueness, or maybe for what it's worth."

"And what do you think that tree is worth?"

"From some reports I heard lately, I'd say about three thousand dollars in lumber."

"And after it's gone?"

"Well, you grow another one."

"To do what?"

"Ah, grow it and cut it down. You know, harvesting of the forests. Effective land management." He wasn't sure where she was going with this line of argument, but he had to give her credit, she'd probably make a sharp environmental lawyer.

"Right. The economic reality of money. Our beliefs around money and finances are simple. Money is like a river. All you can hope to do is reach in and scoop up what you need as it flows by, while your culture wants to dam it up and keep all of it for yourselves. What about giving back to Mother Earth?"

"Give back? In what way?"

"Repay her for what you've taken."

"Repay? Well, no. It's ours to consume. We're the dominant life form on this planet and according to the Bible, everything here is for us to use."

"Bingo! The religious reality. But this is how we view this tree. It's connected by its roots to the ground, and its branches hold back the sky. It has energy like everything else around us. It thinks in its own reality, which is different than ours. Before the Haida cut anything down, we first honor its spirit, through a ceremony to celebrate its life and its gift to us. An exchange of energies. We are caretakers of the land, not its owners. Which is one of our biggest issues when we try to fight for our treaty rights in the court system."

"Because society sees things so differently?"

"Your society does, yes. It bases everything on ownership. We see everything as being in the creator's protection. We're in constant conversation with our ancestors and with the future generations. We must keep our lands healthy, as did our ancestors, as they expect us to do." She smiled and added, "Well, so much for our respective viewpoints. But the way we see it, you have a spirit, so why can't this tree?"

"Because I think."

"And the tree doesn't? There were tests done in the 1970s that showed plants experience fear. When an electrical current is hooked up to them and someone cuts off a leaf, the electrical field goes crazy. In fact, tests showed that when someone just thinks of cutting off a leaf, the electrical field goes up. So who says plants don't feel fear?"

"Maybe there's some truth about talking to your African violets."

"Exactly."

"Well, I have to admit I'm fascinated, disbelieving at this point, but fascinated."

"Fair enough. Like a lot of people, you don't believe in anything you can't see, measure, or prove. If you could suspend the illusion, you'd see spirit does exist, but not in textbooks."

Brook sat for a moment. "Some things I can't see I do believe in, such as intuition. It's served me well in my job."

"Okay then, let's try a little visualization. Close your eyes. Try not to think of anything and let the spirit in, the one Charlie saw. The one that's been with you since you were a child."

Brook closed his eyes. He felt a bit of an idiot, though if his spirit guide had brought him here to meet Chelen, was that such a bad thing? Emptying his mind wasn't so easy.

"Ignore any thought that enters your head. Whenever something comes in, still it and make it drop away. Simply trust me and what we're about to do. I'm going to count to ten and after each number I want you to draw deeper into yourself."

Brook relaxed. Her voice lowered until it became hypnotic and soothing.

"Good. Slow your breathing, and listen to your heartbeat. Nod when you think you're ready."

He was lost in the measured breaths and the thump of his heart. He nodded.

"Now call your spirit guide. Ask it to show you something that might help you to understand why you're here." Her voice was barely a whisper.

Feeling slightly less ridiculous, he silently repeated the words, "Spirit, come to me. Show me what I need to know."

He was suspended in an ocean of dark solitude. Then a breath whisked by his ear.

Brook gasped. His heart stuttered and he turned, straining to catch the movement. A blur of vision, so fast he nearly missed it: the native girl he'd seen in the museum, clad in the regal furs, climbing out of her canoe. Just a glimpse set off a deep hunger within.

"Let go of your senses. Let go of your hearing. Listen to your spirit guide. Trust it."

A brush of feathers on his cheek. Murmurs, nearly singsong, echoed. He longed to see the native princess again, to touch her.

"Don't think about what's happening. Let it guide you. Let go of your ego."

He let go completely and allowed himself to float again. The mystical whispers sifted by. Seductive and beguiling. What if they were lulling him into a false state of security? He pushed the thought away.

A surge of powerful energy screamed past. Tendrils wrapped around him. A face leered out of the darkness and he jolted from the inky depths to an area of deep blue. He gagged at the sickening smell of decay.

"Oh, God," he yelled and snapped his eyes open.

"Don't fight it, trust," Chelen urged him.

He lunged and broke free of the figure, taking several gasps before realizing he was face down on the earth, hands clenched around tufts of grass. "What the fuck was that?"

"The one you called. Your guardian spirit. I know this is hard for you. Belief is so important here. If you think good thoughts, good things will come to you."

Brook sat up. "Yeah, lady, that didn't feel good." He'd thought something bad and it happened. "That ain't no angel watching over me, I can tell you that much. It was like being touched by something dead."

"Stare into my eyes." Fear slipped away as he met her gaze. When he was calm enough, he spoke. "I'm not sure, but I … I think it was trying to show me something here." He blinked as a color flashed into his head. "Blue, something blue and…" He squinted, unable to picture anything else.

"Okay, I think we've lost it. But before the spirit energy leaves completely, take my hand. Close your eyes again and let yourself walk. Go wherever you need to. Trust where you're being led. I'll be here, protecting you."

He stood and took her hand. The warmth sent a comforting frisson through him, as if her spirit were curling about him. In an odd way, very arousing.

Brook pushed away the fantasies. He had to concentrate. The spirit was trying to show him something. He realized that even before the voices started murmuring incessantly.

Closing his eyes, he began to walk, letting his feet and those voices guide him.

Charlie was still in a deep trance as they passed. The murmurs in Brook's head stopped. "I don't know," he muttered. "This spot. Everything went quiet here. I think whatever it wants me to see is here." He moved around a little until he was certain he was in the right place.

Chelen let go of his hand. Maybe she was right, maybe there was something to this spirit and energy thing. He sank to his knees and turned his attention to the ground. It had a crusty sheen to it he hadn't noticed before, like a slug trail. But the space before him was large enough to hold a body. In fact, as he stared, he could discern the faint imprints of a body that must have crushed the decaying leaves and scattered golden spruce needles.

Something glittered, caught by the rays of sunlight. He pushed aside a few leaves and uncovered a deep blue-colored stone. "What's this?"

"Let me see." Chelen peered down at the oddly polished object. "Looks like a lapis lazuli. Lapis lazuli is honoured as a ritual stone in the US southwest, but not in Haida mythology. It's not a local stone. Don't know how it would get here, unless it was dropped by a tourist or something."

As he reached for the lapis lazuli, a caw of a raven broke the stillness of the forest. He pulled free a long black feather half buried in the leaves nearby.

"A raven feather. An omen," Chelen remarked.

A sudden eeriness crept over him as he held the polished stone and the black feather. The air grew heavy. Prickles rose on his neck.

"Do you feel that?" He shivered, even though the heat of the summer sun was making him perspire.

"Feel what?"

He turned to look up. A flutter of wings broke the tension.

"Just a raven. You felt a raven watching you." Chelen laughed. "Maybe he's looking for his feather."

"Oh." Charlie moaned and slumped over.

Chelen rushed to his side. "He's coming out of his trance."

She pulled Charlie off the damp earth. Dirt and leaves stuck to his face. His eyes had rolled back until only the whites showed. His skin was deathly pale under the sheen of sweat. He shook, as if in a mild epileptic seizure.

Brook stood still, feeling detached from what was happening.

"No. I still feel it." He jerked his head up in shock. Dozens of unfriendly eyes seemed to be watching, shadows shifting and calling with hushed whispers.

A breeze rattled the trees, breaking the spell. Nearby, the boughs of a large cedar soughed in the wind. Brook shuddered. There was something about the cedar ...

"You okay?" Chelen asked as she held Charlie against her. "Charlie's not doing so good. Something's wrong. I've never seen him go into spasms like this."

"Yeah, I'm fine now. But for a moment I felt really weird." His skin was still crawling. "I had the oddest feeling. Almost like we were being watched."

Chelen raised an eyebrow in question.

"Like ..." He paused. "This is crazy, but I could've sworn that cedar tree was watching me, trying to talk to me." He tucked the stone into his pants pocket and the feather into the one in his shirt. Charlie was huddled in a fetal position, shaking in Chelen's arms. Brook wasn't sure if she'd heard him, since her concentration had shifted back to the semi-conscious shaman. He went over and touched Charlie's forehead. "He's hot, running a fever."

"We gotta get him back to his cabin. He'll be safer there."

"Safe? From what?"

"Not sure. He looks like he has a cold or a flu, but I don't think so. If we can get him home he can draw from the energy from his protected place."

Charlie shuddered in her arms, spittle foaming from his mouth and down his cheek.

"Help me carry him to the canoe."

"What about his stuff?" Brook stared at the medicine pouch, untied on the grass. "We'll come back and get it in a moment."

He slung one of Charlie's arms around his neck. Chelen did the same. As they dragged him back towards the river, he began to talk in strange, guttural sounds.

Nothing made sense, Brook thought. Nothing seemed real. At least, not in the sense of what he knew as reality. The sooner they got out of this place the better.

They lowered Charlie into the canoe. "I can't leave him here alone, he might roll over and fall into the water," Chelen said. "Will you go back and get his medicine pouch? But whatever you do, don't look inside."

"Sure, no sweat." Brook gulped and hiked back to the clearing, where he bent down to pick up Charlie's stuff, taking caution not to look into the open pouch. No sense in tempting fate, he thought as a sliver of wind swept through the trees. He glanced up and caught sight of a creature standing by the cedar he'd noticed earlier. Covered in brown hair, it was nearly man-sized and seemed to resemble an overgrown, emaciated Ewok. No, its head was slender, and sleek, otter-like. Odd stubby hands grew out of its chest.

The medicine pouch felt alive, feverish almost. As he closed it, the image wavered and vanished. Brook swallowed hard and left as fast as possible.

* * *

Charlie closed his eyes. The clean smell of burning sage wafted around him. The scent of damp earth and the sharp tang of spruce grounded him.

No matter how many times he did this, he felt uneasy about leaving his corporeal body. He took care to set protections, though his quirky sense of humor hoped that no one painted a funny face on him with an indelible marker while he was in the spirit realms. He smiled. *Enough. Time to get serious.* He slowed his breathing until all he could hear was the sigh of the wind, and the movement of the earth below him.

Another breath to scatter the last trace of ego and he was ready. His spirit slipped past the boundaries of flesh and bone. The soil below him was very much alive. Relaxing further, he went deeper, down into the quieter layers, where there was less connection to the physical. This was the spiritual level he usually traveled, but this time it felt different. The energy had changed. Even without his body, he shivered.

Specks of energy whizzed by and through him. Sometimes for sheer pleasure he'd get lost in the flow of planetary life and join in, but he had a job to do first. He stared up at the tendrils of the Golden Spruce's roots. It was only a stump now, but some of the roots still clung to life, and … that was odd.

The spruce tree was anchored into the spiritual realm of the Earth. Why should that be?

Charlie spun around. Everything was disjointed. The fragile lines of energy that tied everything together were severed. The balance was upset, changed somehow.

The tree, his guides whispered. The Golden Spruce was not only creating the disturbance, but held more energy than a Haida prince trapped in it could have accounted for.

He probed the roots, trying to connect, seeking a clue to what happened. Charlie sniffed for clues. This is what he enjoyed: the thrill of the discovery.

As he poked around, a vision flashed.

A raven, a white raven. Clean, and virginal.

Raven had begun life cloaked in white, but his hunger and greed caused him to turn black. Or was this a rare albino, unrelated to Raven? A tendril of fear ran through the shaman. Did

Chelen's white raven come from the Golden Spruce?

Images of the white raven teasing Chelen came to him. Something wasn't right. This was the past, and he hardly ever picked up visions of the past. Maybe because everything was out of order things that had already happened were repeating themselves ... he didn't like it at all.

Charlie followed the white raven as it flew haphazardly, obviously disoriented. It landed on an electrical transformer. An angry buzz coursed through the air. The bird's eyes widened as it quivered horribly. Sparks haloed it. Finally, it fell to the ground. Charlie stared as the soul rose from its body. He recognized a strong spirit, the burst of energy belonging to a being of much higher intelligence.

The white raven's soul traveled until it came to a river so wide Charlie couldn't see the other shore. He had visited it many times, looking for the recently departed. The land of the dead ones. Here the white raven's spirit waited.

Along the banks many of the recently departed that were lost gathered. Charlie looked for Rosemary, just in case, but he knew Rosemary wasn't here. She'd already gone to the other side. A realm no one returned from, unless they reincarnated.

Danger! The knowledge speared through him. His physical body or possessions were in jeopardy. The image of his land otter spirit glared at him, fangs ready. It swam back up. His pouch. Someone was touching his medicine pouch. The otter spirit would defend it, as was his sworn duty. Charlie didn't want to leave the land of the dead ones, but intuition told him what was happening was important.

Brook. Charlie was tempted to let him suffer the fate the land otter would visit upon him. He sighed. He'd have to leave and save the fool's life.

Damn it.

He should let the white man have a taste of native justice, but Chelen would never forgive him.

* * *

Brook straightened at the mocking cry of a raven. Faint noises came from the ancient leather pouch in his hands. He fumbled with the thongs he'd just tied, fighting an irresistible urge to see what was inside.

What did the old man keep in there? Brook lifted the flap and exhaled sharply as mist oozed upward. Tendrils of green and blue spewed from the bag, and something inside moved.

Chapter Six

The pouch was yanked from his hands. Brook turned. Charlie stood beside him, muttering words in some arcane language. The shaman's eyes were glazed and unseeing. Brook hadn't been aware of anyone coming up behind him. He stared at the medicine pouch ... what was in it? As Charlie tied the drawstrings, the undergrowth rustled.

"Thank goodness, Charlie's here with you," Chelen panted, as she pushed through the bushes, her clothes half soaked.

Before she could reach them, Charlie looked Brook dead in the eye. His vision cleared for a moment. "Don't tread on ground you've never walked before. We must leave immediately. Take me home." His eyes rolled back and his knees buckled. Brook caught him as he fell. "Chelen. Tell her I saw the white raven. I saw it die," the old man whispered.

* * *

Charlie slipped back to the land of the dead ones. A large black canoe rested on the shore. A carved *sisiutl* jutted out from the prow and stern, its dragon-like features glaring menacingly. Shadowy spirit beings filled the craft. The ghosts assembled along the edge of the vile water, desperate to embark and traverse to the realms of the spirit world.

A shadowy being in the canoe rose and spread enormous wings. Thunder rattled the ground, lightning flared and the ghosts scattered. *Hiilinga*, Thunderbird, one of the most powerful of all the spirits.

Charlie cowered, but the white raven's spirit remained, unafraid. It leaped on board. The spirits in the canoe could not set foot on this side of the river or else they couldn't return to the spirit realm, but they could enter this world.

Charlie recognized *Xuuadjii*, Grizzly Bear, *Ghuudj*, Wolf, and *Xhuuya*, Raven. The others were too indistinct to make out. All ancients. But why were they gathered here?

The shaman hid behind a rock and waited until Thunderbird's terrible shaking subsided. A swirl of light enveloped first the white raven, then some of the others. The essence of the white raven merged into the larger, dark profile of Raven. Raven, and Grizzly Bear, and Wolf stepped ashore.

Charlie gasped. The vessel, with the shadowy figures of the other ancients, began to return to the far side of the river. He shook his head. This was not good.

Raven, Bear, and Wolf walked past him, heading to the woods that marked the entry to this world. The trio left only one set of footprints.

Raven's.

This had been Rosemary's vision. The death of the Golden Spruce released the white raven, and now Raven himself had returned.

At that precise moment Raven turned his head and stared at the rock where Charlie hid.

"A spy," Raven croaked, waving a wing in his direction. Charlie spun around as tendrils of energy rose and wrapped around his feet, then shot out over the waters of green bile, attaching themselves to the spirit canoe.

"No," he screamed as the roots of energy snapped tight and began to drag him towards the macabre vessel. Raven smirked and disappeared along the trail leading towards the earthly realm. A world Charlie would not be able to return to if he reached the far shore. At least, not in this lifetime.

The shaman struggled, but the bonds held him tight. He splashed into the waters reeking of purulent decay, gagging on the acrid taste.

"Think, damn it, think," he shouted, spitting out mouthfuls of bile. His hand brushed against the talisman of the land otter's tongue hanging around his neck.

He could see the approaching shore. Many figures milled about, among them several old friends. "Come, live with us. It is so good to see you," they cried in welcome.

The land otter spirit appeared just as Charlie came alongside the canoe.

"Sever the lines, fast," he called out, his will to return to the normal world eroding. He wanted so much to stay in the spirit realm, with his friends and relatives. So many he missed. But among them, one person was absent. The one he'd give anything to see again.

A female emerged from the crowd. He recognized the sensuous stride even before he recognized the face and body of Lucy Klintu. She died in his arms, many years ago when he was in his early twenties and struggling to become a shaman. He'd been unable to save her.

Grief welled up from his soul; far too many years he'd spent without her.

Lucy raised her arms. "Charlie, come and be with me. I miss you so." She was as radiant as he remembered. He couldn't go to her; he had to go back, warn the others of what he had witnessed here.

"Lucy, my love. I will return, but not yet," Charlie promised.

"Hurry. I'll be waiting for you."

The land otter snapped at the last tendrils of energy. A shadowy being reached from the canoe to pull him up onto the shore. The sisiutl he'd thought was carved into the prow was no carving. It turned one of its scaly heads and bared its fanged teeth, its breath reeking death.

Charlie broke free and sank into the river.

* * *

They traveled in silence for half an hour, Charlie slipping in and out of semi-consciousness, muttering strange words. Chelen said some of it was Haida and the rest was no language she'd ever heard.

"It's not uncommon for a shaman to speak other tongues when he's in a trance." She mentioned it casually, as if it were an everyday occurrence.

Brook stared at the road as he drove. All the talk about native beliefs and shamanic travels to other worlds was too far-fetched. Not only was it lunacy, but it had no scientific basis. That was what drove him as a journalist; finding the facts, proving the story. How'd he prove this?

He shuddered, creepy sensations washing over him again as he thought about the pouch. He hadn't imagined the mist, or the voices, or the thing that moved inside. Just like he hadn't imagined the strange creature standing under the cedar tree.

Maybe there was a logical explanation somewhere. What about the stuff Charlie lit up? Maybe that had some mind-altering capabilities? He'd have to check it out later. The facts, they were all that mattered.

"How'd he know?" Brook broke the silence.

"Know what?"

"Know I was going to look in his medicine bag."

"Ask him when he comes to. Like I said before, shamans walk in realms we know nothing of. All I know is, I had turned my back for a second and was digging through my pack when the canoe lurched and next thing I know I'm waist deep in water. At first I thought it was you, returning with his pouch. When I did look up, I saw Charlie running past the Golden Spruce so fast I don't think I could've kept up with him. By the time I got to shore, he was gone."

"Run? Doesn't he have a heavy limp or something? I mean, he relies on that cane quite a bit."

"Sure does. He injured his leg a long time ago."

Charlie had barely stirred since he'd collapsed at the Golden Spruce, muttering something about Chelen and a white raven. Brook stared at the pouch and nearly slammed on the brakes when he swore he saw it move again. Charlie mentioned an old shaman gave it to him. No doubt it'd be easy enough to find out the shaman's name and check with the birth registry to see if such a person existed. But what would that prove? He was beginning to doubt his own sanity. He'd not forget the face of the thing that grabbed him while he'd been in the trance with Chelen. A face formed of ancient soils, decaying leaves and decomposed remains.

And the eyes ... No, that was something no one ever forgot.

He pushed it from his mind. Maybe it was safer to think about mythological monsters. "Is there anything in the Haida legends regarding a brownish creature that stands nearly as tall as a man, has arms growing out of its chest, and lips that seem pulled back?"

"Land otter spirit, or maybe *kushtakas*, the sea otter people. Why?"

"It was brief, only a second, but I thought I saw something under that cedar."

"Did you look in Charlie's pouch?"

"No, but it was weird, like I had no control. Almost as if something was forcing me to look inside. Then Charlie ran up."

"Well, both land otter spirit, and the *kushtakas*, can steal your will. Charlie controls land otter spirit, one of the strongest powers to obtain. It may have been on guard, protecting the pouch, or Charlie."

"I don't understand. What do you mean by *controls*?"

Chelen cleared her throat. "Okay, here comes some more of that textbook stuff I learned." She grinned, and he sensed she was trying to lighten her anxiety over her uncle. "When a shaman begins his initiation he undergoes rigorous rituals. He drinks the juice of devil's club, abstains from sex, doesn't cut his hair, and fasts. When he's ready, he goes out into the wilderness looking for the animal spirits he's most connected to. One of the most powerful is the land otter spirit. The shaman must confront this creature, which can control his mind, and must stare at it until the animal is mesmerized. Then he cuts a piece of its tongue and keeps it as a source of his power over the land otter. But he must maintain his daily rituals to stay strong. He does this for every animal spirit he wants to control, so he can use it when he's traveling in the other realms."

"So you believe it was this land otter spirit that was protecting him?"

"Possibly. Or, you could have seen a *kushtaka*. They're reported to call out to people lost at sea, disguising themselves as deceased relatives. Once they've captured their victims they take them beneath the ocean, where they live in their village. The *kushtakas* are elusive, shadowy creatures ... normally you can't see them at all. Other times you can only hear them, and sometimes you'll experience the furriness of your own arms and legs as you begin to transform."

Brook frowned. "Is this kinda like becoming a native version of a werewolf?"

"Similar, perhaps, except they aren't evil beings, just deceptive. There are some defenses against them. Human blood will erase their human shape, and urine eliminates their contamination. Metal will ward them off."

"You mightn't think they're evil, but to me they sound like nasty creatures."

"They're not really. Only a shaman can travel to a *kushtaka* village and attempt to rescue someone."

"Figures." Brook drove on in silence, digesting the information. He'd entered another world in Haida Gwaii. Why the hell hadn't he listened to his intuition and jumped back on that ferry?

* * *

Raven landed heavily by the Golden Spruce tree. Weary, every part of him hurt with an unfamiliar tiredness. He stretched one black wing but it kept kinking on him, wanting to bend at an unnatural angle. If this was aging, he didn't like it. He had to find his immortal stone and try to help his people. His heart sank. Too much for him to handle in his current state. As much as it rankled him to admit it, he needed help.

Closing his eyes he called to all the Corvidae in the area. As each responded, Raven connected with them. After all, they were only versions of him. Each a part of him, linked by dim memory.

One bird told him of three people, two Haida and one pale-skinned, who visited the Golden Spruce recently. The one not of this land, he'd picked up a dark blue stone.

"Where are they?" Raven asked.

"They left by truck earlier."

"Truck? What kind of creature is that?"

The other raven relayed a mental picture.

"I already met other metal creatures with round feet that help the hornet boxes take down the trees and spew noxious fumes," Raven told him. "This truck looks the same, only smaller and red in color like currants."

"Much more than that is different since you last flew in this world. Here, let me show you."

Raven absorbed the bird's knowledge and memories.

* * *

Brook drove up the rough track to Charlie's cabin, just outside Skidegate. An unpainted wooden porch ran around the front and a sooty chimney poked up through the moss-overgrown cedar roof. Charlie was still moaning and muttering. When Brook checked his forehead, the shaman was wet with sweat. Beads of perspiration dripped onto the leather neck thong crusted with odd bits of animal skin and bones.

"Shouldn't we be getting him to the nearest hospital? He looks pretty sick," he asked as they jumped from the truck and pulled Charlie out.

"No, he only looks sick. He's just battling something in the other worlds. I've seen this before, only not usually this bad." Chelen grunted as between them, they carried him to his cabin. Brook suspected she was in denial; he was pretty sure the old man was on his way out.

"You got the keys?" he asked, hefting Charlie's dead weight.

"Keys?" She laughed.

"Oh, silly thing to say. Let me guess, no one would think of breaking into a shaman's house."

"Right. Because you just know he'll find out who did it and send some horrible muck monster after you."

"You kinda read my mind." Brook pushed the front door inward. Around it, and the windows, was stapled some sort of plant. "What's this stuff?"

"Spiny devil's club. It wards off diseased spirits."

"Kind of like garlic is meant to keep away vampires?"

"Yes, that's fairly close."

They entered the dark interior, dragging the barely conscious elder.

"What the — " Brook jumped as something brushed against his head and shoulders.

"And those are cedar boughs, meant to cleanse visitors as they enter."

They rested for a moment in the dim interior. "Tell me, does a modern-day shaman believe in electricity?" He was sure he'd be searching for candles.

"Yes, but only in the room in the back, where his TV is. Charlie would die if couldn't catch his Toronto Blue Jays. Here, where he does his healing work, there's no electricity. It interferes with the natural magnetic energy of the earth."

"Figures."

"But there're candles in the drawer near the back wall, and I think he keeps a flashlight to the left of the door."

"Blue Jays fan. Too bad, and I was just beginning to like the guy." He left Chelen supporting Charlie while he groped around for the flashlight.

He flicked it on and jumped backward. A multitude of bizarre faces stared at him. "Holy," he gasped.

"Yes, Charlie has quite the collection of masks. Now, can you help me put him to bed?" Chelen was struggling to hold up the shaman, whom he'd momentarily forgotten about.

"Ah, sorry."

They moved into another room, Brook straining to hold the flashlight under his arm and carry Charlie at the same time. As gently as possible, they placed Charlie on the edge of the single bed.

Chelen straightened up. "Okay, if you can fire up the lantern, I'll see to Charlie from here on."

"Sure." He fumbled for the matches sitting on top of the dresser, and took the glass casing off the coal oil lantern. He lit the wick and imagined a hundred faces peered at him, eyes glimmering in the flickering glow. Something creaked in a dark corner, and he jumped. "Friendly place. I'll bet he must hold some great parties here," he muttered to himself.

"Go ahead and look around, but don't touch anything. Can you light the rest of the lanterns while I put him into bed?"

"Oh, don't worry. If he has a land otter spirit guarding his pouch, I'd hate to find out what's lurking in this decrepit cabin. Great décor, early twentieth-century shamanic and everything, but definitely not recommended as an up-and-coming B and B."

As he turned up the flame, yet more faces loomed in the blackness. Some with hideous features, others comical, and others locked in expressions of terror, or wonderment.

"What an incredible collection," he said as he slowly circled the room.

"Sure is." Chelen unbuttoned Charlie's shirt and removed his baseball cap. "Charlie picked them up from various tribes around the world. I know he uses some of them in his dances and healing ceremonies. Others are just for his enjoyment."

Brook went to light the two lanterns at each end of the front room. Most of the wooden facemasks were of First Nations design, but he spotted a couple of Japanese theatre masks as well. "So this must be what a shaman does in his spare time," he called to Chelen. "Some hobby. D'you think he'd let me take some photos of these?"

"Maybe, but you'll have to wait until he's awake before you do. He's mentioned some of them are very fragile energy-wise and he wouldn't want your face-puller to steal part of that."

"Face-puller?" He squinted at several more of the masks. One caught his attention, a bird with its face split in half, and inside, a wide-eyed human stared out, mouth gaping. He'd seen several like it at the museum. They were transformation masks, representing Raven shifting into human form.

"When our ancestors first encountered cameras, they thought the boxes were pulling their faces off and stealing part of their soul. Charlie tends to believe that and refuses to have his picture taken, ever. He says it's in the shaman handbook under —"

"Oh, let me guess. Subsection thirteen, paragraph eight, entitled 'Face Pulling, or the Ritualistic Aspects of Photographic Equipment Usage'." They both laughed, knowing that was probably exactly what Charlie would have said if he were conscious.

"But while we're on the subject of picture-taking, there's something you should know. Before you start snapping away at the totems you see in front of some peoples' homes, you'd better ask their permission. Many get upset by strangers taking photos."

"I can see why now. Thanks for the advice." He caught sight of the old stone fireplace. "How about I put on a fire? It's a mite chilly in here."

"Good idea. I'm just about done with Charlie."

Brook didn't spot any firewood next to the blackened grate, so he walked through another doorway and shone the flashlight into that room. "Wow," was all he said as he stared into the shadowy space. Plants of different types hung from the ceiling. He lit a lantern in the corner. Most of the jars on the shelves had handwritten labels. Powdered spruce, hairy rock cress leaves, devil's club, skunk cabbage leaves, crushed sea anemone, bear gall, yarrow, maidenhair fern. The list seemed endless. When he cracked a lid and sniffed at the contents, he gagged on the odor.

"Hey, didn't I tell you not to touch anything?" Chelen stood in the entranceway, hands folded across her chest.

The glow of the lanterns accented her curves. Her hair was disheveled from carrying Charlie. Brook fought the unwelcome throb inside his jeans. Damn him, for letting his testosterone run away with him. How would he be able to kayak with her for nearly a week? He blinked.

125

"Sorry. I've just never seen crushed sea star in a jar before. My curiosity got the better of me. Is Charlie going to be okay?"

"Well, he's resting now. I think he'll be coming around shortly. I'm going to stay, but you should head home. No offense intended. I can start a fire later. Charlie keeps the wood out back."

"I understand. How far is it to where my rental truck is parked?"

"Go back down the road to the stop sign, hang a left and take the second right. That'll put you back on the main road. It's about five minutes from there. Go ahead and take Charlie's vehicle, but leave the keys in it when you're done. I'll pick it up sometime tomorrow."

"I guess there can't be much theft out here." He walked from the room, past Chelen still standing in the doorway.

"There's some. Let's just say being a shaman has its advantages. Like you said, who would steal from Charlie?"

"That's probably under subsection eleven of the shaman's manual."

Chelen laughed. He continued to the front door, and she followed him. Just outside, he turned to say goodbye.

"Thanks for an interesting day, and most of all, for the pleasure of your company."

"Thank you, Brook."

"When will you be ready to go to Sghaan Gway?" Against his better judgment, what he really wanted to say was when can I see you again.

"Well, my grandmother's funeral is tomorrow. I'm not sure, but perhaps I should decline this trip. It really isn't a good time. I know of another guide."

"Well, I can understand that. I'm sorry your grandmother died. But I'd like to spend some more time with you. I trust you and that's important on a kayak expedition. Besides, I was told you were the best." He gave her a long look. "If I'm honest, I'm fascinated. By you ... by the depth of your knowledge. One of the things I love," that last word whispered from his tongue, "is learning about new things."

"Is that all I am to you? A history lesson."

"Far from it. I just meant that something you said at the Golden Spruce earlier struck a chord. About being guided here and meeting you. I guess I need to think about that, and about what happened today." The sudden urge to kiss her was hard to resist. More than anything, he wanted to kiss her. But even if he dared, now was not the time and place. She'd just lost her grandmother, and she had to be there for Charlie. "Look, I ... please don't let me scare you, but ..." His stomach was turning like a nest of upset bees. "I guess I just want to say I'd like to get to know you better. You're a fascinating woman, Chelen."

She paused, staring into his eyes. "Okay, I'll go on the trip. Do you have a preference on what style of kayak, tandem or single? I have two kinds, neckies and the fiberglass feather crafts."

"Single would be fine with me. But you're the pro, so I'll let you decide which would be best."

"Where are you staying? As I said, the funeral's tomorrow, but we could leave the day after. Maybe getting away would be better for me than hanging out here."

"Sure, and if I can help in any way with the funeral, let me know."

"That's sweet of you, but I'll be okay."

Charlie moaned in the background. "Look, I gotta go."

"Sea Raven Motel in Queen Charlotte City, room 303. See you in a couple of days." He took a step back on the porch. "Oh, I almost forgot, when Charlie came running up to me at the Golden Spruce, he muttered something I'm supposed to tell you. Something about seeing a white raven. He said it died."

Her face clouded. Obviously, Charlie's message made more sense to Chelen than it did to him.

"Thanks for passing that on. I'll ask him about it when he wakes up. As for the kayaking,

I'll leave a message at the motel tomorrow night regarding when and where we'll meet. And Brook." Her words were barely above a whisper. "I'll be honest and say that I'd like to spend a bit more time with you too. I guess I'm scared, but I'll explain more on our trip when we have the chance to talk."

He caught the glimmer of moisture in her eyes as she closed the door.

As Brook turned to leave, the hoot of an owl interrupted his thoughts. He jumped into Charlie's truck and locked the door, feeling a bit foolish but safer.

* * *

Chelen leaned on the closed door, clutching it for support as her knees buckled and her heart pounded louder than the biggest deerskin drums. "Oh, Creator, what am I doing? Why did I have to say I wanted to spend some time with him?"

It was painful to say she liked him. Why had she attracted another white man into her life? The first one tore her heart out. Brook wanted to kiss her, and she was tempted to let him.

Pushing the thought away, she hurried to check on Charlie. He still looked pretty pale. What did he mean, the white raven had died? She thought her encounter meant the beginning of changes. First, Rosemary's death, and now, meeting Brook. The white raven dying shone a negative light on everything.

"Lucy?" Charlie's head stirred on the pillow as she heard the truck drive away. She stroked his face and pulled the covers over him before sitting in the chair next to the bed. Charlie seemed to be sleeping now. She leaned back and closed her eyes. No use worrying about Brook. She had to concentrate on Charlie and besides she'd already let Brook pry open a corner of her heart she intended on opening.

* * *

Raven flew along the path of black stones laid so close they looked like one rock. His raven helper called it a highway. Raven was puzzled; it didn't look higher than anything else.

He felt stronger now he'd eaten. The other ravens brought him dying salmon, grubs, and something called a sandwich, stolen from the camper people. A new tribe he'd never heard of. But there was much in this world he hadn't heard about.

He had to find his people, his warriors.

As the sun set, Raven flew into one of the remaining villages. He marveled that humans had somehow captured sunlight and put it into round containers that burned at night, making it easier for him to see. He settled into a tree and watched the gathering of the beasts with the round feet, the trucks and cars. Music came from a building, loud and boisterous, not like anything he'd ever heard before. If the singers chanted to the spirits, they summoned no spirits he knew.

Even the longhouses were different with transparent sections of polished quartz and brightly colored surfaces. Gone were the great paintings of himself or other creatures he knew.

The greatest change was the totems. The carved stories were gone. Replaced with blank totems that trapped the sun's light, and others linked by long vines which he knew from the experiences he'd gained from the white raven were not safe to land on. But not a single watchman stood over any of them. So much had changed it made his head hurt. There was so much to do, and undo.

Raven grew sullen. Why would people listen to such odd music? Or was this the beginning of the winter ceremonials? He had to get inside and see for himself.

A truck pulled up near him with a single male inside. Good, he'd need a solitary human if he planned to slip inside his body. But then Raven recalled how tired he was after his transformation into the Bald Eagle. No, instead he'd just invade the human's mind, similar to how he'd communicated with the ravens.

Raven landed behind the vehicle. He tossed pebbles onto its roof and waited patiently, claws clicking on the gravel.

The door opened. "What the hell is going on?"

Rank, stale odors wafted upward as the man staggered out.

"Hey, you kids cut that out! Beat it, will ya or I'll —"

Raven pulled free from the shadows and drew himself up to his full height. He glared into the hazy depths of the warrior's eyes, expecting to meet resistance, and finding none. He was instantly sucked into the human's mind. It happened so fast, as if the man had no spirit of his own.

"No! What's happening?" Raven twirled around in the torpor of the man's head. He'd wanted to touch the mind in order to understand the world better; instead he'd got sucked into lunacy. As he spiraled down into the muddled, numbing depths, Raven blanked out.

* * *

It was late as Brook climbed out of his truck and slung the backpack over his shoulders before hiking up the stairs to the motel room. He'd swapped vehicles at the museum under the eyes of the Haida Watchmen, and left the keys in Charlie's truck as Chelen asked. His pack felt like a box of feathers. Actually, right now he could carry a dozen backpacks, two dogs, and a small horse. He fought down the guilt and smiled. It was okay to like someone new so soon after Georgina, wasn't it?

132

The sight of Chelen standing in the door to Charlie's cabin with tears in her eyes melted his heart. He'd wanted to hold her and offer comfort.

This was definitely turning into a trip he wouldn't forget.

Fumbling for the keys to his room, he pulled out the stone he'd found earlier at the Golden Spruce. He'd forgotten about it.

"Odd little pebble," he pondered as the light caught the rock, cradled in his palm. Out of habit he locked the door. Hell, if this were T.O. or the Big Apple he wouldn't be taking any chances. Did that make him paranoid? He set the stone on his nightstand. "What did she say this was ... lapis lazuli, that's it."

Beside it, he set the black feather, then headed towards the bathroom, where he peeled off his clothes and stepped into the shower. Tomorrow, he had to himself. He planned to head back to Tlell, and the office of the islands' newspaper. Mist and warmth soon relaxed his weary body. It had been a long day.

When he stepped out of the steamy bathroom, he caught a glimpse of the black feather on the nightstand through the open doorway.

"So, everything in the universe is connected by energy. Do you have any energy, my friend? What would you say if you could talk to me?"

He laughed. "I must be tired. I'm talking to a feather."

He slid into bed, suddenly realizing just how exhausted he was. The events of the day had drained him.

Absentmindedly, he rolled over to the empty side of the double bed and thought of Georgina. "You're just not good enough for me, Brook." Her parting words still carried a sharp sting.

His father's harsh words, spoken over and over when he failed at some task, ran through his mind. If praise was the natural state of the universe, then Brook lived in an unnatural state for most of his childhood.

"Damn." He hadn't realized how much it all hurt.

Did he honestly think Chelen would like him? They were from different worlds. The last thing he saw before his eyes closed was the stone and the feather.

A while later, Brook bolted upright, sweat pouring off him. Paling moonlight streamed through the window. Stupid nightmare. He was making love to Chelen when she turned into a large white raven and then into the creature he'd seen under the cedar tree earlier. *God, how freaky is that?* 3:36 in the morning. He felt like he hadn't been asleep for more than a couple of hours, but the northern sun would be rising soon.

Brook threw back the blankets, sauntered over to the window, and opened it. The light from the nearly-full moon in the clear sky flooded the landscape. Over the ocean the sky shimmered with the northern lights. He smiled. His mother used to tell him that the aurora borealis was the souls of the dead. He'd have to ask if the Haida believed that as well.

Scratching himself between the legs, he headed into the washroom and relived himself, still trying to recall the details of the nightmare.

"Brook."

"What the ..." He jumped at the unexpected summons. A splatter of urine sprayed his leg. "Damn."

Who the hell, or what, was calling him? A chill ran down his spine ...

"Brook, I need to talk. Are you awake?"

"Huh?" He crossed the room and stuck his head out the window. Chelen stood in the parking lot illuminated by the moonlight.

"Will you let me in? I need to talk to you."

"Ah, just give me a minute. I got to put on some clothes." He rifled through his backpack and threw on a sweatshirt and sweatpants. When he opened the door Chelen fell into his arms.

"Is everything okay? Is Charlie okay?"

"Charlie's fine. I'm not."

Brook held her while she sobbed, stroking her hair, surprised by its silkiness. She hugged him tighter, pressing her breasts against him. He was certain she had on no bra, and a hot pulse seared its way into his groin. One of his hands ran down her back. She wore no panties under the black leggings that hugged her curves.

"I … I just need someone to talk to. I had a horrible dream. I dreamt a huge raven broke into Charlie's cabin after you left and plucked his heart out. It was so vivid, so horrible."

She looked up, tears streaming down her cheeks. Then, her words finally registered. She dreamed of Raven. Recollections of his eerily similar nightmare hammered at him. The reality of her body pressed against him chased the thoughts from his mind. Nightmare, who cared about a nightmare when he had a fantasy springing to life in his arms?

He struggled, but couldn't stop his growing excitement. She surely felt it too, and responded by pressing harder against him.

"Kiss me, Brook. I wanted you to kiss me earlier, but I didn't have the courage to ask. Kiss me now."

Each rise of her breasts sent shivers through him. He wanted her in the worst way. Brook closed his eyes and bent his head to hers. A moan escaped her, exciting him even more. His tongue darted out, finding hers.

"I need you," she whispered, her hand sliding downwards. The coolness of her fingers, the firm pressure as she rubbed, sent him over the edge.

"Oh, God," he gasped, the ache too powerful to deny any longer. He peeled off his shirt and pants, and Chelen did likewise. He drank in the sway of those full breasts, the brown nipples standing erect. He flung aside the covers and hesitated. "Darn, I don't have any rubbers."

She slid under the sheets. "Don't worry, you won't need protection," she said. "I won't give you time to get any."

It seemed so natural to have her press him back into the softness of the mattress, ease herself on top of him and slide herself down onto him. She was already wet so he thrust into her. He groaned excited by the subtle domination she held over him.

"Yes," Chelen cried. "Oh God, not yet."

Brook fought to keep himself from exploding, but it had been so long since he'd made love to anyone. Glass shattering stopped him at the edge of orgasm. A large object smashed its way through the window and crashed to the floor by the bed. Whatever it was, it was alive.

Chelen screamed. Brook pushed her off him and shielded her with his body. The tall black figure stood up and spread its wings, dwarfing them both.

Chapter Seven

Glass sparkled in the moonlight. Chelen screamed again. Brook leaped up, grabbing the bedside lamp for a weapon. He cursed at the jagged slivers of glass slicing his feet.

A human-sized raven spread his wings wider, blocking the moonlight.

An eerie wail shattered the air. Brook turned to see Chelen's image shifting. The lips pulled back in a grimace, brown fur sprouting on her naked body, odd short arms growing from her chest while her own arms shrank. She was turning into the creature he'd seen at the Golden Spruce yesterday. A *kushtaka*?

"No!" He'd been tricked, damn it! Brook dropped the lamp. The otter leaped at the same time Raven flew towards him, beak closed in a spear aimed at his heart. What the hell did he just make love to? Not Chelen, that much was certain.

* * *

The sky was beginning to lighten in the east when the modern-day warrior's head jerked back. Raven hurt all over as he finally managed to pull free. He'd never try to go into someone's mind again while they were under the influence of the fire water. It wasn't until the spirits had started to wear off that he could regain enough of his will to retreat. Most of the night was a complete blur. Whatever infected the man's mind – booze, he'd called it – had a disastrous effect on Raven.

He coughed, his lungs hurt, and his head was pounding. The man smoked small versions of the peace pipe all night long, not to mention the building where they held the winter ceremonial had been filled with others doing the same thing.

Raymond Brown slumped over into the front seat of his truck. Beside him was a box of the liquids that smelled of grains, hops, and bitterness, but the drink was intoxicating. It burned his guts, set fire to his mind, and dulled the senses. Why would anyone torture themselves like that?

Raven shook his head. He studied Raymond's face, puckered and swollen, scarred from battles, internal battles haunting his soul. What happened to his spirit? This warrior had no discipline, no training. No belief in anything, no honor for himself. The man possessed no guardian spirit, no connection to the universe. From what Raven had seen last night, there were many others like him. This must be, at least in part, what happened to his people.

He paused to look at Raymond, aged beyond his years, was like an apple, red on the outside and white inside. Raven felt the sorrow. Raymond was still one of his people.

He sighed. A dream catcher hung in the front window of the truck, a crow's feather clung to it with the tip dipped in white paint to make it look like an eagle's.

Raven didn't want to take the risk, and weaken himself further. He closed his eyes and merged with the man again, where he pulled back the matted rug of alien culture and searched for the seed of native essence. He would find it, if it existed.

Raven would deny the man his true culture no longer. He punched his beak through the civilized wrappings, setting the mists of Raymond's heritage free. Raven wanted to do more, but the weariness told him he needed rest.

He could do more though. As he returned to his own body, Raven flung a dream at the dream catcher. Let it help Raymond heal.

* * *

Brook woke up with a gasp and jerked upright, his feet hitting the cold floor. "Holy shit, it was just a dream." He searched the room, just to be sure. In the dim light he could barely see the time: 3:36 in the morning.

"What I'd give for a cigarette right about now." He'd quit three years ago and this was the first time in a while he'd craved one.

It was just a bad dream. Brook laughed as he got up to pee. The room was cold and the curtains billowed in the wind. "What the ... how did the window get open?" He walked over and closed it as he returned from the bathroom, his gaze fell on the empty nightstand. He stopped dead — the feather and the lapis lazuli stone were gone.

His heartbeat thundered in his ears. He flicked on the lamp and scanned the room. No broken glass, no feather, no stone. He pulled back the blankets and in the folds at the foot of the bed lay the lapis lazuli, the feather beside it.

"Nuts, this is nuts. Perhaps you do have some energy after all," he muttered as he replaced them on the nightstand and slid back under the cooling covers.

* * *

Raven flew to the Skeena River, across the great stretch of water that separated his islands from the rest of this world. All the change, the decline of his people; it was all too much to bear.

Raven croaked, the sorrow filling his heart as he flew. Would this have happened if he hadn't become trapped in the Golden Spruce and abandoned them when they needed him the most? His eyes narrowed. He'd not abandon them now.

Raven needed to restore his people to their former glory.

Before he retrieved his immortal stone, he had to do this. Begin the cycle of the return of the ancient ones. He must awaken the spirit beings.

Finally, he reached the vast land on the other side of the strait that was home to his people's enemies, the Nisga'a and the Tsimshian. Along the Skeena River he flew until he came to the jagged rock next to the shore. His wing threatened to buckle on him again, reminding him how fast old age was setting in. He settled on the opposite riverbank, took several deep breaths, and crowed three times. Once to the heavens, the second time to the earth, and a third time to the waters in between. Those three pitched tones, unheard for many centuries, penetrated not only time and place, but reached realities that once were common on earth. Not since Raven had first visited Rose Spit and found the clamshell with the featherless pink beings inside had he tried this spell. He couldn't repeat such a great feat today, but he had to start the process.

His breath crystallized in the cool air. Long moments of silence ticked by. Nothing happened, though he was certain this was the transformer rock of the Snag.

Stone grating on stone broke the morning stillness. Raven glared across the water to where the boulder shimmered, its mottled gray shape beginning to soften. Another rasp of rock, and it wiggled as its lines shifted. He smiled to himself. Yes, he had picked the right rock. It blistered and shuddered as it transformed. The creature that emerged scraped its way to the water's edge, lifted its head and stared across at Raven. Elongated, jagged teeth revealed themselves and reptilian eyes submerged as it slid beneath the waves. Its long tail, lined with barbs of hardened flesh and rock, slapped the surface before vanishing. Bubbles betrayed its presence as it headed towards Raven. For the first time in hundreds of years, the Snag swam the Skeena River.

The bubbles stopped just in front of Raven. Then, slowly, the hideous head rose, pebbles embedded in the flesh. With the river flowing past and water streaming from its bulk, the ancient creature regarded him with emotionless eyes. The Snag used its massive head to ram the canoes of the local tribes long ago. Now the beast would sink other crafts.

The Snag was close enough that Raven gagged on its rancid breath. It wasn't happy to have been disturbed from its slumber. Raven held his ground, even though the beast could spring from the waters and swallow him whole.

"Swim across the wide waters and into the Yakoun River. Find the canoes of the pale-skinned ones. They have fouled our land and made us weak," he croaked.

The slitted eyes blinked, and wordlessly, the Snag slipped underwater. Raven watched as it moved down the Skeena towards the strait.

It had begun. He called and gathered the other ravens again. They would become his eyes and ears, help him find the one he sought.

He had to locate the pale-skinned human and trick him into returning his immortal stone. The ancients decreed he couldn't steal it back. A foul trick that was, as they knew how good he was at trickery. Curse them.

Chapter Eight

A warm breeze stirred through the open door, temporarily cooling the stifling heat as Brook walked into the reception area of the islands only newspaper, the *Northern Islander Report*. It was the only newspaper on the Charlottes. The small room was crowded with clippings pasted on the wall, books lined along the floor, bundles of newspapers piled in a corner. Early on in his journalism apprenticeship, Brook worked in the same kind of office.

He smiled at the memory of those younger days spent with the *Guardian* in Gibbons, Alberta. An experience he'd never forget, nor want to. He'd learned so much working there.

He shivered in the summer heat. In the middle of all the chaos, a man looked up from one of the two desks. He grinned. "Hi, my name's Brook Grant and I was wondering if I could go through your archives. I'm looking for any stories you might have run on the Golden Spruce" He hoped the gentleman wouldn't ask for his ID. He didn't want to let on he was a reporter.

"Doing research, hey? Sorry about the heat in here, the AC went on the fritz last week and like everything else it takes forever to get parts from the mainland. Well, enough of the apologies. Bob Burns is the name my parents hung me with." He rose and offered Brook his hand, an infectious smile lighting his face. "I don't get too many visitors in these parts, but sure, do come in. Just ignore the mess. The archive room is in back. I spent the last two months putting it all onto the computer, wanted to make this business a little more attractive to prospective buyers. Right now though I'm in the middle of a hot lead story for the next issue, due this afternoon." He glanced at his watch. "In fact, I'm late. Please, come this way."

Bob directed him behind the counter and into another small room tucked around the corner. As they walked past Bob's desk Brook glanced at the computer screen.

Native Elder witness to sport boat crushed in Yakoun River. Claims Snag did it.

Extremely rare White Raven killed by encounter with electrical transformer.

He stopped and stared in disbelief. "Hey, you're right, interesting stories." He wanted to ask more about the lead article, but Bob was obviously pressed for time.

The story about the white raven; Charlie told him it was going to happen. How did the old shaman know?

"I have to apologize. Normally, I'd sit down and chat with you. But I've saved a rough draft, so if you want you can read it while you do your research. Tourist, are you, Brook?" Bob smiled under his mustache and removed his sherlock

Holmes style deerstalker cap, revealing the baldness underneath. He wiped at the sweat gathered there.

"Just passing through."

"I figured so. I know everyone around here. Well, seeing as I've delayed the press run for today's issue, we don't get much hot news in these parts ... other than Mrs. Johnson winning the Friday night bingo, again. Fifth time this year. So maybe another time. Go ahead and help yourself to a coffee. Been brewing for a few hours, but still, it's not too strong. Do you know how to access the data?"

"I'm quite familiar with the program. But, thank you." He took the chair Bob indicated and immediately located the draft of Bob's articles.

Hank Johnson and his grandmother, Margaret, witnessed the destruction of the sport fishing boat The Tyee Hunter, owned by Bill Manley, earlier today. It is believed the vessel went down in the Yakoun River with all hands aboard.

The Johnsons reported seeing an object that Margaret claimed was the legendary Snag, which normally haunts the Skeena River and has been rumored to sink unsuspecting canoes. When interviewed, she said she saw the Snag swimming in the middle of the wreckage. She described it as a large creature, reptilian in nature, with huge slitted eyes and green toad-like skin.

This comes right after several people have reported seeing a man-sized black raven, and the most unusual sighting of an albino raven.

Brook sat for a moment in thought. "What insanity. Snags, Kushtakas, Shamans, Ravens. These islanders are crazy," he mused. Still, there had to be a grain of truth in there somewhere. He searched back through a few issues until he came to the article involving the Golden Spruce and scanned it, finding nothing he didn't know already.

The opening of the front door and the thud of heavy boots stopped Brook in his research.

"Bob, whose vehicle is parked out front? The rental, a Chevy Blazer."

He recognized the gravel voice almost immediately. Officer Miles Courtney. Thankfully, the computer in the archive room couldn't be seen from the front desk and judging by the tone in Miles' voice, the cop was not looking to take him for coffee. He remained hidden.

Brook could see Bob, though, and the fellow glanced in his direction. Brook shook his head.

"Why don't you call the rental outfit? I'm a little busy right now," Bob replied. "Some tourist parked there. I think he's gone off hiking, maybe along the Pesuta trail. Though why anyone would want to look at some old shipwreck is beyond me. Anyways, he wandered off with a backpack."

"That frantic tone in your voice usually means you've got a hot article to fiddle with. I'll bet you got wind of the incident involving the fishing boat." Courtney grunted. "I can't have you printing that, you know. It'll only panic people."

"Sorry, no can do. I don't get many lead stories, other than the local human-interest crap, and I've done enough of those to make me puke. The only other exciting news this past week was that albino raven getting fried to a crisp by a power pole, and what Raymond Brown says he saw. It's wild, claims he met a raven as tall as him, and the thing talked to him."

"Now that's a load of bull. Only thing ever talked to Raymond was the bottom of a bottle."

"Maybe so, but he swears he's giving up drinking and wants to start up a native warrior program for reformed alcoholics, something called 'Raven's Work.' Even phoned and asked if I'd run some PR for him."

"Raymond quit drinking? I don't believe that in a million years. The bottle and him have been married forever. Look, Bob, you can't go around spreading vicious rumors like this. Ever since the Golden Spruce was cut down, I've been getting nothing but crazy incidents from people. Seeing spirits, visions, you haven't heard the half of it. They're pretty upset about the whole thing, and I hate to think what'll happen if they read about the Snag sinking a white man's boat. Incite them into a frenzy, then we'll have a real battle on our hands. D'you want to see the Feds come in here like they did down East with that reserve's battle over the golf course?"

"Look, Miles, I talked to Margaret myself earlier. I tell ya, she saw it all. Her face was still white as snow. It's my duty to get the story to the public. Damn it, I'm a reporter. It's my job."

"Hey, Bob, get off your high horse and look at reality for a minute. The Haida are pretty cranky over the fact it was a white guy took down the Golden Spruce. Being one myself, I have some idea where they're coming from. You get that warrior blood fired up and there's no telling what could happen ... to any of the white folk around here, yourself included. Tell you what, can you at least tone it down a little? Maybe drop the hype about the Snag. Is that too much to ask?"

Brook watched Bob's face for his reaction. He knew what his own answer would be.

"I hope that wasn't a threat of violence, Miles. But okay, I see your point. I'll tone it down."

Brook felt his admiration for the other journalist drop. He'd never let small-town politics interfere with a story, never had when he worked in Gibbons. It was something that eventually got him promoted to the Vancouver paper before he moved on to the *Toronto Star,* and then the *New York Times.*

"Thanks, Bob. Say, has there been a reporter from the big city snooping around lately? Blond, thinning a little on top, stands about five-ten. If you see him, let me know, and don't let him know you know anything. The fewer loose lips the better."

"Sure."

Brook heard the officer leaving and the cruiser start up and drive away. He stood up and walked to the doorway of the back office. Bob met him there.

"So, you're a reporter, are you? I kinda figured it. I could smell a fellow newshound a mile away."

"Yes, I am. Can you promise to keep this off the record?"

"Guess so."

"I just don't want anyone to know that I work for the *New York Times.*"

"That right? You sure don't sound American."

"Correct on that one. Moved there recently from the *Toronto Star.* I've also worked for Vancouver and Alberta papers. I came up here for a holiday about eight years ago." He reached into his pocket and pulled out a business card. "I'll trust you to keep this quiet. I'm doing a little digging into the incident with the Golden Spruce. I figure the natives might have had something to do with Gordon Chatwick's death. I thought I'd check it out, and wouldn't you know it, I already had a run-in with your friendly constable. Miles can be a little pushy, don't you think?"

"That's just the way he is. Born-with-spur-stuck-in-butt, he should have been named. Did you find anything interesting out there? I haven't had the chance to go up to the site yet myself. Although I wanted to ... sure got the natives riled up. Not only that, but a few crazy things have been happening since that tree got cut down." Bob fumbled in his vest pocket and pulled out his own business card. "Keep it, and if you know of anyone who might be interested in owning an island newspaper, I've got this business up for sale, so pass it around. And yes, my lips are sealed. It crossed my mind that the Haida would get pretty upset by what happened to the Golden Spruce, but it never occurred to me they might have done Chatwick in. I'd be damn careful poking around, if I were you."

"I haven't found any evidence of that, yet. But I couldn't help catching part of your conversation. Did I hear you say Raymond claims to have seen an oversized raven?"

"Yup, that's what he said. Whatever he saw has done him a world of good. There's not many natives out here that drink, but Raymond was one of them. The experience changed his life. I saw the look in his eyes, and he was serious all right. Something's definitely changed inside, given him the balls to quit the booze."

"Interesting. Have you got his address?"

"Not offhand, but I'm sure I can find it for you."

"I also couldn't help seeing the title of one of the stories you're working on. The white raven being killed by an electrical transformer."

"Yeah. Too bad, though."

"Oh, why's that?"

"Well, from what I've gathered from the natives, a white raven is a sign of change and beginnings. But as a reporter, I know it's nothing but an albino version of a normal raven. Rare, I'll grant you that. And funny that it would show up just after the Golden Spruce ruckus, and then this other incident with the fishing boat happens."

As Bob chattered on, Brook stuck his hand in his pockets looking for a pen so he could jot down Raymond's number. Instead, he found the lapis lazuli he'd picked up at the Golden Spruce. After the weird dream, or whatever had gone on last night, he'd felt a compulsion to bring the stone with him.

"Here's that number you wanted. Hey, what's that you got there?"

"Oh, this. Actually, it's about the only thing I did find up at the Golden Spruce." He held it up to show Bob.

153

"It does capture the light magnificently, doesn't it? That's quite the rock."

The words came from a third voice. Bob and Brook both jumped and turned to stare at an elderly gentleman standing just inside the front door. It was anyone's guess how long he'd been there.

"I'm sorry if I startled you. The door was open so I just came in. I'm glad I did. That's quite the rock you have there," the stranger repeated. "Could I take a closer look at it?"

"Do I know you?" asked Bob.

"I … ah … am just visiting the Crow family on my holidays. My apologies, but I couldn't help overhearing your conversation. The body's getting old, but my hearing's still sharp. Now if I can just get the rest of the equipment to work." The old man laughed and tried to straighten his back. "I'm very interested in that gem you got there. You see, I'm a collector. Rock hound, you might call me."

"Sure," Brook blurted out and before he realized it, he was walking around the counter. His intuition was going off again, telling him something wasn't quite right about the old man. But the need to comply with what he was asking was as overwhelming as the urge to open Charlie's medicine pouch. Shivers ran down his spine at the remembrance. The longer he stared into the old man's eyes, the more he felt compelled to hand over the stone.

He stood very close, blocking the doorway, some internal urge making sure he wouldn't make a break for it.

The old guy smiled, but it only added to his sinister appearance. His eyes had that beaded, almost rapier-like quality of a bird of prey. Apart from anything else, it worried Brook that Bob didn't recognize him. Something was definitely wrong here.

The man scrutinized the rock, holding it against the sunlight streaming in. It sparkled in the reflection of his dark eyes. "Yup, it's a lapis lazuli all right."

Now Brook had relinquished the stone, the urge to obey was subsiding. He should step back out of courtesy, but didn't. What had come over him? He could afford to take no chances with the stranger.

"Lapis lazuli is a semiprecious stone with no real value. Just a rock, really. Did I hear you say you found it up by the Golden Spruce?"

"I did. Under some leaves to the left of the stump. I've been told it's not native to this area. Must have been dropped by some tourist, I figure."

"Would you like to go for a coffee? It's nearly noon and I'll bet you're hungry. I know of a Raven legend regarding a rock just like this one. Maybe if I can tell you a good enough story, you'll buy me lunch, sell me the stone, or both. Are you a collector?"

Brook shrugged. "It just caught my eye, I guess."

"Well, I don't have a lapis lazuli in my collection. Maybe I can convince you to part with it? What do you say?"

Again the odd compulsion washed over Brook, increasing in intensity. His stomach growled, as if it had been hours since he'd last eaten. "Sure, I'm always game to listen to a story, and if you can weave a good enough yarn, perhaps I'll even give you the rock. I've no real attachment to it."

Whatever made him say that? He hadn't felt hungry moments earlier, nor was he ready to give up the stone. Since the old guy had been holding it, the features on his lined face seemed to have grown younger. Brook stuck out his hand, palm upwards. "If you've finished, sir?"

"Oh, yes, of course." With a frown, he returned the stone to Brook just as Bob cleared his throat.

"Hang on. Before you go, Brook, I've found that article you wanted." He motioned Brook over.

As he broke away from the stranger's stare, Brook felt the compulsion fade. When he turned to Bob, the crusty editor gave him a hard glance.

"We'll just be a moment, sir."

"Sure, no hurry," he snapped.

Out of the man's earshot, Bob whispered to Brook, "I'm going with you for lunch, if you don't mind. There's something about that chap I don't trust."

"You, too? I got a funny sensation the second I saw him."

"I call it reporter's instinct. Not only that, did you see the way his eyes sparkled when he held that stone in his hands?"

"I sure did. I think it's far more valuable than he's letting on. But didn't you have an important lead feature to do?"

"I do have to write that article, but for some reason I was hungry the minute that guy walked in. I've never set eyes on him before, but I'd rather not leave you alone with him. Oh, and for your information, as far as I know, there is no Crow family living on the islands."

The two of them of them walked back to the front office.

"I've elected to join you for lunch," Bob announced. "My guts are growling. The River House is just up the street. Has a great view of the ocean, as well as some pretty good food."

"Sure, the more the merrier," the old man grumbled. His expression said he wasn't happy about having a tagalong.

Brook gave Bob a quick wink.

As the three of them entered the café, Brook noted the old man walked in a peculiar way. Stiff, as if he had two prosthetic legs. He also seemed to let them take the lead, like he was studying what they were doing and trying it out for the first time.

"Hi, Bob. How's your day so far? I see you've got company," the waitress greeted them.

"Hi, Cynthia. How's the young one doing? Yes, a couple of guys I met this morning. Brook here is a fellow reporter and Mr. ... ah ... I don't believe we caught your name."

"You guys can call me Marten. Marten Crow. Like I said earlier, I'm a rock hound, so I just putt around and collect stones, that sort of thing."

"What would you like to order, gentlemen?"

"I'll go for coffee, your clam chowder, and a ham and cheese sandwich," Brook said.

Bob gave his menu to Cynthia. "I'll have my usual."

"I ... uh ... didn't bring my glasses. Can you tell me what's on the menu?"

"Sure, I could practically recite it from memory." Bob laughed and reeled off the list of dishes.

"Coffee, the clam chowder, and two salmon sandwiches with fried potatoes sounds good."

"Holy," said Brook. "You're certainly trying to get your money's worth."

"Let's just say I have a big appetite. Now this story involves Raven and something called the immortal stone. The stone holds Raven's immortality and it is placed at the base of his

158

throat. If he ever lost it, he would become mortal and could be killed. He would also begin to age at a very rapid rate, as time is not friendly to those who have cheated it. Well, Raven did lose his immortal stone, and how that happened is open to speculation. But here's the version I know."

Brook was even more intrigued by Mr. Crow. His eyes would widen and squint upwards, his arms a-flap in constant gestures. Already, he felt himself in the presence of a consummate storyteller. "Does this legend involve the Golden Spruce? I've already heard two different accounts of it."

"Yes, it does. There are probably many variations, since the tale changes from being handed down, year after year, by different speakers."

As the waitress brought their meals and coffee, Brook and Bob listened attentively to Marten's story.

"Prince Kiidkayaas of Sghaan Gway set out on a quest to find a shaman who could cure his people of a mysterious sickness. In a place called Ttannu he met a man called Kungii of the Raven clan. In exchange for food, Kungii would lead the prince to this powerful shaman. But during the journey Kiidkayaas and his slave Wago tricked Kungii into revealing his true identity. Kungii was in fact Raven, the great transformer and trickster. After a great struggle,

during which Raven wounded the prince grievously, Kiidkayaas managed to reach into the bird's throat and steal Raven's immortal stone. Now, you see, the wily prince could force Raven to take him to find the one who could cure his people. The great northern shaman, Xatsinoo.

As Raven flew with Kiidkayaas astride him, snow began to fall, and the prince's knife tightened against Raven's throat. "Where do we fly to, Raven? I grow tired of this game."

"Patience, dear prince. You know that we are bound for Llaanas."

Raven clicked his beak in satisfaction. The snow he had called down was weakening Kiidkayaas. "Indeed, the snow becomes thicker. You are dressed for the southern weather. Hide among my feathers and they will help to keep you warm."

The prince shivered. "Keep flying."

At last, Raven tucked his wings in and landed. Winds howled around them as they set down in deep snow.

"I see no village," Kiidkayaas said as he dismounted, shivering in the cold.

"Ah, but you must be careful, dear prince. Xatsinoo has placed a spell to hide his village."

Kiidkayaas shook his head. "What now, Raven?"

Raven eyed the leather pouch around the prince's neck. He was sure the boy had tucked his immortal stone in there. "You will need to cover your clothing, as a southern prince would not be welcome here." He moved to a rock and produced a fur cloak, a headdress, and a pair of moccasins.

The prince donned the offered clothes, but stopped as he spied Raven glaring at his pouch, which he'd lain on the ground in order to fasten the heavy cloak. He snatched the pouch up and placed it back around his neck.

Raven shifted his glare to the prince. "We shall approach on foot, so as not to arouse any suspicion."

He turned and began to strut towards the village. The snow had already started to drift, and before long the prince was lagging behind.

"Wait," he cried, "I can't keep up to you."

Finally, Kiidkayaas looked over Raven's shoulder. As he did so, the raging snowstorm suddenly diminished, but instead of any village, he saw only the waters of the Yakoun River.

He faced Raven, knife in hand. "There is no village. You have tricked me."

"Ah, brave prince, you should not have looked so hard. There is a village here, and now you will have a very long time to look for it."

"What?" He tried to move and realized he couldn't. "What is happening to me?" He looked down at his feet. Tiny roots were spreading, anchoring him to the earth.

Raven cawed. "I have tricked you at last, foolish prince. The spell is not hiding the village. It is, instead, in the moccasins."

"E-i-i!" Kiidkayaas screamed his agony. He couldn't pull his feet from the moccasins as the roots had begun to grow up into his flesh. His skin took on a mottled woody hue, blood gelling into sap, slowing his mind. Pain transcended pain as his body thickened.

Raven plucked the pouch from the paralyzed prince's neck and quickly swallowed the stone he found inside.

"Safe," he crowed at the doomed warrior. "No one out-tricks Raven. I would have helped you, prince. But you are far too arrogant for your own good. A little time spent thinking about such behavior will perhaps teach you a lesson."

Kiidkayaas stayed silent, but just as bark was forming over his face, he stuck out his tongue. Nestled there was Raven's lapis lazuli stone.

"It is not I that is so foolish, Raven. I, too, can play tricks. Turn me back to what I was." The words came out with great effort.

"No!" Raven screamed and spat the fake stone from his mouth. It was too late to reverse the spell he had cast. The spruce tree he'd created had nearly finished trapping the prince and Raven's immortal stone. Raven had doomed himself to die.

162

He leapt for the small space where Kiidkayaas's face remained and flew inside the tree. The trunk bulged outward for a moment before solidifying again, black feathers fluttering to the snow.

That summer, the spruce tree containing Raven and Prince Kiidkayaas sprouted golden needles."

Bob leaned back in his chair after clearing his plate. "Now that's definitely a story worth listening to. I think, Brook, you could be out some lunch money. I've got to use the washroom, but I'll be right back." He rose and left the table.

Marten's face lit up with a big smile, but Brook shifted uneasily. One part of him wanted to hand over the lapis lazuli, but another told him to hold on to it. It would always remind him of Chelen, especially after that dream he'd had last night. He had a sudden urge to talk to her.

Something else was bugging him, gnawing away at his guts. Something about Marten's tale didn't jive with the version Tom Wilson told him at Ninstints. He needed to compare notes, and in the meantime, the compulsion to hand the rock over to Marten was overtaking him again. "Well, lunch is on me. Great story. But I've decided to keep the stone as a memento of my trip."

Marten sat still, his face turning a deep shade of red, his eyes burning into Brook with a fiery intensity. He feared the old man was about to explode, he looked so angry.

"Ah, good afternoon, Brook."

Brook turned, reassured by the familiar tap of a cane on the floor. "Hi, Charlie. Hey, come on, grab a seat and have a coffee. I'm glad you're looking so much better."

"I see you've company." Charlie's eyes settled on Marten.

"The usual, Charlie?" Cynthia stopped by the table.

"Make it a beer, heavy on the root," the elder said as he pulled out a chair. He had on the same baseball cap and denim jacket. He was obviously not into dressing for any occasion.

Marten swallowed twice before responding, "Look, Brook, I've just realized I've something important to do."

Brook's senses tingled as Charlie and Marten glared at each other for a few more moments before Marten rose.

"Perhaps we'll get a chance to talk again, Brook. I'm sure I'll see you around," he said dryly as he left.

Brook stared after him, pondering what had just happened. Marten and Charlie seemed to have some sort of old grudge against each other. In any case, it seemed he'd just made his second enemy on the islands.

"What was that all about?" he asked.

"I'm not sure. Strong energy around him, very strong." Charlie frowned. "But something else ... almost as if he was trying to block me out. Odd."

Bob came sauntering back. "I see our strange rock hound has transformed into one of the locals. How are you doing, Charlie? You know this fellow, Brook?"

"Yeah, we went up to what's left of the Golden Spruce together the other day. Chelen and I had to drag him back to his cabin when he took a bad turn. As for our mysterious Mr. Crow, he just got up and left."

"Chelen Davidshaw? You know her? Very pretty girl, that one."

"That she is. I've hired her as a guide. I want to go to Sghaan Gway and I was told she was an expert on the area."

"You've made a good choice. I hear she's an excellent guide and knows the islands like the back of her hand."

Charlie was strangely quiet.

"You okay, Charlie?" Brook inquired. Perhaps the elder was still recuperating from the episode at the Golden Spruce. Brook wanted to ask him about the white raven and how he'd known it was going to die before it actually happened. But he didn't want to nose in on the story, especially since Bob hadn't published it yet. He'd ask Charlie about the white raven later, after the article was printed.

"Well, I've more or less recovered from my shamanic travels, if that's what you mean. Just trying to pinpoint that guy's energy. There's something puzzling about him. As if we've met before. Only where?"

* * *

Raven fumed as he stood outside the café, kicking at bits of grass and rocks. His powers of hypnosis were weak. But he fooled Brook, nearly had him convinced to part with the immortal stone, he was sure of it. If only the Haida elder hadn't interfered. Had Raven stayed any longer, the shaman would have uncovered his disguise, for it had taken all of his energy to block him even for a little while.

The old man was the *ska-ga* spirit who'd spied on him when he'd absorbed the white raven's spirit. Only a medicine man with great powers, or great luck, could have saved himself.

Well, the shaman had survived, and he was suspicious of Raven. Normally, he enjoyed the challenge of tricking shamans, but trickery involving them was much harder because he had to fool their animal spirits also. Raven hadn't even found the energy to transform back into himself and fly away when he'd held his immortal stone. It was a struggle to transform into Mr. Crow in the first place, especially after flying all that way to the Skeena River to awaken the Snag. Raven sighed. Conserving energy was something he wasn't used to. He needed to retrieve his immortal stone from Brook before anything else. Just by holding the lapis lazuli for those brief moments, he'd washed a few years off his body. He'd wait until Brook was alone, maybe on the kayak trip he'd mentioned ... at least his incredible sense of hearing was still intact. There would be plenty of time then for him to get the stone back, even if he had to use a more direct approach. And afterwards, even the shaman named Charlie would tremble in fear before him. Yes, things would be very different once he was whole again.

Smirking, he shuffled up the street into an alleyway. There he closed his eyes, pulled the human skin off, bunched it up, and shoved it into a garbage can. At least he'd got a meal out of the deal; he'd tricked Brook into that. He leaned against the wall for support as the world spun around him. He clicked his beak in frustration. It used to be nothing to throw on the skin of another creature, or to fly great distances to far lands and awaken transformer beasts.

With another sigh, Raven stretched his wings and lifted skyward. He knew where to spring his trap. There he'd eat, sleep, and wait for Brook.

Chapter Nine

Brook spent the rest of the day hiking out to the wreck of the Pesuta, a barge that ran aground in 1928. Not much remained of the two-hundred-sixty-four foot vessel. Still he enjoyed relaxing on the beach, combing for shells. When he returned to his hotel that evening, he found a note awaiting him. "Meet us at Howler's at seven. Across the street from the tourist shop where they never heard of Martha Stewart."

The scrawled handwriting could only have been Charlie's. Brook was curious to know if Charlie had found out anything about Marten Crow, and looking forward to seeing Chelen. He hoped everything went well, or at least as well as could be expected, at her grandmother's funeral. He checked his watch. He had forty-five minutes.

He showered and shaved, then dressed in clean jeans and a cotton shirt. The last time he'd been this excited about a woman was with Georgina, and look how that had turned out.

Brook sighed. This trip was supposed to be a getaway. What was he getting himself into? It would be better to play things by ear with Chelen. He was supposed to be investigating a story, for heaven's sake, not chasing women.

As he covered the couple blocks to Howler's café, the salt smell of ocean pervaded the air. The main street reminded Brook of his old hometown of Gibbons, Alberta. Small ma-and-pa type shops, a credit union, Royal Canadian Legion, local hospital, several charter companies and a grocery store. No big-name fast food franchises, though he'd heard about the legal battles between Haidabucks, the small coffeehouse in Masset, and Starbucks regarding their name and logo. He was glad the little guys won.

He stopped at a corner newspaper box and grabbed a copy of Bob's paper, reading as he walked. The story about the white raven was the main lead. The body of the bird was going on display at the Port Clements museum. But the Snag incident had been reduced to a minor piece on the third page that merely stated two fishermen had died when their boat crashed on some rocks. RCMP investigating, charges may be pending. Alcohol suspected.

"Coward." Brook sneered and tossed the paper into the garbage. Even in a small community, politics sometimes got in the way of the truth.

He stopped in front of the Raven's Gallery gift store, the window display was organized chaos. Whoever owned the place must be an eccentric, he mused and walked across the street to the café. Brook paused in the doorway of

Howler's, his attention distracted by a black truck with the logo of the Haida Watchmen parked across the road. The Watchmen were everywhere, hovering in the background. Keeping an eye on the islands and the people.

Inside Howler's, he glanced around and laughed. If Martha Stewart hadn't spent any time in the gift shop across the street, she obviously never came in here either. The interior of the café boasted a heavy glass door, green and yellow walls and decor somewhere between art deco and Spanish. He was a few minutes late, Charlie and Chelen were already sitting out back on the patio sipping on coffee.

"Hi, guys. As soon as I got the message I showered and rushed over. How's it going? Charlie, I do have to thank you for stopping by when I was dealing with that unusual old man," Brook blurted out.

Chelen's eyes looked puffy and red, but her pupils dilated and he knew she was glad to see him. A thrill of desire curled through his belly.

"I'll have a coffee and a hamburger with fries and gravy," he asked the waitress as he sat down, the aroma of greasy burgers alerting him to the fact he hadn't eaten since lunch with Marten Crow and Bob. "How are you doing, Chelen? I hope the funeral went well."

"Yes, it did," she said bluntly. He smiled in sympathy, and then turned to her uncle.

"Thank heavens, you're looking a whole lot better, Charlie."

"Trust me, it sucked to be me the other day. I've had some rough experiences on my shamanic travels but that was one of the worst. I nearly didn't make it back alive, and I'll explain why in a minute. But first, Brook, can you fill me in on what you know about Marten Crow?"

"Sure, but what can I tell you? Except that when he turned up, I was at the newspaper in Tlell about to show Bob Burns the stone I found by the Golden Spruce."

Charlie's mouth fell open. "Stone? What stone?"

"Do you still have it?" Chelen spoke up. "I'd forgotten about it, what with Charlie getting ill and everything happening around the funeral."

"As a matter of fact, I do." He reached into his pants pocket. "I brought it along. I wanted to show it to you earlier, Charlie, when we bumped into each other at lunch, but you still didn't seem like yourself." In fact, Charlie had downed his root beer in one gulp and shuffled off, leaving Brook and Bob to discuss their strange lunch companion between themselves.

"Even so, might've helped if you'd told me about it then," Charlie growled.

"It's a lousy semi-precious gemstone. I didn't think it was such a big deal." He held it over the table, the polished navy blue rock shining in the neon lights of the café.

171

Charlie ran his hand over his face, scratching at the day-old stubble sprouting on his cheeks. He took the lapis lazuli from Brook and closed his eyes momentarily. "Semi-precious it is, harmless it ain't. I wish you could feel what I do. It all begins to fit now."

"What fits? Actually, Marten Crow was very interested in the stone, too. Bob didn't like him either, though, said he'd never seen him around the islands before."

"Figures." Charlie hefted the pebble in his hand. "So what did this Mister Crow want with you?"

"That rock, in exchange for some legend regarding Raven and his immortality stone. Originally, I agreed to give it to him, but changed my mind and bought him lunch instead. Seemed to be the least I could do. He started to get red in the face, and I thought he was going to flip out when you arrived."

Charlie shook his head. "Now what I'm about to tell you I know you won't believe, but I'm going to tell you anyway. Chelen's grandmother had a nightmare the night she died. I was there. She said she saw Raven walking away with Wolf and Grizzly Bear following, but they left only one set of footprints. At the time, I was unsure of the meaning, but knew it was a bad omen. Later, Chelen told me about running into a rare albino raven, and I took that to be a sign of changes coming, though just how big those changes were I didn't realize until I journeyed in the other worlds.

When we went to the Golden Spruce, the first thing I did was try to pick up any emanations from the area. I got a vision of the white raven after it left Chelen. It was disoriented from the flash of her camera and landed on an electrical transformer. After it died, I watched its spirit travel to the land of the dead ones. There, I ran into Raven."

"The real Raven? Creator God, the big cheese?"

"Yup."

"I'll bet that's when you got sick, wasn't it?" Chelen put in.

Charlie turned to her. "Somehow, the downing of the Golden Spruce upset the usual balance in the other worlds, releasing both the white raven, and Raven himself. He must have been trapped in the tree, along with the prince. In the land of the dead ones I saw the white raven's spirit merging with Raven, and then he, Bear and Wolf left the spirit world and entered ours, leaving only one trail. That's what I stumbled onto when I went into my meditative state."

"Are you trying to tell me this Creator from native legends, the one and only Raven, has been released or brought back to earth, or something weird like that? Then what about Prince Kiidkayaas?" Brook interrupted, wondering what kind of whack job he was talking to.

Charlie smiled. "Yes, Raven. I didn't run into Kiidkayaas, and up to now I haven't been able to locate him, which in itself is unusual."

Brook narrowed his eyes. He wasn't buying a line of this insane reasoning. "Look, I know you travel to spiritual realms, and that's cool. You deal in things I've never heard of, nor even imagined existed. But remember my background is different, so when you're talking about Raven, black or white, a mythical native version of something close to a God, strutting around ... yeah, I have a huge problem with that. This goes way beyond my boundaries of credibility. You honestly expect me to accept that your Creator, the Raven, the Main Dude of Haida legends, is wandering around in this realm?"

"Not only is he wandering around, but from my journeys to the other side, it seems for some reason he's waking up certain spirit beings."

"What do you mean by spirit beings? Are we talking about things like the Snag?"

Chelen studied him. "Where did you hear about the Snag? It's not a very common legend."

He thought for a moment. He couldn't really explain being in Bob's office without revealing why he was there in the first place, and he hadn't the heart to go on deceiving her. "Sorry

Chelen, let me backtrack for a minute. I'm actually a reporter with the *New York Times*. I was at the island newspaper researching reports on the Golden Spruce and its demise. The guy who owns the paper was working on the story about the Snag and chatting to the RCMP about it."

"I'll bet you thought a native killed Chatwick, didn't you, Brook!" Chelen glared.

"I could lie and say no. But yes, it did occur to me. At least, at first."

Chelen's temper seemed shorter than usual, but with her grandmother's death playing havoc with her emotions, he could understand. Whatever he'd felt earlier as he met her eyes was driving him crazy. He wanted to comfort her and make the pain go away.

Charlie intervened. "Look, calm down, you two. I can safely say no native is involved in killing the idiot who cut down the tree. I'm not certain, although I've a hunch who did kill him."

Brook sat quietly. He wasn't sure if he was ready for the line of reasoning Charlie was sure to take.

The elder smiled. "Brook, you really should start considering the possibility Raven might actually exist. After all, not only have you met him, but you bought him lunch."

Chelen's eyes bugged out. "What!"

"Marten Crow? Now, I've heard it all. I know Raven's supposed to be some sort of shape shifter, but that's really pushing it. Marten's just a harmless old man, a bit of an eccentric kook, who was grubbing about for a meal and rambling on about some immortal stone." He was beginning to seriously doubt the sanity of the people here. Maybe Charlie had more than just herbs in those little jars back at his cabin. Whatever he was on, it was definitely good stuff.

"Unless he was desperate to get the stone back and wanted to make sure he could convince you to give it to him," Charlie said.

"Give me a break! If this Raven dude is as powerful as you say he is, why would he have to even ask? He'd just take the stone from me."

"Don't know for sure. Some legends say he can't just take it back; it has to be offered to him. Anyway, it's not his style. Raven's a trickster, so he was probably trying to trick you into it. If he really is missing his immortal stone, I would guess he's pretty weak. In any case, when I sat down with you at the café I was getting very weird vibes from Mr. Crow. He was trying to block me out, shield his thoughts to keep me from discovering who, or what, he was. This much is for sure … things in the spirit world have been greatly disturbed since the Golden Spruce was cut down."

"Speaking of being disturbed and unsettled, I had the strangest dream the night before we went to the Golden Spruce." Chelen spoke up. "I dreamt I went over to Brook's hotel to talk about something and Raven burst into the room and attacked us."

Brook nearly gagged on his coffee. "What? I had nearly the same dream, but after we'd been up to the tree. I got up in the middle of the night and heard you calling me through the window. I let you in, we talked and … " He didn't want to admit in his version of the dream they made love. "Ah, let's say we had a romantic situation develop. Raven burst through the window. You screamed. I leaped out of bed. I turned to look at you, and you'd changed into one of those *kushtaka* creatures. Then Raven came at me."

A faint blush crept into her face. Had her dream been along the same steamy lines as his? His pulse quickened at the possibility. "Some coincidence," he added. "Our two dreams were so similar."

"Not really … we could easily have the same, or nearly the same, dream. Dreams are just the mind's way of dealing with the events of the day. Often they're from some of the thoughts we have just before we go to sleep," Chelen answered.

"Aren't you a walking encyclopedia," he couldn't help teasing her. "Actually, you could be right. I've read something similar to that. But

I'm having a real hard time with all this talk about Raven being alive and walking around. I mean, god-like creatures don't just pop out of trees and go on walkabouts in other people's skins. As a journalist, I guess I need concrete proof of his existence."

Charlie held the lapis lazuli stone before Brook. The shaman had been quietly studying it for the last few moments. "Well, what do you think this is? A figment of your imagination? I think this could very well be Raven's immortal stone. There's some mighty strong energy emanating from this rock."

"I'll tell you what it is. It's a bloody rock, and that's all it is, a rock." He politely took it from Charlie and put it back into his pocket.

"I guess I can't expect you to believe what I know to be true. Some of us just have to learn the hard way." Charlie's words had a hard edge to them.

Dismissing the veiled warning, Brook turned to Chelen. "Now, when and where do we meet for our trip tomorrow? Chelen?"

"Sorry, I was just thinking about that dream. It sure is eerie, to have nearly the same dreams." Her gaze was soft as it met his.

He felt his temperature rise as she held him in thrall.

"Earth calling Brook and Chelen, earth calling Brook and Chelen." Charlie laughed.

Her face flushed a little deeper. "Meet me at the Skidegate ferry terminal around seven tomorrow morning. You'll leave your vehicle there, and we'll take the *Kwuna* across to Moresby Island and unload the kayaks at Sandspit. I've got everything ready to go, including tents."

"Great. Just hope you don't snore."

"Snore! The only one snoring will be you, from exhaustion. I'll pack all of the provisions, so just bring your backpack and something for sore muscles. Oh, and try not to fall behind too much. I hate making guys look bad." She chuckled.

He was relieved to see her finally joking a little.

"Well missy, them sounds like fighting words. We'll see who can keep up to whom."

As he headed back to his room at the Sea Raven, the sun was beginning to set over Queen Charlotte City, the fading rays sending streaks of turquoise, magenta, and crimson bleeding into the water. He paused to appreciate the show. His mind wasn't totally on the incredible sight playing out in front of him. Something bothered him about Marten Crow's story, and it irritated him more after Charlie's insistence Mr. Crow was really Raven.

It was all outrageous, of course. And yet … some part of him said he'd be a fool to dismiss it all as the imaginings of a storyteller's mind.

Charlie Stillwaters was a bonafide shaman. He'd met enough mystics to know they possessed certain abilities beyond his ken, and as a reporter, he'd learned long ago to trust those little twigs of intuition.

Later, in his hotel room, he reached for his journal and read through Tom Wilson's version of Raven's story. It might have been eight years since he was at Ninstints, but the legend still entranced him.

After his conversation on the ferry with Henry Richardson, he'd made several notes on his laptop afterward. There might also be a clue there.

He remembered his urgent instinct to flee as the ferry docked, a premonition that coming back to Haida Gwaii heralded some sort of turning point in his life. The haunting visions of the totems that plagued his sleep in New York. Those dreams stopped once he'd reached the islands. Something had changed. The old Brook Grant would never have entertained crazed notions about some old guy being Raven in disguise, or even toyed with the idea that a creature such as Raven could actually exist.

Sitting up, he jotted down the details of the tale he'd heard from Marten Crow. Then he compared the three interpretations of the legend. Tom's version said virtually nothing about the events purported to cause the formation of the Golden Spruce, other than the prince was rumored to be trapped in a golden spruce up north.

And what had Henry said on the ferry? Brook glanced at his laptop. The prince and his grandfather were leaving their home, driven away by a fierce snowstorm, when the prince turned around and stared longingly at his old village. And so the prince lost his soul, and was transformed into a tree that turned golden from his grief.

Marten's version, on the other hand, went into greater detail. It elaborated on things Henry mentioned, such as the identity of the prince's companion. According to Marten, the prince's grandfather was in fact none other than Raven appearing as a man, which would make sense as they'd both flown north together. Was this where Henry's version of the story originated from?

But Marten Crow's telling also contradicted things Henry had said. According to Henry, the prince and his grandfather had been leaving the village when the prince was turned into a spruce tree. Marten said Kiidkayaas and Raven were walking towards a village.

What's more, Marten said looking for the village wasn't what cursed the prince, but the spell Raven placed on the moccasins he gave him. Raven working his famous trickery again, Brook thought with a chuckle.

The three variations of the legend were different, but so what? As Marten Crow said, myths changed in the telling. What was he missing?

There had to be something. Some anomaly, some clue ... He glanced over his notes once again. Nothing leaped out at him. Go back to the basics, he thought. He'd been looking at the differences between the three legends ... maybe he should start examining the similarities?

When it came to him, it was so obvious that he groaned. Raven.

Both Tom's and Henry's stories said nothing about Raven being trapped in the Golden Spruce with the prince. Henry hadn't mentioned Raven at all, a peculiarity for sure. How come Marten Crow was the only one of the three who mentioned Raven?

The totem at Ninstints clearly showed the man and Raven locked in combat. So someone else must have known Raven was involved. One more time, Brook ruffled the pages of his journal. Tom said the totem was erected after the slave, Wago, returned with tale of Kiidkayaas and Raven battling for Raven's immortal stone. The totem probably depicted only the events Wago was aware of. The slave, like the rest of the people of Ninstints, didn't live long enough to see the completed totem. Out of over three hundred recorded as residing at Ninstints in 1840, by 1884 only thirty were left. Whoever the carver was couldn't have known that the prince and Raven were imprisoned in the spruce tree.

Well, maybe that was it. Who else but Raven could know Raven had been trapped in the tree with the prince?

Brook closed his journal and flipped off the light. He'd had more than enough mythological madness for one day. Being a reporter was sometimes too much like being a detective. Quickly he drifted towards the oblivion of sleep.

"The Yakoun River." The totems with the Ovoid eyes whispered in his dream.

He sat upright in bed, the words repeating themselves like a needle stuck on a vinyl record.

"Only the voice of the snowstorm whistled through the forest and across the waters of the Yakoun River."

In the darkness he fumbled to switch on the lamp. Blinking in the sudden light, he grabbed the map of the islands from his nightstand. The answer stared him in the face. Raven had indeed flown towards the north with the prince, but instead of delivering him all the way to Llanaas and the shaman-cum-sorcerer, Xatsinoo, he took him only as far as the banks of the Yakoun River. Those were Marten Crow's words; no one else mentioned anything like that, or about the trick with the moccasins. Only Marten said both the prince and Raven had become trapped in the Golden Spruce tree Gordon Chatwick destroyed.

It appeared as if Raven had indeed fooled the prince, at least partly. And if Raven did exist, then being true to his character, he'd find some way to brag about his trickery. Raven had a big ego, and like many con artists and serial killers, he'd have a hard time not gloating about his feats, however subtly.

Which was exactly what Marten Crow did at lunch.

Maybe, just maybe, Charlie had a point about Raven being real. Brook shut off the light and slipped back under the covers. This was developing into more than a news piece about a crazed environmentalist's destruction. Only who'd believe the story if he wrote it?

Chapter Ten

Brook woke on time and met Chelen at the docks. The day promised to be clear and beautiful with a warm sun beaming down. Before they left Sandspit, Chelen packed the hatches of the two kayaks full of essential supplies and life jackets. Then they set off for Sghaan Gway, kayaks gliding smoothly through the water.

They paddled past towering headlands towards the ancient village of Cumshewa, which Chelen indicated would be their campsite for the night.

"Once, over twenty longhouses were occupied there." Chelen spoke. "A former Eagle crest town, although many Raven crest dwelt here also."

Brook knew that The Haida were primarily of the two lineages.

The isles were draped in layers of silken mists, until the sun strengthened and burned them off. Brook caught glimpses of abandoned logging camps and scarred clear cuts dotting the coast. Still, many first growth trees with age-old coats of moss and ferns lined the shoreline as they passed.

Chelen was right about one thing; he had a hard time keeping up with her. She was a strong kayaker. He hadn't forgotten the strokes, but his technique was rusty. Too bad he'd had no opportunity to properly prepare and practice a little first. Perspiration darkened her cap, as Brook tried to march the rhythm of her shoulders rising and falling with the strokes of the paddle. Her shirt was drenched, and whenever they were side by side, he caught glimpses of her nipples jutting against the thin fabric. It made for a tough time trying to stay focused on his task, and enjoy the beauty of the trip. What would those breasts feel like in his hands, against his lips? Stop it, he grumbled under his breath. It was hard to not slip into some erotic fantasy. It had been way too long since he'd been with a woman. God, what he needed was a cold shower.

As they paddled, Chelen shared the history of Haida Gwaii, filling him in on everything from native settlements to non-native intrusions. Her grandmother passed the knowledge on to her, she told Brook. Ttanuu, where they would camp on their way back from Sghaan Gway, was one of the last and largest villages abandoned when the native population crashed to less than a thousand in the late 1800s. "The name meant Sea Grass Town, and it had two rows of longhouses with over sixteen buildings, and thirty totems. Modern Haida once threatened archaeologists and forced them to leave the dead alone." She bristled. "Our dead stay here, and the ones that are taken away will be returned," she vowed. The Haida had already repatriated many remains.

Today, only stumps remained of the once-imposing longhouses, and even those were hard to find under the onslaught of regrowth.

He gave Chelen lots of space to be alone with her thoughts. She still seemed abnormally tense; probably being here reminded her of her grandmother. His thoughts returned to yesterday. Could Marten Crow indeed be Raven?

How could he even ask that question? Never mind start to believe it might be true. There was no concrete proof, of course, but how could you begin to prove that an adult-sized Raven was actually eating salmon sandwiches with you at a café, disguised in a human skin? Not to mention, what happened to the poor human who once owned said skin. Still, all the evidence he'd digested last night, suggested, crazily enough, that maybe Charlie had a point about Mr. Crow. Details like the moccasins and how the prince fooled Raven into entering the tree, things like these regarding the prince's and Raven's activities during the time that the two had been alone, could surely only have come from first-hand experience. Things only someone who'd taken part in the events that had evolved into mythology could know.

Brook recalled Marten Crow's odd behavior at the restaurant: his large appetite, his inability to read the menu, the way he seemed to study everything and behaved as if he was learning for the first time — all little things that now seemed to fit into place. What if Charlie was right?

As they traveled on, Brook prickled with unease. If Raven was alive, and here, what would he do? Why did he want Brook's plain old blue pebble so badly? Unless ...

Brook stopped paddling. Unless he really did have Raven's immortal stone.

The lapis lazuli was in a pouch in his backpack. He should have left it behind in the hotel room. He'd never meant to bring it with him, but something compelled him to grab it on his way out the door.

"Hey, do you give up already?" Chelen called as she began to leave him behind.

"Not on your life." His kayak leaped ahead as he dove the paddle into the rolling waves. His legs were already aching from maneuvering the pedals and his shoulders screamed from the repetitive arm movements. It hadn't taken him long to become reacquainted with the searing pain of raw blisters, especially after dipping them into salt water.

"Impossible," he muttered as he caught up to Chelen. All this talk of myths and the past was getting to him, just like she was. This wasn't reality. Reality was kayaking to Ninstints with Chelen.

* * *

188

"You're unusually quiet tonight," Brook said after they'd stopped for the night amid a stand of cedars near Cumshewa. The day had flown by even though he was tired, but if Chelen was worn out by the kayaking she didn't show it. "Are you thinking about your grandmother?"

They already had supper, a delicious plate of freeze-dried, rehydrated lasagna. Something that would ordinarily turn his stomach he'd gulped down with relish, and now he sipped at his coffee as the sun set. The evenings were long here, and the sun rose early in the morning. He'd miss that when he went back East.

Chelen sighed. "Yes, Rosemary's spirit has been with me all day, and especially here. She was one of the last to be born at Cumshewa before the village was closed. It was here that we took white slaves and burned their ships. That was before the plagues, of course."

Brook had read about the exploits of Koyah and his plundering of the Resolution. An explorer, sixty years later, found the old ship's flag proudly displayed like a grisly scalp.

"I have to be honest. A lot of what I'm trying to deal with is more about you. Especially the dream we talked about at the café."

"Yours sure sounded similar. But you never got into any great detail." Brook stood and added wood to the fire from the pile of driftwood he'd collected earlier, pungent aromas

189

of cedar and spruce smoke filtering around them.

"You said in your dream you woke up and heard me calling your name. After you let me in we made love, and at some point Raven crashed into your hotel room. Well, in my dream I had gone to your hotel room to talk to you about the Golden Spruce."

She fell quiet. The moon had barely cleared the trees, casting pale silver light. The surf crashed in the background, filling the crisp air with the tang of salt water and seaweed.

Fear shadowed her expression when she looked up at him. "Much more than that happened in my dream. Before Raven burst in … I didn't tell you, couldn't tell you … we were also making love."

He gave her a long look. Did she have the same passionate fantasy he did? "Why didn't you say something in the c-café?" he stuttered. The heat from the campfire seemed to suddenly increase. Sweat beaded on his forehead at the memory.

"I guess I was too embarrassed to mention it in front of Charlie. And besides, I barely know you."

"I see your point." His voice softened. He'd certainly never dreamed about Georgina like that. "Did it feel as good for you as it did for me?" he blurted out, and realized he should have been a bit more subtle.

Chelen clammed up and turned away from him, but not before he'd glanced into her eyes.

"Look," he said, "I'm sorry if I've upset you. That wasn't my intention. It was rude of me."

"I think I'm tired. It's been a long day and I'm turning in now."

"Wait. Talk to me, Chelen. I need to know what's going on inside you." She was running away, trying to escape. He had to pin her down and get the truth before the moment slipped away.

"It's so hard to explain, Brook." Moisture welled in her eyes. "It would take too long."

Despite her reticence, he couldn't help pushing for more information. "We have all night, and all week, so try me. Tell me about your history. Your ancestors seemed so poor, yet your stories suggest they were happy. They left no written language to tell us what they thought about their world."

She sighed. "We weren't poor. We just didn't have any money."

"The differences between native and Western ways of thinking, I guess." The native ways didn't make any sense to him.

"Right. The differences between you and me, Brook."

"But we live in a multicultural age. Do we have to fear what we don't share?"

"Ideally, no. Trouble is, you live in such an individualistic state. In your world, there's no community and no one is connected to the universe. And in your world, tell me, how many are truly happy?"

"That all depends on how you measure happiness, I'd say."

"Exactly. You're always living in the future, looking for material gain."

Brook shrugged. That was one of the reasons Georgina left him. A journalist's salary didn't provide what she thought she deserved.

When he didn't speak, Chelen rose and ducked inside her one-person tent. He followed her. She was crouched just inside, unrolling her sleeping blanket. He sat outside, cross-legged, facing her.

"But is that so bad?"

"We all deserve a comfortable existence. But you use whatever's at your disposal to enrich your life. Always taking."

"I work for things, yes. Don't I deserve what I earn?"

"But you never give back to Creator. You consider yourself one microcosm in this world, individual and unique. But you're like a piece cut out of a photograph. Western civilization is always trying to break everything down to its most minute form."

"Isn't that the way the world works?" Now he had her talking, he was enjoying discovering how she viewed the world.

"Your world, maybe. Our culture is oriented more along the lines of Eastern philosophy. How is everything connected, how will one thing affect the next. We view life more as a hologram. If you look at only one piece of a hologram, it still reflects the complete picture."

"I'll take your word for it."

"It's kinda like metaphysics. The whole universe is a spider's web, and where the web intersects it's connected by crystals, and each crystal reflects the ones around it. Each piece is a whole and sees the others as whole. To remove one changes nothing."

"I've read stuff like that, sure."

"I can't tell you how many nights my grandmother would sit by my bed and drill the native ways into me. She was smart, though ... wanted to do more than protect me from the white man's brainwashing. I think she knew we'd begin to rebuild our culture one day and that someone needed to know the old ways, yet be open to learning the new. That was something she couldn't do. But with her death, I've realized she wanted me strong enough in our customs so that I could integrate into yours."

"And she did a great job, if you ask me."

"Well, thanks. But none of us can truly deny who we are inside. Our two cultures are so far apart, in so many ways, that it's tough to live in both. I mean, your people live mainly in the present. But we also live in the past, because we view ourselves as a self-contained part of a much larger whole."

"Yeah, I get the idea of connection. But can it work, in the real world?"

"Sure it can. Our band council thinks first for the communal good of our people, and secondly for the good of the individual. We make our decisions, though, based on the bigger whole of our ancestors. You see, we carry our ancestors, our spirits, with us. That's why I know where I came from, where I am, and where I'll be buried. Can you say that?"

"Never thought of it in those terms, I guess."

She stopped making up her bed and sighed. "So you see, Brook, I look at reality in a completely different light than you. Neither viewpoint is incorrect, just a matter of perception and that's why our cultures don't get along."

He stared for a long moment, unsure what to say. "I'll head off while you change."

He rose and poked at the flames of the campfire. She was right. He'd no idea where he'd be buried, and until now hadn't cared. Brook didn't feel connected to any greater oneness with the universe. Maybe that was part of what he was missing, no connection to his soul. But hadn't he felt a connection to something bigger than himself on the ferry?

Maybe that's why he came back ... Maybe that's what had scared the hell out of him.

Chelen stepped out of her tent wearing only a long T-shirt that accentuated the curves of her legs, and sat down beside him, near the fire. The silence stretched between them. He gulped.

"You've really got me to thinking," he admitted.

"I don't often meet outsiders I can discuss native world view with. So if you're interested I'll go on, but if it gets to be overload, let me know."

"I'd never feel like that," he said honestly.

"Okay ... we believe that we don't die, but simply enter other realities. This world is only one plane of existence."

"Enter other realities? How? Isn't that done through the winter spirit dances?"

"That, and other ways the shamans know. We believe in reincarnation. After we die, our spirits are reborn into the next generation. Our ancestors, all of them down through the generations, guide us. In essence, we're in constant dialogue with them. At the same time, we realize we're stewards looking after the land and all within it for future generations. We're entrusted with this sacred duty."

"Well, I suppose someone needs to guard these islands for those to come. No wonder your people get so upset at the logging, and all that."

"Right. Western-thinking people treat the earth like a commodity. Once the dollars are gone, so go the workers, but we remain. We've been here since eternity, will be as long as the spirit winds speak."

The flames threw flickering shadows across her face. He blinked. For a moment he saw others face behind her features. Nonsense. He shook his head to clear the thought.

"Where will you be, Brook? After this story? I'll be honest, I'm attracted to you, and I'm scared to get hurt again."

He swallowed and searched for the right words. Everything was happening so fast, too many buried feelings awakening. He was concerned with her views on white society. Justified or not, it was the culture he'd been raised in. Maybe, in the real world, such deep-rooted differences would come between them. But finally she'd admitted what he'd suspected all along: her barriers had to do with more than a mere conflict in upbringing. If he really wanted to figure her out, he had to gain her trust.

"Who hurt you before, then?"

She swallowed hard. "Hell, this still isn't easy to talk about." After a deep breath, she continued, "I met a logger who was here to do some contract work a few years ago. Doug McCafferty was his name. We fell madly in love and got engaged. He promised to stay after

196

his job with the logging company ended, and for about a year we were the happiest couple. Then the logging contract expired and within the month, he packed his bags and left. Said he couldn't take not working."

"And you think I'd do something like that?"

"Won't you? After this assignment, where will you go? There's always another story waiting." She stood and looked down at him. "It won't work, Brook. We come from two different worlds. But I have to admit, the fantasy was pretty good."

Brook moved towards her. He couldn't explain why he felt so drawn to her; he sure as hell wasn't ready for a relationship. But Chelen was like an addiction, overpowering his rationality. And yes, damn it, he wanted to see where the attraction would take them. Better to let her lead the way though, if she decided she wanted to.

She turned towards the tent, then back to face him. "Do I want to be involved with you, Brook? No. I've learned my lesson, and I don't want to take the chance. But I was raised to always tell the truth. And the truth is, my body and my heart betray me every time I look at you. I've been wrestling with this ever since I met you."

She disappeared into her tent. Brook made sure the fire was on its way out and the kayaks and backpacks secure before he entered his tent and unrolled his sleeping bag. Then he found himself standing outside her tent. She'd just let some of her walls down, and he figured it was about time he did the same.

"Chelen, can I come in? There's something I need to say."

"Sure. I'm decent."

He slipped inside to sit beside her. She was curled up beneath her sleeping blanket and he caught the streaks of wetness on her cheek in the weak glimmer from the lantern.

"Look, I hear what you're saying about being cautious. I've some issues of my own. Just before I came here, my girlfriend left me for another guy. He was what you'd call your typical Western-minded male, full of money. I guess I wasn't meant to be her Prince Charming. But I sure didn't expect to come up here and find some connection to you, or any woman, for that matter. I only wanted to be alone, and that was one reason I took on this assignment." His throat closed up as he realized what he'd just admitted to himself for the first time. "I didn't expect to find anyone like you, nor be this attracted," he whispered hoarsely.

Chelen rolled away from him, soft sobs shaking her shoulders. It broke his heart to sit there and do nothing.

"Can I hold you? Nothing more." He couldn't believe the words came from his mouth. What if she told him to get lost? And if she didn't ... what would it be like to hold her?

She stiffened and then gave a barely perceptible nod. He stretched out beside her and she turned towards him, into his arms. After she'd fallen asleep, he brushed aside a stray lock of her hair and reached over to turn off the lantern. Darkness closed around them. He continued stroking her hair while another sigh escaped her and his eyes closed. They were in a wood-sided house, smoke from the fire filled the air, delicate seashells and eagle feathers adorned her hair as he held her naked under a pile of furs.

He blinked and opened his eyes. What was that ... déjà vu? Some sort of memory? Brook eased away from her and stood up. He was no good for her, she would never accept him as a partner. He sighed as he went outside; somehow he was never good enough. He stood by the dying fire for a while listening to the waves caressing the sand of the shoreline. Later, Brook lay inside his tent, the wind soughing in the branches, lulling him almost to sleep. All around him the air hummed. Spirit winds, he imagined, bearing the breath of her ancestors. When he finally slept, he dreamed of Chelen and the Haida who'd walked these shores.

Of totems staring out to sea, topped by the three enigmatic Watchmen, predecessors of the modern guardians of the old sites, their vigilant eyes scanning everything. Were they still out there, watching him? Did they know something he didn't?

* * *

Late the next morning, Raven waited at Koona, or Skedans as the pale-skinned people called it. He watched as one of his daughters and the yellow-haired one who held his immortal stone paddled their kayaks towards the beach.

Raven thought about his experience with Raymond. What had happened to the Haida? He remembered and looked at the ground, kicking at shards of seashell.

Was what he was doing right? Trying to turn everything back to long ago? At the same time, the people had many new inventions to make their lives easier. At the lunch meeting with Brook, Raven had been surprised to see all the different things. Everything from the sunshine-captured-inside-glass containers to music from large boxes that couldn't possibly hold all the singers inside them. What magic shrank them? The hot beverage he'd drunk had kept him up most of the night. What right had he to upset it all?

But the sensations of weakness, especially when he was inside the buildings, remained. He knew it had something to do with the buzz generated by the tools and the thing called electricity. It powered everything, but the hum kept him from thinking clearly. Perhaps it also kept him from being in touch with the spirit worlds. Raven glared. Did it do the same to his people?

He stared up at Skedans' remaining totems. Only Sghaan Gway had more poles still standing.

In the background, just north of the abandoned village, the drums of Skedans still played. The booming produced by the pounding of the surf in the caves, reminding him of the old ways. How he missed the sight and the smell of lazy smoke curling from the longhouses, the droning of the endless winter chants, the thumping of the rawhide drums. The dancers dressed in the costumes of the animal spirits that possessed them, some even wearing representations of Raven, their Creator. The dancers would cavort in wild abandon, possessed by their *sghaay haw*. Seized by the ecstasy of the spirit world, they prowled like Wolf and strutted like stiff-legged Stork or Blue Heron, until they dropped in exhaustion. The elders looked on, dreaming of their youth, and over it all, the endless, pulsing drumbeats. He used to like to show up and trick the people into feeding him. Raven smiled. He'd played some good tricks in his time. But it appeared the best one of all had been played on him.

Somehow he had to make amends to the people for not being there when they needed him the most.

But first the stone. He had to get his immortal stone back.

Raven flew up into a tree behind the totems and stood very still, blending into the forest, the aches in his body reminding him of the present. His feather tips even bore tinges of gray.

* * *

Chelen and Brook beached the kayaks on Louise Island and spent some time exploring the twin crescents of shoreline protecting Skedans Bay. The totems loomed against the dark forest. The morning's journey did nothing to ease the relentless ache in his muscles that had already throbbed last night. Brook rolled his shoulders back and forth a few times in an effort to release the knots.

"Koona was one of the larger villages, but it was abandoned after the last smallpox epidemic swept through in 1862," Chelen told him. "A shaman foretold the coming disaster and said if the Haida were to have any hope of surviving, they must consolidate and live in just Masset and Skidegate. Less than eight hundred survived."

"I can't even begin to imagine that. It must have been devastating to the ones who lived."

"Even more so for us, since our society was oral based. So much knowledge was lost, as if our culture was wiped clean, like a blackboard."

After checking in with the Watchmen, they ate lunch near mortuary poles that inspired artist Emily Carr. Today, only crumbled remains marked the village site. Much could be said for preserving antiquities for others to view, but it wasn't the Haida way. They preferred to let nature take its course. Still, it seemed such a waste.

He could do a little preserving, though. He grabbed his old 35mm camera, preferring it over the newer digital versions. The blue sky had darkened and what looked like a brief summer thunderstorm was moving across the horizon. "Okay if I take a few pictures?"

"Sure. I'll make sure the Watchmen don't scalp you for using your face-puller."

"I admire the Haida for setting up the Watchmen Program. The people who safeguard the old sites are providing a great service, and besides, it takes guts to protect what you believe in."

He focused the camera and lined up the shot, musing that something was different about Chelen today. After last night he'd expected her to be cold and awkward around him, or perhaps sullen and withdrawn. But so far she'd been warm and almost affectionate. The thought gave him pause. Maybe he'd gotten through to that hidden part of her that she kept locked away. Or maybe she was sensing what he was beginning to realize, that whatever was happening between them might not have been planned, but it sure was real.

He aimed the camera at one of the leaning totems. A bunch of ferns sprouted from near the top, crowning it with a green cap. He took several flash shots, the emerald gloom of the forest and the mixed rays of sunlight, along with the menacing shadows cast by the approaching storm, all adding to the atmosphere of the images. He imagined, just as Charlie said, the spirit world being unsettled. If these Watchmen could talk, would they tell him what really happened up at the Golden Spruce? What if the restless entities that had been disturbed should be left alone to sleep? Myths never meant to be brought back to life?

Pushing those notions away, he walked up to Chelen and pointed his camera at her. "Smile."

"Hey!" She tried to hide her face, but he was too fast. "I hate having my picture taken."

"Most people do. D'you think we're going to get nailed by the storm?"

"Many of them brew up and then just blow away. I sure hope this one doesn't come ashore."

He decided to test the waters, so to speak. See how she would respond to some mention of their little tryst last night. "Hey, you'll be safe in my arms." He steeled himself for her to flinch, or turn away from him, but she surprised him.

"Thank you for holding me last night, Brook. I've slept alone for so long, I'd forgotten how good it feels ... to be held."

"Just holding you was more than I could have hoped for." He stared into her eyes, almost forgetting to breathe. All he could think of was kissing her.

No, what he wanted was not possible. Instead, he put his arm around her. "See, I'm not such a bad guy once you get to know me."

She smiled. "That's just it. You're too damn nice," she accused and pushed him away.

Grinning, she returned to fixing lunch. Brook took a few shots of the seaweed drying on the rippled sand exposed by the low tide.

He soaked it all up: the beach, the ocean, the forests, and Chelen. When she wasn't looking, he stole more images of her, trying and failing to capture that elusive quality that made the woman special.

As they ate, he wanted so much to reach over and touch her. Nothing sexual, just to feel connected to her in some small way.

A rumble from the heavens broke the spell. "We'd better move it." He wolfed down the rest of his lunch. His heart hammered in his chest, not out of fear of the thunder grumbling overhead, but from the realization he wanted to take their relationship to a whole new intimate level. Logic said it was too soon and he should be cautious, but something he had no control over drove him relentlessly on.

"We'll shelter up the beach until the storm passes. We can make it as far as Lyell Island tonight if need be," Chelen said. "But I've another place in mind if the weather clears later. Lyell is not a place I want to visit. Too many bad memories."

"Sounds good." Lyell Island was where the Haida had made a stand against logging on the Queen Charlottes. It hadn't ended well for the natives. He'd worked on some of the news articles, and that was one of the reasons he'd originally come out to Haida Gwaii. At the time, he didn't understand why someone would risk a jail term over a few trees.

Brook inhaled a waft of the cedar-laden air. Now, he understood. "I'll bet that has to do with the logging fiasco, doesn't it?"

"You got it. Many of my relatives and friends were involved."

As the lightning and thunder split the heavens, they waited in the shelter of the trees. After the sky cleared, they set off. Brook glanced at the next storm, skimming by just to the north of them. He didn't relish getting caught on the water if it came their way.

* * *

Long after the two humans left, Raven shook his feathers. Every bone in his body hurt. His vision blurred, like he'd been blinded and doused in ice water at the same time by the lightning box the man pointed everywhere. Was this what happened to the white raven? A chill ran through him. The blinding bursts sent his mind reeling. Raven stretched in an attempt to work the kinks out of his stiff joints. What powerful tools the humans created: strange lights, roaring metal contraptions, it all made him very tired. He knew now nothing of myth and ancient magic could exist in this age ... not even him. The humans possessed the magic.

Scrunching his face, Raven considered what had to be done. He must get rid of these new inventions. They had given the Haida the ability to be greater than he and kept them disconnected from the spirit world. How could he convince them to believe in and respect him again when they had ammunition that rendered him useless?

He watched the man and the woman paddle into the distance. Raven was barely able to straighten up his one wing any more. He was aging far too fast for his liking, and feared he certainly hadn't the strength to head into battle while Brook possessed that flashing weapon of his with the power of the god of the shining heavens.

Raven grinned. No, he hadn't the strength, but he knew of others that did. Others he'd woken that he could count on. They could do what he needed to have done. Right now though, he needed to rest. He was too drained to even fly down to the beach.

Yes, clearly he must return his people to the old ways. And once he got his immortal stone back, he knew exactly who he had to wake up next.

Sruhlru Jaad, Foam Woman. She possessed the power to recreate the past.

Chapter Eleven

"We'll camp here for the night," Chelen declared as her kayak glided towards a looming island. Since leaving Skedans they'd managed to avoid the worst of the squalls and made it safely past Lyell Island. Brook enjoyed the steady rhythm of paddling even though his body ached beyond belief. He loved being on the water.

"Why here? It doesn't look like much," he gasped, thankful to be ashore for the day. So far he'd struggled to keep up to Chelen's pace.

"This is Hot Spring Island, and after spending days in a cramped kayak, sweating your guts out, I'd think a relaxing dip in the thermal pools would be a nice break."

"Well, since you put it that way." He couldn't wait to stretch his legs, ease his aching back, blistered hands, and whatever part of his anatomy still possessed any feeling other than pain. If Chelen was sore she sure didn't show any signs of it as she scrambled out of her seat.

They set up camp away from the water's edge, Chelen being careful to pull the kayaks well up the beach. "They're great craft, though you must take care of them, like children."

The earlier storms had cleared, leaving behind a sky washed in pastel pink, purple and a dozen shades of blue. They presented their passes to the Watchmen on duty and struck out along the trail to the hot springs.

As they approached, the sulfur fumes stung his nostrils. He stopped momentarily. Everything began to spin in a murky haze.

"You okay?"

"Just tired, I guess, or maybe too much sun." He began walking again.

Peals of laughter rang out. Brook looked down at his feet. Moccasins? His legs were bare. What the ...

"Brook?" She shook him as he staggered drunkenly. "Sure you're feeling good?"

He glanced back down at his feet. Just his old blue hiking boots. "I ... ah ... no, something weird is going on here. I feel like I'm sleepwalking."

Over Chelen's shoulder he saw two natives running up the trail. A female decked out in fine fur, eagle feathers hanging from her hair and necklaces of shell beads and precious abalone clicking delicately. The male followed, clad in a loincloth that looked like it might have been woven from reeds, his head bowed in subservience. *He must be a slave.* "Did you just see that?"

"See what? There's no one else here. Brook, I'm getting worried about you. I think you overexerted yourself. Did you drink enough water today?"

"Gallons. It's not that. I'm seeing things. I can't explain it. It's ... this place, I've ..." Visions of the hot spring pool entered his head. "I'd swear I've been here before. On the other side of this hill is a cliff-side pool overlooking the sea and it flows down to a smaller pool, steps away from a rocky beach. There are several areas on this island where hot water comes to the surface," he said matter-of-factly.

"Yes, how did you know? They're therapeutic, for curing rheumatism and other ailments. The Haida have been coming here for hundreds of years, and to us, it's a sacred site. The island used to be reserved for the shamans and the nobility. Here, I better hang on to you."

"Good idea." Her strong arm went around him and a quiver of awareness ran through him at the touch of her body.

"Sure you want to go for a dip? If you decide to pass out in the hot springs there's no one to help. In any case, I'm sticking close to you."

"Oh yeah, let's see ... the choices are sit here in my sweaty clothes or join a gorgeous woman in a hot tub au naturel and risk drowning in scalding water." He peeled off his shirt. "No contest, you win. If this is how I'm meant to go, then so be it. It's been a nice life."

Keeping his shorts on, he stepped into the pool and lowered himself into the hot waters up to his neck. Every burning muscle screamed, "Thank you."

"Are you coming in? The water's awesome." Twilight settled in as the sun sank into the sea, melding the indigo slopes of the neighboring islands with platinum water. Despite the captivating surroundings he couldn't help staring as Chelen removed her T-shirt, revealing a sleek top that hugged her like a second skin. He swallowed twice.

Laughter rang out again. The native princess he thought he'd seen on the trail earlier stood beside him, stripping off her clothes. First her cedar cape, painted in the images of the eagle and denoting her clan and rank, then the short leather skirt that had been concealed under it. Unbraided jet-black hair fell like twin curtains of midnight over her shoulders, barely covering the full breasts, like the ones he'd been thinking about most of the day whenever he caught a glimpse of them trapped under Chelen's T-shirt. Abalone and tiny shell beads nestled in her cleavage. Lust seized him, ripping past tired flesh and making his blood throb. His native princess stretched, arching her back, smiling.

A splash sounded as she slid into the pool behind him and reached out to touch him. He wanted to pull her to him, feel the brush of her nipples against his chest. Instead he felt the tickle of her hair against his back, sending a shiver through him. What the hell was happening to him?

Chelen shook him, her voice breaking the spell. "Hey, what's up?"

In a blink, the mirage vanished. Chelen's image blurred with the other woman's in the pool. Steam swirling around him. What was going on? Was he losing his mind?

When he opened his eyes, he found Chelen watching him. He couldn't see much of her under the water other than the outline of her body.

"What's up? I dunno. She was so real, so ..." How could he say, "So much like you," when he didn't know what Chelen looked like naked? The visions of the Haida princess were so lifelike, so much like Chelen. His dream of her naked in his arms sprang into his head, sending the blood rushing to reawaken parts of his anatomy. It had been far too long since he'd been with a woman, and his body betrayed his desire. He was glad he'd kept his shorts on.

"Who was real?" she breathed in his ear.

"I've no idea. This is strange, but I keep seeing visions of two natives, cavorting along the trail there, and here in the pool."

"Hey, take it easy with that imagination of yours. I'm gonna get jealous if you start hallucinating about another woman."

"No, I'm quite serious."

"Either that or that's one of the most original come-on tactics I've ever heard," she joked, but her eyes darkened in concern. "Could be all sorts of explanations. But my grandmother Rosemary used to say that time is never what it appears to be."

"See, I don't get that. Surely time is a fluid progression, one minute leading into the next and once it's done, it's gone." If he focused on Chelen's words, maybe the visions would go away. He imagined he heard moans behind him, and he didn't dare turn to look.

"To you Westerners, maybe. For us, time is a different issue altogether. Tell me, Brook, what time is it?"

He glanced over at his watch. "Ten-forty-three Pacific time, One-forty-three Eastern time."

"See, to me it's the end of the salmon run. I'll need to begin smoking fish soon for the winter. The berries for the most part should be picked by now, and it's nearly time for the spirit winds to come, along with the winter storms and ceremonials. To the Haida, time is a cycle. Everything runs in a continuous cycle. That's the way of the earth. You're born, connect with a past spirit, become an adult, grow old, die, become dust, and join the fellow ancestor spirits until you're called down to be reborn again. This is the way we think. Nothing has a beginning or an end. Everything I've talked about with you deals with connection. Every breath you take washes energy into the heavens. Every breath changes part of who you are and when you wake up in the morning you're different from the man who went to sleep."

Brook exhaled a deep breath and watched it join the channel of the universe, mingling with the mists from the hot spring as it disappeared into the cosmos. "What do you see behind me?" he asked her.

"Nothing. Well, other than the ocean, and the driftwood on the beach, and the steam from the pools."

He turned around. Chelen was right, yet the sensuous sighs still floated on the sulfur-laden air. As much as all this turned him on, it was beginning to scare the crap out of him.

"Are you sure you can't hear that?"

"What?" She cocked her head. "All I hear is the waves."

"A slave and a Haida princess, that's what I keep seeing. It's so vivid. I can hear them making love."

She gave him a long thoughtful look. "Well, there's a time and place for everything. The shamans used to come here to experience visions, and maybe in a past life you were one of us. It would explain some of the connections you're experiencing."

"A past life? That's too spooky. Except that could be why I've such a strong link to the totems at Sghaan Gway. I felt a compulsion to come here years ago, and again when I heard about the Golden Spruce being cut down."

"Possibly."

Brook leaned over the rocky enclosure separating the hot spring from the cold waters of the ocean. Her breath warmed his neck as arms folded around his body and the graze of erect nipples along his back sent a jolt through him.

"Don't turn around. Just let me feel you against me."

Slender hands slid along his chest. Her fingers curled through the hair and teased his tiny masculine nipples, hardened in the evening breeze. Her body brushed against him. He didn't know which woman he turned to kiss. He didn't care.

Her lips were pliant and inviting. Immediately, he pulled away. "Sorry. Not sure what came over me. I'm being driven wild by these images of the past. By your closeness. Holding you last night was incredible." He blurted it out. He hadn't been ready to go this far, this soon.

"For me, too. I've been resisting this all day, wondering what it would feel like to kiss you. I wanted to last night. It's been a long time since I've been with anyone, Brook. Maybe all these weird experiences you're having are due to me, projecting my desires onto you. Mentally seducing you."

"Oh, you're doing that all right. And more."

She smiled seductively. The relationship was racing ahead, faster than he'd ever dared hope.

He wanted her, more than anything else, he wanted to make love to Chelen.

"I've a bottle of wine back at our campsite. Care to head back and crack it open over dinner?" Her voice, husky with desire, broke the tension.

"Sure." She blew him away. Last night she broke his heart by telling him things could never work between them, and today she was making passes at him. Would he ever understand women?

They rose from the steaming waters, the chill of the night air prickling his skin. In the background the passionate cries of the phantom native princess resounded in his ears. Only who was the slave and who was the master?

Chelen's breath rose on the crisp air. They fixed a quick meal and settled down with the bottle of wine. Wood smoke hung lazily in the still night, the snap of the campfire chasing away the darkness and easing Brook's pent up energy. He savored the static charge of sensuality building like an approaching thunderstorm, filling the present with an unsettled calmness.

The alcohol eroded his borders of rationality, and his fears. Not that he needed anything to strip away his inhibitions. He hadn't seen any more hallucinations since they'd left the pool, but the lust-filled groans of the two natives lingered, though not as hot as the memory of

Chelen's kiss. He couldn't remember the last time a simple kiss had set his libido sizzling.

The campfire's heat warmed his leg while her hand moving over onto his thigh ignited chills of arousal. Enticing, demanding. Her fingers communicated she wanted more than friendship, much more. Ever the guide, Chelen led him, and he was more than content to let her. That in itself was thrilling. Besides, he definitely didn't want to push himself on her. Tonight he would go as far as she wanted and no more.

She drew closer. Hot blood coursing through him, his mouth hovered over hers.

"I've been fighting the attraction all day, trapped between not wanting to get involved and wanting to be with you," she murmured. "I'm afraid to kiss you again."

Was she for real? Brook reached forward, brushed her face. She gave life to his fantasies. "Me too."

"Yes. But what if, in a past life, that was us making love by the hot springs?"

"A week ago I'd have said no way, but now I could almost agree. You've shown me so much about native beliefs that I'm beginning to doubt my own sanity. This is crazy: you, me, this whole trip … especially you. But yeah … it could have been us."

God, he wanted her. She was so close he could smell the intoxicating aroma of cedar and spruce clinging to her clothes and the cloying hint of fermented grapes from her mouth, feel the heat of her breath. Her expression lured him, in spite of her words. "I'm so afraid to kiss you. What if what we think we feel isn't real?" He traced a finger over her lips. "Yet I can't stop."

He lowered his head to capture her lips. Suddenly, it was like coming home and there was no going back.

A deep moan escaped her. Brook grasped as the wine-taste of her washed over him, freeing a sea of desires. He moaned and pulled her closer.

The movement of her hand on his jeans, tracing the inside of his thigh, pulled him back to reality. What was he doing?

"Are you okay with this?" Her eyes were alive with her need for him. Her hand rested so near to the focus of his ache for her. Her fingers played, stealing his breath with the intensity of his arousal.

The anticipation left him trembling. "Yes."

"Then make love to me," she begged. "I can't promise this will last, so let's just make the most of this time together."

He pressed his index finger against her full lips and they parted slightly, signaling acceptance. Her tongue licked his finger.

Hot, wet. It suggested she wanted more than to lick his finger. He ran his fingertip, wet with her saliva, over her chin and to the base of her throat. "I want to taste you here, with my tongue. And here." He moved his hand down over her right breast.

She closed her eyes as his finger traced around her nipple. It was already hard, unfettered by underwear. The nipple responded, hardening even further.

"Oh, God." She shuddered.

"And here. I want to taste you here." He roamed lower, towards the juncture of her thighs. Even through her jeans he could feel the wetness. If one night was all he had, he wanted to fill each moment with memories.

As his hand moved back up to her waistband, Chelen stopped him and leaned in to kiss him again. It was like being fed a thousand volts of current, one seductive spark at a time, fusing his essence to hers. Like having a lightning bolt pass through his body. The psychic bonding of souls.

She pressed his hand downward, encouraging him to continue touching her through the denim barrier. Her other hand slipped up his thigh and rubbed against his hardness trapped in the confines of his pants. His fingers moved in unison with hers. *This is happening way too fast.* The thought skittered across his mind.

He rose, and Chelen allowed him to take control. Did some part of being dominated thrill her, scare the hell out of her, as it did him? They were rushing headlong down the breathless river of no return, almost against their will.

* * *

As he pulled Chelen to her feet, a part of her protested. She pushed it away and tried to ignore it. This wasn't Doug, it was Brook. It was insanity, but it was right. Every instinct told her that.

"Follow me to the tent," he whispered.

Chelen prayed he was different. Her heart couldn't take another crushing blow like the last one. His touch, and her reaction to it, shocked her.

Doug's kisses had never done that to her. She longed to be possessed, to be taken hard and fast by this virtual stranger.

The glow of the campfire mingled with the moonlight against the nylon tent walls. Brook bent to kiss her again and began to unbutton her shirt, his hands unsteady.

"No. You undress first," she gently ordered. She wanted to watch his body be revealed. She wanted to take him. She would not be denied.

In the dim coolness, shadows leaped. She tossed her own clothes into a crumpled pile in the corner, his following quickly. Goose bumps ranged across her skin, the scent of her arousal intensified in the close confines.

There was no retreat now and no denying the ache inside her.

"Just a minute," he said as he ripped open a foil package and quickly slipped on a condom. That simple, practical action restored her reason.

Should she do this? Could she really open up to a stranger? Let him touch her soul? Because he would.

Chelen had to have him — now. She would claim satisfaction for the yearnings inside. She pushed him back, straddled him and sank herself onto him. Arching her spine, she plunged down, accepting his full length.

"Oh," was all she managed to gasp as a shudder vibrated through her. A quiver, like the first spill of a dam bursting, sweeping away her sanity. "No," she moaned. "It's been too long."

Time lost its meaning as she thrust down on his hardness. Her hands pinned his shoulders and she shook, surrendering to the waves washing over her, savoring each movement of him inside her. Each convulsion triggered an answering shudder running through him.

"Oh God. I'm …" The orgasm paralyzed her, his thrusts sending barbs of sensation through her. Fear and pleasure collided and merged before bursting inside her like fireworks. Chelen surrendered herself to the emotions sweeping through her. Tears sprang to her eyes with the intensity of the experience.

"Oh." He convulsed, driving himself deeper into her before he collapsed in ecstasy. Arching her body above his like a bow, she cried out and collapsed into his arms. His heart hammered against her breast.

Never had making love torn apart every fiber of her being like that. Chelen pressed closer to his sweat-slicked chest. Was it him, or was it just her yearnings and the length of time since she'd been this intimate with someone?

He pulled the blanket over their still entwined bodies to ward off the chill and held her tight. The rhythm of his heart in her ear felt even more right.

She'd only wanted one night. She hadn't expected it to be this overwhelming. What had she gotten herself into?

She snuggled into the warmth of his body. Outside, thick fog rolled in, drowning out the background sough of the surf and the sighs of the ghosts making love under the cedars while sulfur mists swirled heavenward, cutting them off from the rest of the world.

Chapter Twelve

The tent flaps snapped in the dawn breeze. The coolness of the empty space beside him woke Brook. Sunlight had barely begun to penetrate the shadows under the trees, and he rolled over, squinting in the dim light of early morning.

"Chelen?" Still lost in that place where reality and dreamtime coexisted, he let his eyes close, sleep tugging him back under its thick blanket. His dreams had been reruns of last night, making love with Chelen, over and over.

His hand stole across the covers, but he was alone, lying there with that weak but satisfied feeling that comes from making love all night long.

It had been too good. No, Chelen had been too good. Letting him break down her defenses. And in doing so, she'd touched places in him that he didn't know existed. Making love to other women had never been that intense. He only hoped it wasn't too soon, that this wasn't a rebound thing. It would suck if they both ended up getting hurt again.

No. This felt way too good, way too natural. It had to be the real thing.

In the back of his head though, another thread of doubt lingered. A childhood memory of the little boy who had never been good enough for his father. His eyes opened wide. The same dread as had assailed him on the ferry struck again.

"Chelen! Chelen!" he hollered as he rose, shivering in the gloom. No response except silence to fuel his anxiety. He stuck his head out of the tent while struggling to pull on a shirt. Panic clawed at his guts, chasing away the last vestiges of sleep. "Chelen?"

Dense fog had rolled in from the ocean. He could barely see in front of him. Last night's fire had burnt itself out, the dark ashes gleaming dully in the moisture-laden air. She hadn't got up to start a fire.

"Damn." Diving back into the tent, he scrambled into the rest of his clothes, trying to shake the grogginess from his limbs. It must have been the lovemaking that had left him so weak. He slipped into a pair of tight sweatpants … they weren't his, probably Chelen's. He didn't take the time to find his own. But if she didn't have her sweats on, what was she wearing?

The apprehension he'd felt on the day of his arrival returned threefold. He gagged, swallowing the bile that rose in his throat. Something was very wrong. Staggering outside he tripped on the tent flap, eerie stillness greeting him as he stood shivering in the cloying dampness. The heavy curtain of fog muted any rustling of leaves or squawking of gulls, and weighted his hair, plastering it against his face. Like being caressed by a wet haddock rather than something supernatural like the Haida believed. It was too cold for Chelen to wander off, especially without sweats. She should be snuggled up beside him, sleeping. Hell, he should be sleeping.

The warm security of his blanket called to him, and he longed to crawl back under it. Perhaps he should. His fear was probably all nonsense. Chelen was most likely fine. Maybe this was one of the weird dreams he'd been having. He'd wake up and the woman would be there in his arms. Turning, he took a step back towards the tent, simultaneously arguing with his body's urge to slide back under those delicious covers and his very real fear that Chelen was in danger.

The trepidation weighed in the back of his mind like the beginning stages of a migraine. A voice of impending danger sang through the haze that clouded his clarity. He'd only had a couple of glasses of wine last night, so he couldn't be still be drunk or hung-over. Mind you, what with the kayaking and the dip in the hot tub, maybe he'd been badly dehydrated. The wine did hit him pretty quick.

No, something was definitely wrong. *"Sleep. Enjoy the morning sleep. After the fog lifts, you can get up."* A seductive voice whispered through the fog. Brook tipped his head to the side, listening. The voice lulled him, sapping his energy, coaxing him back to the tent. He shook his head to rid it of the insistent urging.

"Perhaps this is a dream," he told himself. "Relax."

"Chelen!" he yelled again, fighting the pressure that deadened his arms and interfered with his thinking.

No. He wasn't sleeping and he wasn't dreaming. Nor was there any Haida princess and her slave running around the island. Hell, he couldn't even believe his eyes anymore. What he could do was trust the prodding of his intuition and allow it to guide him. He took two more steps towards the tent; it was so much easier to move towards it. Inside, he bent over and dug through his backpack and tucked his hunting knife into the elastic band of the sweatpants. His camera, he noticed, had been pulled from its case and the lens shattered.

Taking a deep breath, he headed back towards the shore, each step like walking through quicksand. The rock-strewn beach was still and the tide had gone out while they'd slept. The fog embraced him, their campsite disappearing into the nebulous mist. Then he spotted what looked like the two kayaks on the beach, right side up, their delicate fiberglass bottoms resting against the harsh rocks.

"That's impossible," he murmured, "we set them upside down last night, far from the water." But as he got closer he realized that one of the long shapes lining the beach was not a kayak but a drift log.

A muffled splash echoed in the gray blanket of the fog. A paddle? Was that the sound of a paddle? Another couple of steps brought him to the waves' edge, where he strained to see across the waters. Mists moved in and out like white sheets on a clothesline. Was that the shape of a kayak, bobbing a few yards off shore?

"Chelen!" he called, loud enough for her to hear him. Another splash, as if she continued to paddle. On the back of his neck, his skin tingled like a thousand bugs crawling out of his hair. He swung around and glared at the veiled vegetation lining the beach. Every shady space concealed a foreign presence, and under each bush lurked eyes, as if something or someone was watching him. With a great effort, he tore his gaze away and struggled to his kayak.

"Go to sleep. She'll be right back." the voice whispered.

"No. Go away," he yelled as he scooted inside the kayak. The paddle weighed a ton. He barely managed to push away from shore. Was it a dream, after all? He didn't have the time or spare energy to pinch himself.

Just ahead he could see the outlines of Chelen's kayak.

"Chelen! Wait!" Her body shimmered in and out of the morning mists, but she never moved to acknowledge his voice, as if she were sleepwalking. "That's it. She's sleepwalking. She has to be."

As he approached the kayak, drawing away from the supposed safety of the beach, his strength began returning. The fog that seemed to be dimming his thoughts parted and he glanced back towards the shore. On the beach, as the mists weaved in and out, the apparition of a huge black bird-shaped object appeared, strutting on the sand. It hadn't been there earlier, he was certain. Then the fog closed around him again, cutting him off from the land, and from Chelen in the kayak somewhere ahead of him. Sweat broke out on his forehead. It would be so easy to become disoriented on the open sea. He redoubled his efforts to reach her. The kayak loomed suddenly out of the mist, three meters away from him. It floated motionless while several dark shapes cut through the water, under his kayak. Fish, he thought at first. Big fish.

Moments later, Chelen screamed as her kayak tilted to one side. Shadows surrounded her. Whales? No, whatever the things were they were hairier, and they certainly weren't fish. Probably seals or …

A shudder ran through him as the strangeness registered. No. The creatures were the stuff of nightmares, they didn't exist, they weren't real. Wild splashing accompanied Chelen's terrified scream as she thrashed at the beings with her paddle. He swore he'd seen a dozen hairy hands reaching up and grasping her kayak. He couldn't be certain in the shifting fog.

Something jostled his own craft, sending spears of electrifying fear to his heart. "Sweet Jesus, no."

A caw, the voice of a raven, came from the shore, slicing through the cloying thickness. Its mocking cry stripped away the last of his tiredness. Rage seethed in his heart. Damned if he'd let the creatures have her. Not Chelen, not ever.

The water was still alive with frothy bubbles and ripples of movement as Brook pulled alongside the upside-down craft. Where was Chelen? He flipped the kayak over easily. Damn it.

The drawstring on the kayak's skirt that should have held her safe inside was torn.

"No! You bastards." He shoved the empty kayak away. Shock held him immobile until something jostled him again. He could only stare in disbelief as a pair of hands reached upwards and whatever was attached to them latched onto the rim of his hull. Coarse brown hair covered the arms. The kayak dipped as a face peered up over the bow, revealing the creature, or one just like it, that he'd seen at the Golden Spruce. Its grotesque lips were pulled back from its teeth in a grisly grimace.

"*Kushtaka.*" Brook stuttered in terror. "No. No, I don't believe in you." He lifted his paddle and swung it as hard as he could, half expecting it to cut through thin air. What he struck was not imaginary. Blood spewed over the bow as the supposedly mythological beast cried out in shrill horror and sank under the waves, clutching its bloody head.

Other hands reached up and clutched the kayak, high-pitched screams shattering the calm. Before Brook could bring the paddle down again, the Pacific loomed up at him and whatever was beneath capsized him. The water teemed with *kushtakas* as he kicked free of the kayak. *Chelen? Where is Chelen?*

Something grabbed his heel and tried to pull him under. "No! I don't believe in *kushtakas*." He kicked at it with his free foot. Breaking the surface, Brook pulled in great draughts of air.

What was it Chelen said they feared? Metal. His knife. He jerked the blade from its holster. Salt water closed over his head, the coldness stiffening his fingers as he slashed at whatever still held him by the ankle. Jabbing wildly, he kept chanting the same message over and over like a madman's mantra. "No! I don't believe! This isn't real! I don't believe!"

Whatever held him let go, and both of his legs kicked free. Red clouded the water.

Lungs bursting, Brook swam upward. Other *kushtakas* swarmed towards him, trying to cut

231

him off from reaching the surface. He slashed at them, too, until he finally broke away. Gasps of air mixed with gulps of salty water. He coughed wretchedly, choking as he fought to stay afloat. Shrill screams rent the air and the *kushtakas*, or whatever they were, disappeared. Crimson spirals hung in the turgid water. Hypothermia took only a couple of minutes in the open sea, and he felt his hold on consciousness weakening. The cold water leaching the warmth of his body.

Chelen?

"I don't believe," he muttered, as he floundered past the two abandoned kayaks. He allowed the pull of the crashing surf to steer him toward what he hoped was the shoreline. A raven's call was the last thing he heard as darkness clouded his vision and frigid waters closed over him.

* * *

"There's more than one way to trick you."

The odd voice spoke in Brook's throbbing head. The crash of spume against rock... he must have managed to wash ashore. He fought to open his eyes, swollen by the sting of salt water. Through the haze the familiar outline of an oversized raven shimmered. It stood gloating over him, with one bent wing and grayed tips to its feathers.

"Chelen?" he rasped, forcing the words past the agony in his throat.

"Somewhere you can't reach her. Now give me the stone. My patience is running out."

"In my backpack, take it, you can have it."

Triumph gleamed in Raven's eyes as he rummaged through the pack, hurling things every which way until the shiny rock twinkled in his beak. Throwing his head back, Raven opened his mouth and allowed the stone to fall back into his throat, to rest in its former spot.

Brook struggled to remain awake, fascinated at the transformation taking place before his eyes. One bent-up, crippled wing began to straighten itself and the silvery tinges darkened to jet black. For a moment the bird before him turned into Marten Crow, then back to Raven.

"Ah, Brook. You should have given me my immortal stone when you had the chance at lunch the other day. It would have been easier that way. Instead I was forced to compel you to bring it along on this journey. I could pull your heart out through your ribcage, but a little suffering before you die for the misery you put me through only seems fair. Don't you agree? Goodbye, Brook."

Raven stretched his wings wide, and flapped once or twice before he lifted upwards.

Brook tried to sit up. He had to go look for Chelen ... she was out there in the frigid waters. His body refused to obey him and he slumped over, the grit of the beach rasping against his cheek. His eyes closed against his will and he faded away.

* * *

At last, he had regained his immortal stone, and the strength was already returning to him. He'd wasted enough time on the pale-skinned man. Raven stretched his wings, reveling in the powerful, rejuvenating sensations of flight. Now, he was ready to truly help his people.

He would awaken Foam Woman. She would know how to bring about the return of the Haida and the old ways.

* * *

The grate of crushed seashells underfoot roused Brook again. Someone, or something, jabbed at him. Had Raven come to finish him off? His eyes were swollen, his mouth dry, his head pounding. He tried to sit, but every bone and muscle in his body protested. Just that simple movement sent pain stabbing through him. Not only did this feel like the worst hangover he'd ever had, but his teeth were chattering, confirming just how cold and wet he was. He had to get warm, find some dry clothes. Even as he thought it, he slumped back over and lay still. At least it didn't hurt to do that, much.

"Now, this is one sad-looking character," said an unexpected but welcome voice that pierced his stupor.

"Charlie?" Brook groaned. As he rolled over, his stomach rose up in his throat. "Oh, I think I'm going to be sick." He lurched up and leaned sideways, hurling out the Pacific Ocean he'd swallowed.

"You know, sucking back sea water is not a highly recommended sport around these parts."

Brook wiped his face with his hand. "Trust me, it wasn't intentional." The earlier events replayed themselves in his mind and he looked up, saw that the fog had lifted and a gray sky loomed overhead. How long had he been out? Then he spotted Charlie's beached kayak, along with his and Chelen's.

Chelen?

Her kayak was there. Everything that happened; it must have been a dream. He could have sobbed with relief. "Chelen!" he cried. Where was she?

Charlie frowned and went very pale. "You mean she's not with you?"

"No. I mean, yes. She must be here somewhere. Her kayak's not gone, after all." He had to rescue her, had to get her back.

Charlie crouched down beside him, his face intent. "Now think, Brook, have you seen Chelen this morning?"

"No. I don't think so. I thought I did, but it was just a dream. Her kayak's there, isn't it?"

"I found her kayak. And yours. Drifting out there on the ocean. Brought them with me."

Oh, God. It wasn't a dream.

"Charlie, Chelen's gone. They've got her," he blurted out. Brook wanted to collapse into the middle of the mess he'd created and cry, but he hadn't the energy. His guts heaved again, only this time there wasn't anything left to throw up.

"Who's they? What are you talking about, Chelen's gone?" Charlie shook him. "You're starting to babble, man. Get a grip on yourself."

He stared up into the shaman's eyes. "I believe, Charlie. They've got her. The *kushtakas*."

"What!"

His head pounding, Brook relayed what had happened that morning. "Is she still alive, Charlie? We have to get her back!" He clenched his sides, trying to conserve some body heat as he shivered uncontrollably.

"First, we need to get you to a fire and dry you out. I know you're concerned about Chelen, but right now I think you've got hypothermia." Charlie stared out at the ocean, his face mirroring his inner anxiety.

"I'm more than concerned about her. Because ..." Brook choked on his words. "Because I really care for her, that's why. I'll do anything to get her back. Anything."

"Well, you just may have to do that. Let me secure your kayaks and then you can take me to your campsite. Get some heat and hot food into you. Later, while you're packing up, I'll journey to the *kushtakas'* village and see if she's there. I hope she is." Charlie helped him to his feet and together they walked over to the kayaks. "I was afraid something like this might happen, and that's why I'm here. After you two left, I began to search for the prince and do some looking into the lapis lazuli you found at the Golden Spruce. I didn't come across Kiidkayaas, or Raven for that matter, but found plenty of evidence that Raven is up to his old stunts. The one thing he needs to survive is his immortal stone, which meant you weren't safe. Hence why I'm here."

Next to Brook's kayak was the paddle he'd used to club the *kushtaka* over the head. But nowhere on it, or on the kayak, was there any sign of blood.

"Speaking of Raven," Charlie added, "do you still have his stone?"

"No. That's what Raven came here to find, and he's got it."

"Dammit, now we're in trouble."

"How'd you know where we were, anyway?" Brook asked, his head beginning to clear.

"You wouldn't believe me if I told you."

"Try me. After what's been going on this morning, I'd believe anything." He gagged, spitting up more of the ocean.

"Ah, a convert. Actually, I talked to the tree spirits, and they told me your whereabouts."

As they headed to the campsite, Charlie explained further.

"Since you two left, I've been searching the spirit lands. And before long I discovered that Raven had been very active, waking up several entities, including the *kushtakas*. It piqued my curiosity, so I visited the land of the tree spirits. They have eyes everywhere and they told me Raven had flown ahead of you. Seems he's desperate to save his people at any cost and for that he needs his immortal stone. Right now, he's on his way to see *Sruhlru Jaad*."

"Who?"

"Foam Woman, or Drift Ashore Woman, as she's sometimes called. She's the one who gave Raven his powers, and she has the power to recreate things. That's where Raven set off for after he retrieved his stone this morning ... Foam Woman's valley, to wake her up so he can change things back to the way they once were. Seems he can't handle the way the world is now and feels responsible for the Haida's demise as a people."

"So are you telling me what I think I'm hearing? That Raven is going to wipe out everything that's occurred since he got trapped in that Golden Spruce with Kiidkayaas, and return things to how they were before the white man came?"

"You're very bright, Brook. We must stop him. By tinkering with the established order,

Raven has set in motion changes and events far beyond his control. Even within the trees themselves, things are very unsettled right now."

"What do you mean, changes?"

"Well, I'm not sure. But things are evolving unexpectedly out there."

Brook stared into the greenery of the forest, where lushness cloaked every branch, but his mind wasn't on the natural beauty around him. This trip, that he'd hoped would be a retreat from life, a chance to heal his shattered ego, had evolved into a bizarre adventure that got crazier at every juncture. He held his jaw tight to keep it his teeth from chattering so violently, afraid he'd crack his teeth. Home. Why couldn't he just go home?

"Do you want to see Chelen back and alive?"

"Of course I do." His heart sank as they arrived at the camp, where the bottle of wine still sat by the fire's ashes. His world view had changed radically within the last few hours, and he'd changed just as much since he met Chelen. The harsh reality of her beliefs come to life haunted him until he wanted to sit down, hold his head in his hands and cry. Instead, he glared at Charlie. "More than anything I want her back, safe with me."

"Then, whether you believe or not, if the *kushtakas* have her, we'll have to go and intercept Raven. He's the one who's awoken the spirit beings. If we can defeat him, then all will return to the normal way of things. But if we let him win, there's no telling what else he'll bring back from the past."

Immediately, Charlie set about gathering wood. In Brook's tent, clothing and belongings were strewn about. The immortal stone wasn't there. Raven's visit had been no dream and the proof was right in front of him.

"He's definitely got the stone. It's gone," he called through the canvas. "Wait a minute. Didn't Chelen tell me only a shaman could travel to the *kushtakas'* village? Are you going to rescue her?"

"Well, I sure intend to give it a try. But with Raven in possession of his immortal stone again, I don't have the power to go up against him and the *kushtakas*. Like I said, if we can get to Foam Woman's valley in time to stop him, then everything should return to the way it was before he showed up in the modern world. Which should also mean that the *kushtakas* should return to where they were before this all began, and Chelen should come back to us."

"That's an awful lot of shoulds. I need her back, Charlie."

"Well, theoretically that's the way it's supposed to work. But then, theoretically, communism works incredibly well. In reality, it sucks. Anytime you get someone in absolute power, they corrupt absolutely and the whole system evolves into a dictatorship. In the spirit world, nothing is definite. It's always in a state of flux, and that's the only constant thing."

"What do you know about communism? I wouldn't have thought that was part of the shaman's manual?" Brook pulled on his jeans and a warm sweater, and then crawled around the tents, collecting their gear. The scent of their lovemaking lingered. Well, that much was real anyway, he thought. Nothing else seemed to make sense any more.

"I've got cable. It's amazing what you can learn on those educational channels when there's no Bluejay ballgames on."

The spit of kindling catching fire suggested that Charlie was getting a good blaze going. Brook emerged wrapped in his sleeping blanket and seated himself beside the fire pit, rubbing his hands together as close to the leaping flames as he dared. Just donning dry clothes made a world of difference in his attitude and he thawed out as he let the heat lick at him.

"I'm going to journey to the other realms and see if I can locate Chelen. You need to get some rest and warm up. Stay here and guard my body while I'm gone."

"I'll make something to eat, and let me guess. Page fourteen of the shaman's operational manual says time required for an altered state rescue is dependent on unknown variables."

"You catch on quick, I can say that for you." The elder smiled as he crossed his legs and closed his eyes. "Just put the coffee on. I'll probably need some when I come back. And oh, in case you forgot, don't go near my medicine pouch."

"Trust me, I'd sooner swim in a moat filled with alligators than touch that thing again." Brook fed another log into the fire.

After an hour or so, Charlie was still in his altered state and Brook, having eaten and consumed some caffeine, was feeling much better. The shivering had stopped altogether and while he had the chance he packed up the tents. He wasn't sure if he could trust where Charlie was going to take him. Hell, he didn't even know if he could trust the old man period. But at this point he didn't have a whole lot of choice. Chelen. Was she still alive? What if she wasn't? No, he couldn't go there. Think positive, he had to think positive.

Once he had everything stashed away, Brook sipped at the dregs of the coffee, saving a couple of cups for Charlie. The whole experience, being here on Haida Gwaii this time, was a dream, some kind of glitch in his imagination. If someone had told him a week ago that he'd be preparing to go backpacking through the woods with a Haida shaman looking for a Raven god-figure so that he could rescue a native girl he'd fallen in love with, after she'd been captured by some otter-like creatures that lived beneath the sea, Brook would have laughed his head off and told the person they were a stark raving nutter.

Only now, who was the stark raving lunatic? Because now Brook had to go and rescue Chelen from one of the most powerful god-figures in Haida mythology. How could a man who'd never measured up to anything in his father's eyes, be expected to succeed?

He should go home and forget it, why waste the effort? Pulling his blanket over him, Brook leaned back, folded his hands behind his head, and sank into the spongy moss.

He could have done just that at one time, but not now. This time too much was at stake. For Chelen, but perhaps also for his whole world, if Charlie was to be believed.

* * *

Charlie picked his way through the layers of the other worlds. Everything was unsettled, like freshly turned sod. Things forming and reforming, dissolving into itself and emerging as something else. Chaos had awakened and disturbed the ordered existence of the universe.

"This is Raven's doing," Charlie muttered as his spirit journeyed. "I fear he's sticking his beak into matters he knows nothing about."

The shaman's spirit settled on the shores of the land of the dead ones. Many newly arrived souls paced restlessly, unable to cross the waters, longing to go to the other side. He glanced around, but Chelen wasn't here like he'd hoped. At least from this place it would have been a simple matter to retrieve her. There was one place to go next, but first he wanted to investigate something. He looked down at the trail where he'd first seen Wolf and Bear's footprints merging with Raven's, just as Rosemary dreamed.

He touched one of the prints and felt himself drawn away to another world. He'd been there once before, many years ago when he was an aspiring shaman collecting one of his animal spirits. Howls split the hush of the valley he found himself in. A full moon hung in the sky. In this place, the moon seemed to be always full.

Another chorus of howls sliced the air, coming from everywhere it seemed, shattering the stillness of the night. He stood on a high cliff, and the yelps echoed around him in a crazed, high-pitched lament. Begging for the return of a loved spirit, mourning the lost soul of one of their kind. Compassion and fear filled Charlie's spirit. He wanted to join his voice to the haunting cries and let his soul sing freely.

Amid the trees, shapes moved. They were hunters and would know if someone stalked their grounds. The mists swirled as they broke the forest's cover: black wolves that prowled like jaguars; white wolves that paced to and fro, restless like snowflakes driven before a blizzard.

Common brown wolves merely sat on their haunches and glared at him, howls ripping their throats. But the gray alpha male with the ice-blue eyes didn't appear.

That was the sprit beast Charlie had seen merging with Raven, in the swirl of light that enveloped the white raven and the other spirit beings in the canoe, when he'd made his earlier trip to the land of the dead ones. That was the one he'd captured as a totem spirit long ago.

A large gray female stood on a rock beside the pack. Alone.

"He is not here." Her thoughts assailed him. Rage, tinged with sorrow vibrated in the tones of her mind speech. *"My mate is not here. We are unsure of what to do."*

*Empathy filled his heart as he w*atched the creature bow her proud head before she pointed her muzzle to the sky and let out a soulful pain-filled cry. The anguish in her voice spoke to Charlie tales of their past: their times together, the hunt, moments of passion, raising young ones, all gone.

As well, that howl told Charlie everything he needed to know. His wolf spirit was gone. Raven's work.

"Return him to us, shaman." A chorus of yelps splintered the night.

Charlie recognized the urgency behind the demand. "I will do what I can to return your mate to you." He needed to leave this place and continue his search.

Charlie's spirit drifted off to a land near the ocean, where he searched in the wintering dens. All empty. Then he made for the river's edge, where the great white Kermode spirit bears gathered every fall to gorge on the returning salmon. But no torn carcasses or fish heads littered the shore, and nowhere was the plodding form of the grizzly bear to be found. Instead many dying salmon littered the waters and riverbanks.

"Eat us, please, give us mercy," they begged Charlie. Suffering, as they flopped frantically in their death throes.

Another one of his animal spirits gone. Its disappearance smacked of more of Raven's doing.

Charlie sent his spirit into the water, certain he knew where he'd find Chelen, but Wolf and Bear had deserted him and he didn't have the time or energy to look for them at the moment. He would have to attend to that matter when this was all over and his niece was safe. As he descended into the river's depths and headed towards the open sea, thousands of salmon streamed by, intent on their journey to the spawning grounds.

He kept swimming down until he came to several caves. Even here, the *kushtakas* were restless, several milling about. He hid behind a rock. If they saw him, he'd be captured and they'd try to make him one of them. Below their realm he swam and carefully ascended until he surfaced inside one of the caves, where he looked around and went on to the next. Finally, he found the one cave that held the bodies of the newly captured. The *kushtakas* had been busy, all the captives would be transformed into one of their kind. It would be too late if Chelen had already gone through the transformation.

His heart leaped in joy at the sight of Chelen, sitting in a corner talking to an elder. Everywhere guards patrolled. No way could he fight them all. Closing his eyes, he pulled the tongue of the land otter from his pouch and draped it around his neck. His form shimmered, his lips pulled back to his nose. Coarse brown hair covered his body and his arms shifted until they grew not from his shoulders, but out of his chest. Disguise complete, he strode quickly over to Chelen.

"It's so good to see you, Rosemary," she was saying to her companion, an elder who was really another *kushtaka*. They often took the form of departed relatives, in order to fool people into their realm.

"Come, there is a white man here to see you," he hissed at Chelen. Hair was beginning to cover her body, but her lips hadn't pulled back yet. She was changing, but it was still not too late to save her. The *kushtaka* with her glared at him.

"Brook? He's here?" She stood up.

"Follow me," Charlie ordered, and moved toward a group of rocks. Chelen followed on his heels. The *kushtaka* pretending to be Rosemary kept them under a watchful eye. Did it suspect he wasn't really one of them? He had to be quick or it would cry out an alarm.

"Where is he?" Chelen asked.

Charlie stared into her eyes. "It's me, Chelen."

"What? Charlie? But you're a *kushtaka*. Where's Brook? I want to show him to Rosemary." She spoke slowly, as if drugged. Over her shoulder, he could see the other *kushtaka* rising to its feet. Damn, he had to be quicker. In order to leave with her he'd have to get them both past the guards, and since he doubted he could do that, he had to stop the transformation process as quickly as possible. There was only one way.

"Listen to me, my niece. You've been captured by the *kushtakas*. The one you've been talking to is not your grandmother."

Chelen looked over her shoulder at the hairy form heading towards them. Her eyes widened. "Oh God, Charlie, the last thing I remember is getting up and leaving the tent. Voices. I'd heard voices outside and went to investigate."

"They've captured you, and tried to get Brook as well, but he escaped."

"Is he okay?" As she spoke her eyes cleared, shaking off the *kushtaka* spell.

"He's safe with me. We'll be heading off soon to find Raven. He's responsible for all this. He's planning on turning the clock back by a couple hundred years, and he's gotta be stopped." Now the *kushtaka* was searching the rocks, trying to locate them. Failing in its search, the creature veered towards one of the guards by the entrance to the cave. "Now we're in trouble. Look, I can't take you out of here, there's too many of them. You'll have to stay until I find a way to defeat Raven."

"I can't stay. This place is horrible."

Charlie pulled the land otter's tongue from around his neck. As he did so, he shed the animal spirit's form. "Put this on. My guardian spirit will transform you into a *kushtaka*, like I was. They'll think you're one of them. For now, you'll be safe. If you're found out, the land otter spirit will fight for you. Now go."

She donned the talisman and her form shimmered and changed, just as several guards approached their hiding place.

When she walked right past them into the center of the cave, none of them even glanced in her direction. Thank the Creator, they'd been fooled. Charlie closed his eyes and allowed his spirit to dissipate and be drawn back to his body.

Wolf, Bear, and now Land Otter spirit … some of his strongest allies were gone. What should he do? It wasn't possible to go up against Raven alone and win. But there was another ally: the spirit of his pouch.

He sighed. The pouch was supposed to be created from the skin of the creature whose spirit was too great to be contained. Too strong was the animal's spirit to ever attempt to wear it around the neck. Charlie shivered; it would require all the energy and courage he could muster. Some spirits he could sit down with, drink beer, spill chips, and play poker. Some, he'd only be in the same place with if he possessed a bazooka, a machete, and a small armed nuclear tactical missile. This was one of the latter. The spirit that guarded the entrance to the valley of Foam Woman, where he knew from the trees that Raven was headed.

In Eastern Canada they called him Wendingo. Here, he was called Buhkwuss, Sasquatch, or simply, Wild Man of the Woods.

Chapter Thirteen

Brook lurched upright. A glance around told him it was past midday so he must have slept for at least a couple of hours. Most of the fog had burnt off, as it usually did along the coast. He looked, but couldn't see Charlie anywhere, although the aroma of freshly brewed coffee lingered. The shaman must have come out of his trance a while ago.

Brook grimaced and shook his head in frustration. "Not again," he muttered. "I fall asleep and people disappear."

To his relief, Charlie came strolling out from behind some trees, sporting a rather sheepish expression. "Hey, even shamans have to answer the call of nature," he growled. His limp seemed worse this morning.

Brook studied the old man; something seemed off about him, as if it was Charlie, but not Charlie. The medicine pouch was missing from its usual place around his neck. Charlie never took the thing off. Except, maybe, to go to the bathroom? Then again ...

Charlie bent over the fire and stirred the coals. Brook moved quickly behind him and drew his knife. One hand gripped the elder around the neck, while with the other he held the steel blade of the knife to the old man's throat. His actions would trigger a response if Charlie was who Brook feared he might be.

"Hey, are you crazy?" he sputtered as Brook released him. He didn't transform into one of the creatures that captured Chelen, or into Raven. Charlie was the real thing.

"Sorry. You didn't have your medicine pouch on and I thought you might be a *kushtaka*. Chelen told me what metal does to them."

Charlie laughed, half coughing and spitting. "I guess we've definitely made a convert out of you, haven't we?"

Brook put his knife away. "I didn't want to take any chances. Did you find Chelen?"

"Yeah, I did. The *kushtakas* are holding her in one of their villages below the sea. My Land Otter spirit is watching over her. She'll be okay, for now."

Thank heavens, there was hope, no matter how slim, that he could get her back. "Then let's grab a bite to eat and get moving." Brook was suddenly full of energy. "We've a bird to fricassee and a damsel to rescue."

* * *

Brook and Charlie spent the better part of the day paddling back up the coast in the kayaks, retracing the route Brook and Chelen had taken. Her empty kayak bobbed behind them, tethered by a short rope. When they reached Lyell Island, instead of skirting around it, they veered

252

between it and Moresby Island, along Darwin Sound to a place Charlie called Qinggi. The abandoned village guarded the trailhead to the valley where Foam Woman lived, he said in the few words he spoke. "Legend has it that after the great flood, Raven was found soaking wet and despondent, so he was adopted by the tribe. Raven returned the favor by summoning four different tribes of men from the ground. That's how the various tribes, the Haida, Tsimshian, Tlingit, and Kwakuitl were born."

"Nice guy. Some way of rewarding your rescuers. Awaken some new neighbors for you to fight with." Brook laughed.

"Always the trickster." Although for his age, Charlie was a surprisingly strong paddler, he was unusually withdrawn and intent, and didn't bother responding to Brook's humor with his usual sarcastic remarks.

This was a side of the elder that Brook had rarely seen. Several times he would stop, close his eyes and send his spirit ahead to investigate every break in the trees. The trailhead was not only rarely used, but purposely hidden so outsiders would never find it.

Once again, the weather began to turn ugly, an approaching squall whipping up the water. From the roiling clouds grumbles of thunder rumbled closer and louder. A thunderhead looming on the horizon sent apprehension rippling through Brook as they kayaked into a narrowing chasm. Rock walls rose straight out of the sea, churned white surf dashing itself on the granite crags. Brook wondered if the storm would strike at any moment, or blow over. If it didn't pass them by, they'd be hammered into the sheer cliffs edging closer on each side.

Anxiety twisted like a pent-up cobra in his stomach. Where was Chelen? Was it possible she really was a prisoner in some otters' village below the tossing seas? Was she okay?

Finally, Charlie smiled and pointed. "The trailhead."

Brook beached his kayak by Charlie's and heaved a sigh of relief. They pulled the vessels up on a narrow strip of sand and flipped them over beside a stream cutting a path through the woods to the ocean. The normally small waterway was threatening to erupt in fury. For the first time, Charlie looked nervous, and he knew it wasn't from the storm bearing down on them. The shaman was unsure and afraid.

"We'll set up camp here tonight, in the forest," Charlie decided. "The spirits are very restless. It'll be a long day of hiking tomorrow, and first I'll need to open the entrance to the valley we seek."

He pulled some grayish-looking grass from his pouch. "I'm going to smudge the area to clear it of any harmful spirits, and then smudge us. We are being watched, but I can't tell by what. If you should get up in the night, do not pass these trees. This is the edge of your safe boundaries." He walked up to certain trees and incised them with a sigil using his knife, muttering apologies to the tree spirits.

"And what if I forget?" Brook asked in mild curiosity.

"Then in most likelihood, I'll be hiking alone tomorrow." Charlie smiled and patted his medicine bag. "My remaining animal spirits will be on guard during the night. Oh, and Brook, you may hear me talking to spirits later. If you do, it would be wise to stay inside your tent, and don't dare to look out."

Brook didn't even want to ask why. "What about you? Aren't you going to get some shut-eye?"

"I have some preparations to make and some spirits to honor. I often go without sleep and food during times like this. I need all my focus on my task, and I can't be distracted by mundane pastimes like resting, eating, and the elimination of body fluids."

Brook stared as the shaman pulled a long tunic that looked as if it had been freshly oiled from his backpack. He then produced several rattles, and what appeared to be hollow bones, one of which had a dragon of some sort carved on each end.

"A soul catcher," he muttered in response to Brook's inquiring look. Charlie placed a necklace of claws and assorted animal parts around his neck. "These are amulets containing the powers of the spirits I've collected, all except the Land Otter, which is protecting Chelen right now." He pointed out other scraps of petrified triangular flesh that vaguely looked like they could be from the tongues of some unfortunate creatures. Next he smudged charcoal all over his face, and then took off his baseball cap — for the first time in Brook's presence — and undid the knot of hair underneath it. He shook the long hair loose, letting it unravel well past his shoulders, like some ancient guru hippy.

"Ah, this doesn't look like one of your regular meditative spirit journeys."

"It isn't." The normally jovial shaman was deadly serious. "Some of my spirit animals are gone. Raven's meddling, I suspect. Normally, it takes six to eight days of fasting to create the trancelike state I need to capture a new animal spirit, but I only have tonight." He sat cross-legged, hands resting on his knees, and closed his eyes.

"Before you go, Charlie, do you believe in past lives, like Chelen does?"

"Of course. Why do you ask?"

"It's just that when she and I were at the hot springs I kept seeing visions of a Haida princess and her slave. Is it possible I could have been native in a past life?"

Charlie sent him a probing look, and then grunted once. "Very possible. There's always been a residue of native energy around your being that I've been unable to trace. But I was willing to leave that alone, since I suspected it was merely a result of the threads that soulmates cast so strongly between themselves."

"Soul-mate threads?" Just when he was beginning to start believing in some of the incredible things that were happening to him and in the world around him, Charlie threw something new into the mix.

"I didn't want to say anything earlier, but when I sensed the strong connection between you and Chelen I knew it was more, much more than physical attraction. True soulmates is what you are. In all the universe each of us has only one soulmate. These souls cast strong spirit threads between them which travel unseen, pulling each soul to their inevitable meeting. But that I imagine you already realized, even if you don't believe in such matters."

With that headline-news bombshell Charlie smiled and closed his eyes again. "See ya in the morning, and remember this."

"What?"

"Black, I like my coffee very black, think tar and cut back the water content."

Brook laughed. This was more like the Charlie he knew.

The shaman went limp and for a moment Brook swore he saw a shimmer rising from the body before he was gone, his shaman's spirit venturing to whatever lands or realms he needed to travel to. As the daylight waned, Brook pitched the tents, built a fire and cooked some supper, which he ate sitting alone beside the crackling logs. Chelen's absence was a tangible essence in the cedar-drenched twilight. Was she his soulmate? Had they met before in a different time, roamed Haida Gwaii as princess and slave? More than anything, he wished she was sitting beside him now, telling him about her world and turning his beliefs upside down. The circumstances of her disappearance left him reeling, with the logical, Western part of his brain insisting on rational explanations. But wherever she was, she wasn't here where she belonged, with him. For the first time in his life he was truly lonely. How could he feel whole when half of his soul was someplace else?

Time drifted and eventually, when the rain started falling, he went to bed, excusing Charlie's earlier curtness. Whatever Brook did, or didn't, believe, clearly the shaman was up against something very serious. How would you go about battling a god?

Outside, lightning lit the sky and thunder shook the ground. Brook imagined the spirit world was angry. He woke up a couple of times in the middle of the night, listening to the trees thrashing while more bursts of thunder shook the earth, the rain pounding his flimsy roof until he feared it would collapse on top of him. At one point, he swore he heard voices coming from just outside the tent. One was Charlie's; the rest were more guttural and animal-like. Reflections and shadows moved along the canvas walls, twisting shapes of things not meant to be seen by man, shadows resembling the images on the totems. The elder was right: it wasn't safe to be out there, nor did Brook want to be.

Charlie was out there, amongst the madness, communing with the spirits. Brook heeded the elder's wishes and his own inclinations. He burrowed deeper into the sleeping blanket, shuddering with admiration and fear for the old man. What the man must have experienced in his training to become a shaman, Brook couldn't even imagine.

As he tossed and turned, he longed to reach out for Chelen, fold her into his arms, snuggled up beside him as she'd been the last two nights, her soft breath on his neck, the silkiness of her hair caressing his chest. But most of all, the mingling of their souls.

Connection. She'd spoken of it so many times since he'd met her. Connection to the earth, to the universe, to each other. Especially to her. She was a part of him. She'd experienced things he didn't know existed and opened windows too long shuttered in his heart. Brook prayed to whatever spirits were listening, be they native or Christian, that she would come back to him and that Charlie would be safe tonight. If everything she'd told him about energy and connection was true, then given the state Charlie had been in after his earlier encounter with Raven in the spirit world, Brook wondered if the shaman could use a hand. Or in this case, some white-light energy.

The walls of the tent suddenly sucked inward and he felt his body crushed against the earth. Brook struggled to breathe as a horrible stench pervaded the confines. Visions of a large black beast hovered over him. No, not him, Charlie. The shaman was in trouble. Brook was seeing through the old man's eyes.

Brook had to help. All he could think of doing was to send Charlie the white light energy he'd just thought of. Like the shimmer that had risen from the shaman. "Wherever you are, Charlie, accept this as my spirit offering," Brook mumbled, closing his eyes and focusing on Charlie's form as he'd last seen it, with his blackened face and hair hanging down.

The air within the tent and outside grew very still.

* * *

Charlie stood before the entrance to a cave, the forest looming all around him. This cavern was not deep in the ocean, it was not *kushtaka*. Foulness issued from it, the rankness of rotting meat and unwashed bodies. The gagging stench of sweat confirmed the lair was home to the one he sought — Buhkwuss.

His spirit wavered, recoiling from the entity within, and he clutched at his medicine pouch. Without his strongest allies he was way too vulnerable to be facing what awaited him. So many preparations he could have made to ensure his success, but time, which mattered little in this realm, hadn't permitted him.

He entered the darkness of the grotto, the moonlight streaming in from behind him providing the only source of illumination. Something cracked underfoot, whiteness gleaming in the gloom. Bones, old bones lay scattered everywhere. Some with scrape marks scored on them, some hollow with the marrow sucked from them. Drained dry, long ago. The bones of his ancestors, of fellow shamans who had fallen in the course of their duties. The leather pouches, beads, and necklaces of puffin beaks, torn apart and strewn everywhere, seemed to mock him. *Maybe this was a mistake.* He wasn't strong enough to win this fight.

A mist of fetid breath wafted against his face from the blackness, and twin orbs of bloodshot red hovered before him. Then a part of the dark moved. A whole wall of darkness lumbered towards him. *Too late to change my mind now.*

Revulsion overwhelmed him, closing his throat as sweat, old urine and other putrid smells assaulted his senses. Even worse, Buhkwuss had glands that spewed a chemical meant to induce fear in its opponents, and the knowledge did little to assuage Charlie's apprehension. If he'd had a meal earlier, it would be spewed on the ground about now.

The beast was mindless, intent only on destruction. A creature of the most dangerous kind. Unpredictable. It stared at him, unblinking. Charlie stared back. If he'd thrown up earlier it would have torn him apart. He slipped easily into the beast's mind, reading its thoughts. It advanced towards him, and he held up his pouch.

"This pouch is made from the skin of one like you. Another step forward and I'll make another to decorate my other hip." The Wild Man of the Woods didn't need to know it was one of Charlie's ancestors, not him, who'd captured the original beast which was this one's son. He felt the reaction of the pouch to the proximity of its kin. The savage beast snarled, sniffing the dried flesh of its offspring. "Bad move," Charlie thought. "Very bad move."

The buhkwuss shuffled to a stop in confusion. It swung its head back and forth with indecision. No one ever spoke to it in such a fashion, Charlie figured. Now it was time to use all the balls he had, or lose them. Its loathsome appearance, its sheer bulk and ungodly smell, were usually enough to employ the main weapon at its disposal: terror. It growled, obviously unsure what to make of Charlie's cocky stance.

The shaman squinted into the depths of the buhkwuss's eyes, fighting to prevent himself from sinking into the depravity of its soul, focusing on putting it under his spell. Moments, in a timeless realm, stretched longer than seemed possible. Charlie's eyelids grew heavy … if he blinked, he was a dead man. His limbs faded into numbness, while his spirit sagged. He was losing the upper hand. Buhkwuss was winning. Sweat beaded on Charlie's forehead. If he wasn't careful he would become another bone tossed into the refuse pile.

A smile broke the hairy beast's face, jagged yellowed teeth, cracked from crushing bones and sucking marrow, gleaming in the faint light.

A reverberation in the background told Charlie Thunderbird was restless, exercising his wings. And then from somewhere Charlie heard his name, drifting in the gloom, echoing unbidden in his thoughts. *"Charlie, accept this as my spirit offering."* Charlie latched onto the thread of thought and drew in the trail of the white-light energy, letting it flood him. The light strengthened his flagging spirit and his shoulders lifted. He stared even harder at the formidable beast before him, narrowing his eyes in concentration. Buhkwuss' eyes blinked once, and then flickered. The beast was unused to such mental contests and to being defied. It staggered a few steps, swaying on its feet. The great head tipped forward, the eyes fluttering closed as it fell asleep.

"Thank you, Brook," Charlie whispered, releasing Brook's spirit energy to return to its owner's body. He reached forward, plucked a lock of the creature's matted hair and placed it into his medicine pouch. Wasting no time, Charlie retreated from the stinking cave and let his tired spirit journey back to his waiting body.

* * *

Next morning, Brook looked about as he crawled from his tent, relieved that the storms had dissipated. To say he hadn't slept very well would be an understatement. He'd bet Charlie hadn't slept at all. The shaman wasn't anywhere to be seen, either. Apprehension curled in his gut. Where was the old guy?

A shrill yelp drew his attention. The old shaman, naked as the day he was born, was standing in the chilly waters of the stream that ran down to the beach. He pulled something from his pouch and flailed himself with it.

"What the devil was that all about?" Brook asked him when he returned.

"Just my usual morning ritual. I bathe in ice water and whip myself with devil's club. It's part of being a shaman."

"Devil's club, what the heck is that? Anyways, I get the same kind of exhilaration from drinking four cups of coffee and reading the newspaper." They laughed together. "I'm presuming it went well last night?"

"A version of ginseng, not of the Panax family of plants. You could call it Siberian Ginseng. Never ate it myself, probably has similar effects. The sharp thorns along its stem make excellent ..."

"Charlie?" He didn't have time for his prattling this morning.

"Oh, yeah, last night. As well as can be expected, and I'm still alive. Don't think I would've made it if you hadn't sent me your energy."

"It was weird. I sensed you were in trouble and tried doing what you did when I saw your spirit rising."

"You saw my spirit essence leave my body?"

"Believe it or not, I did."

"Very interesting. There's more about you that you haven't discovered, young Skywalker." Charlie laughed. "Usually only those gifted in areas of shamanic ability can see spirit essences, but thank you for the assistance, at any rate. Now we need to hurry. I'll explain along the way."

They hiked for most of the day, following the stream from the beach up into the forest. Charlie set the pace, and Brook found it hard to keep up.

The older man was sweating, as if he was running a fever, or struggling to keep something under control, but he was still in better shape than Brook, leaving him with burning muscles and fighting for breath.

When they reached two gigantic cedars that appeared to be growing from one trunk, Charlie rubbed his hands together. "Now, the fun part begins. These are portal trees. They allow us to leave the dimension you know so well, and enter another, one of the worlds I sometimes frequent. My journey last night has, among other things, opened up the entranceway."

Charlie stepped boldly through the portal and after a moment's hesitation, Brook did the same. He experienced a disconcerting dizziness and the odd sensation of walking through a filmy veil of some sort. The forest beyond didn't look any different, but a little farther on they passed an ancient grayed totem that he swore he hadn't seen from the other side of the portal. It stood leaning at a precarious angle, as if it hadn't many more years before it was doomed to fall to the forest floor. The three Watchmen that normally stood in silent duty at the top of the pole were displayed individually here, each being devoured by a different creature. Beasts he'd never seen carved on totems before. Spirits, perhaps, from the other realms Charlie had mentioned, realms he'd never care to visit. Trepidation sent frissons of fear through him.

The message was quite clear: even those that merely watched weren't safe in this place.

"Who's depicted on that totem? I'm no expert, but I don't recall seeing those figures anywhere else."

Charlie nonchalantly walked past the relic. "And you won't. It marks the trail we're about to travel on as sacred ground, and home of beings older than most European civilizations. It also warns you to stay away because the route to Foam Woman's valley is well guarded."

"Oh, very nice. A real touch for the tourists, I'm sure."

Charlie's face looked haggard but he smiled in response. As far as Brook knew, the shaman hadn't eaten since the day before yesterday. "This trail is not for non-natives, or non-shamans, to know anything about. Hopefully, last night's exercise worked and I've put most of those spirits to sleep for the duration of our expedition. I also got the begrudging support of a new animal spirit, one of the sentries along the trail, that's agreed to safeguard our journey to the valley. But you must stay on the path, and keep me within sight at all times. There are those who give their word but can't be trusted to keep it." Sweat streamed down his brow. "It's taking a great deal of energy to keep this being in line … it persists in trying to fight me off. If I'd had more time to properly prepare, I'd have greater control."

"Ah, this animal spirit sounds like some of the politicians I write about. Exactly who, or what, is it?" He stepped a little closer to Charlie. "I may not be First Nations, in this life anyway, but trust me. I can keep a secret. Where are we going? I mean, does this place really exist in our world?"

"In the central midwest he's called Omah, down the coast Quamault. We call him Buhkwuss, or Wild Man of the Woods, but you'd probably call him Bigfoot, or Sasquatch. And don't worry, I won't have to trust you. You'd never find this valley again, nor its entranceway. Let's just say that you won't find any golden arches here, although keep your eyes open and maybe we'll spot Elvis." The elder's humor was grim, mirroring his expression.

"Does where we are really exist though, or is this some shadowland, like in our dreams?"

Charlie gritted his teeth as the track steepened. "It's kept under a spell of concealment, but this realm is real enough. And if you're wondering, the ticket to this attraction is definitely no deposit, no return."

"Holy."

"Die here and your soul will not return to your body on earth. Die here, and you'll experience horrors you never knew could exist. Message received, zero distortion?"

"Check, got it, memory forever." Brook stepped back in line behind him. Every so often cracks rang out in the bushes beside them, and a hint of repulsive body odor washed over him from behind. Once, he swore he heard the thud of something following them. "What the hell was that?"

"Don't look back and whatever you do, keep your eyes on me, don't lose sight of me. This is not a tourist stop." Charlie repeated his warning.

Farther along, Brook caught a glimpse from the corner of his eye of something loping alongside them. The figure was three meters high, black and hairy with arms hanging well past its knees. It seemed to have no trouble keeping up with them and appeared as if it could probably maintain double their current pace for days. It sure fit the descriptions he'd read of Sasquatch, and he wasn't about to stop and ask for its autograph. Charlie hadn't been kidding about this Wild Man of the Woods stuff.

As they drew ever closer to the valley, Brook made sure he stayed on the shaman's heels, his eyes glued to Charlie's backpack and the trail in front of him. He sure couldn't afford to make the same mistake as Prince Kiidkayaas and look back.

* * *

They walked for another couple of hours until they reached the head of the valley, Foam Woman's home. Brook gazed down on its heavily forested slopes, obviously virgin first-growth timber, where no loggers had ever

269

ventured. The scents of pine and cedar drifting on the breeze were refreshing, rejuvenating, as was the absence of any desecration.

Charlie breathed deep and let out a sigh. "We're here, and safe, for now."

Turning, Brook caught sight of the sasquatch's bulk looming against the line of trees, its eyes on the forest they'd just left. "Some escort we've got there. Does it park your car for you, too?"

Charlie laughed. "Well, he ain't no Toto, but he'll stay behind to guard the trail and keep it open. So let's follow the yellow brick road, shall we?"

A gentle wind stirred as they walked, blowing constantly and from all direction, warm, moist and full of energy. Its origins weren't from the earthly realm, Brook sensed, but somehow tasted of the past, of other realities, other worlds. The wind was full of voices with a magical quality that hummed in his ear in a pleasing melody.

As they descended, the strange feeling intensified. The colors were too brilliant, the scents too real, somehow. Like the stories of fairyland. Everything seemed to have an eerie presence about it. Brook couldn't quite place it, but not only were the trees increasing in size the deeper they penetrated this surreal world, but the varieties were also mingling more, growing side by side until the whole forest contained no stands of one single species. Just as they passed a Douglas fir that spread more than ten meters across, Charlie stopped.

"We're here." He spoke in a reverent tone.

The song of the wind vanished. The valley grew still.

Then Brook heard something so faint, he almost missed it. He stopped breathing for a moment, to be sure the sound didn't come from within himself. It emanated from everything around him. A low, calm breathing.

"You are now in the presence of the oldest beings on our planet." Charlie spoke softly.

Brook looked around. "Where? All I see are …" He gazed upwards. "Trees."

He whispered the last word as the overpowering truth captured his breath. Neither of them spoke. The huge trees dwarfed them, silencing them with the awe of their presence. Many, like the Douglas fir, boasted massive girths and reached so high into the sky that their topmost branches were barely visible. Each tree moved of its own accord, like a living being, shifting its branches in its own individual rhythm. Not as regular trees moved, slaves to the fickle whims of the winds, but to their own heartbeat.

The last time he'd felt anything even close to this was when he'd stood before the cedar tree in his youth, filled with sympathy for its plight. The eerie sensations of being watched at the

Golden Spruce, he realized, had been correct. Maybe it wasn't only the *kushtaka* he'd seen under the cedar there that had been studying him. Perhaps the tree had been checking him out also.

He approached an enormous cedar.

"If you're going to touch any of them, you must ask permission first. They're very sensitive to touch," Charlie cautioned.

Touch it? He'd never thought about touching one, or like the environmental protestors he'd seen in the news, actually hugging a tree. He'd done something similar before though, with Chelen beside the Golden Spruce. Wasn't hugging this stately tree something she'd have done if she were here? She'd be enchanted by this place.

Heart aching, he turned to Charlie. "Can I touch that cedar?" He nodded toward the tree in front of him.

The shaman smiled. "Don't ask me. Ask the tree."

He stood before the venerable cedar. "Ask the tree? How will I know if it agrees?"

"Just try it."

"Okay ... " He drew in a deep breath. He must be out of his ever-loving mind to even think about talking to a tree. But why not? "May I touch you and feel your bark?"

From inside the trunk, a baritone whisper sounded in his mind, vibrating through him. *"Yes."*

"Wow." It spoke, the tree actually spoke to him. A strange joy flooded him, followed by a serene, settling peace. He extended tentative hands, pressed them to the rough skin of something he'd never really thought of as sentient. The bark of the cedar was warm, moved under his palms, pulsing, like a heartbeat. He looked up in awe ... he was communing with a living, breathing tree. What else would amaze him on these islands? Nobody would believe him if he tried to tell them about this experience. But then, maybe some things weren't meant to be shared.

He hadn't felt this same inspiring insignificance since he had gone canoeing to do some whale watching. He'd got a little too close to a gray whale and it had headed straight for his flimsy craft, diving at the last minute to swim underneath him, fifty feet of massive mammal. So close, he swore he could reach down and touch the barnacles clinging to it. Run his hands over it, if he hadn't been holding onto the edge of the canoe with white-knuckled fingers and clenching the edge of his seat with his butt cheeks in fear. He knew then, as he did now, that he was in the presence of an intelligent being.

He held his breath, afraid to offend the elders. The effect of thousands-of-years-old trees alive and breathing was unsettling, and at the same time, soothing. They meant no harm that he could discern. Here was the truth of what Chelen talked about, being connected to the universe, the reality of each plant and animal containing a spirit.

"Charlie, the *sghaana giidas*, the spirit beings, when they travel on the winds and return to Haida Gwaii every fall ..." He hesitated, trying to sum up what he was thinking.

"Yes."

"I mean, the wind noise stopped when we entered this forest. Is this where the spirit beings, the spirit winds, come from? Is this the source?"

"One of them. The *sghaana giidas* are very strong in this valley. With all the logging I don't think they have many places left to go to, since they don't inhabit regions disturbed by man. All I really know is that they and the *Dida Cwaa Nang Qaaruns* are part of our connection to the universe. Part of another reality that exists alongside ours, and is connected to it. Maybe this place simply exists to ..." He stopped abruptly, clearly listening to something Brook couldn't hear.

Charlie turned. "He's here. Raven's here. Come." Motioning for Brook to be quiet, he guided him through the forest, moving carefully around several of the trees. In one clearing Brook almost trod on a small cedar. He glanced around: it looked odd and out of place, the only sapling on the forest floor. As he skirted it, he swore the youngster moved, studying the humans, just like the large trees did. Before he could snag Charlie's attention to point out the sapling, Charlie grabbed him. "There he is. Raven himself. And look who's with him."

The legend that had come to life filled his vision. The mythic Creator that had spirited away Brook's woman and turned the most erotic dream he'd ever had into a nightmare stood before him. The same bird figure that left him to die on a beach. Raven had stolen his soul-mate and Brook wanted restitution.

The word came so naturally, it was the truth. Somehow all this craziness about Haida slaves and princesses was real, a reincarnation of himself and Chelen … it was the only explanation. He had to get his soulmate back, and soon.

Pushing his heartbreak away, Brook focused on Raven. The big bird was hunched, eyes closed, head bowed before a woman who wore a flowing gown of vivid sea-blue edged in the white-water foam that crested retreating ocean tides. From where Brook stood, he couldn't see her face, but he didn't have to guess who she was. He could only pray that Foam Woman was talking some sense into the damn bird, and could somehow prevent him from dragging humanity backwards by a couple of centuries. Civilization might have its faults, but he sure as hell didn't fancy regressing to the more primitive aspects of history. Too bad advancement had to come at such a price, but why couldn't progress and preservation coexist? If he got out of here alive, with or without Chelen, he'd have to shift his mindset, and his way of looking at the world. The real world, the only one he knew. He'd help to save places like this valley.

Charlie nudged him out of his daydream. "Watch Raven," he said. "This is better than I thought. Perhaps I can catch him off guard. I need to slip into a meditative state. I'm hoping to attack him on a plane of reality other than this one." He stared hard into Brook's eyes. "As a last resort, if I fail you'll have to look into the medicine pouch and use whatever presents itself. It would be your only chance."

Brook eyed the pouch and cringed. That was the last thing on earth he wanted to do. "Will it help me?"

"Don't know. That depends on you."

"On me? On what?" But he feared he knew what Charlie's answer would be and almost recoiled in panic.

"On whether you've courage enough to handle it. In this dimension you can manifest your own reality."

"I can't," Brook muttered as the ghost of his dad's voice returned to haunt him. "I can't."

He said it to himself. Charlie had already slipped into his altered state and was beyond hearing.

* * *

Chelen looked up from her seat on the rocks, near the water's edge. Today she and Rosemary were weaving cedar baskets, a slow task that involved all of her concentration. But concentrating was so hard to do lately. Yesterday, they'd begun the long process of smoking the salmon, drying them on racks in preparation for curing in the smokehouses. Rosemary rarely left her side.

She smiled. This was good, life was good. As it should be, yet something was bothering her ... what was it? It was important that she remember. Who had visited her the other day? Yes, someone visited her. It was so hard to think, sometimes. Why was that?

Occasionally, she was able to go walking along the beach by herself. The drums would pound, announcing the arrival of the warriors in their canoes, and she watched as they disembarked. She supposed one of them would become her husband someday and eyed each man as he stepped ashore. Rosemary had told her once to trust her heart, that she would know when *he* came. And every night, Chelen dreamed of her soulmate. Dreamed that she'd already met him and made love to him. The other braves held no interest for her.

Her hand brushed the talisman around her neck. A piece of dried Land Otter tongue. Rosemary wanted her to get rid of it. Why would her grandmother care about some withered old talisman?

Charlie, Brook?

Memories flooded her. It was Charlie who came to see her, he'd given her this talisman to protect her, to stop her from becoming a *kushtaka*. The fog in her mind cleared. She was in a *kushtaka* village under the sea. Rosemary wasn't Rosemary … Charlie had told her so. It was a *kushtaka*, using her own memories to seduce her.

More importantly, where was Brook?

They'd made love all night long. What happened after that? Her memory was blank.

Brook had surprised her with his talk of visions of the native princess and her slave. Chelen also had memories from a previous life. She'd had the visions too. For the last couple of nights, in the dreams that had haunted her, the fur-clad maiden who she knew to be herself walked with a prince from the Halq'emeylem tribes to the south. Captured in a raid, he'd fallen in love with her, and she with him. No princess could marry a slave, only other royalty, but she would set him free someday. She would

278

never be free of him, though. He'd made her a slave to his heart. Her and Brook.

Lovers in a past life, in many lifetimes. The soul never forgot.

She missed him ... Brook, her warrior. What had Charlie said? He and Brook were looking for Raven. Raven had done this, caused her to be brought here, where the old ways still reigned. It wasn't really so bad, living life as it used to be, as it should be.

Just then the *kushtaka* bearing Rosemary's image came walking towards her. So far, the talisman her uncle had given her was working, keeping her from turning into one of them. But she feared it wouldn't last much longer. Every day it became harder to remember what life was like, another life outside this underwater village.

She put on a blank look and smiled at Rosemary. It was time to weave, and tomorrow she'd begin boiling the oolichans to make grease for the coming winter.

* * *

A sudden flap of wings and a sinister caw chilled the atmosphere of the enchanted woods. Raven. Where was he? Brook looked about him. Raven was gone, and so was Foam Woman. Another flap of wings came from behind him. He spun around just in time to see Raven click his beak twice and Charlie fall over like an overcooked strand of spaghetti. The elder convulsed twice and went limp.

"My, what a shame. Poor fellow, looks like he had a heart attack. Must have been from the shock of finding out I wasn't meditating, but only waiting for you two to show up. Let's see if I can revive him, shall we?"

Raven's thought sank into Brook's head. They had been set up, tricked by the best trickster in the world. With a deft maneuver, Raven reached down and speared his beak into the shaman's chest. He pulled the heart from its cavity, still beating. He'd done this many times before, Brook could tell.

Raven flung the bloody heart at him.

"Oh God," he gasped as it splattered at his feet, staring in fascinated horror at the feebly beating heart. Disbelief froze his thoughts.

Raven tore the medicine pouch from Charlie's still body. "Here," he teased, tossing the pouch at Brook. "See if you have the courage to look inside it, white man."

Brook gagged, revulsion clawing at his throat. Shock paralyzed his thought process, along with the harsher reality that it was now up to him. He continued to gape at the heart, wiping his mouth. Raven's act was so callous, so gross.

What had the creature done to Chelen?

"As you see, I'm feeling much more youthful now. I have you to thank for finding my immortal stone." Raven's image shifted easily into a much younger version of Marten Crow.

Brook stared at him in stupefaction. Opening the pouch would cause madness. Wasn't that what Charlie had said when he first met him? But the woman he was falling in love with was gone, and now, Charlie was gone, too. He had nothing to lose except his own sanity, and that was hanging by thin tendrils of rationality that were slowly snapping away.

He found the strength deep within a place he never suspected he possessed. He did have what it took to succeed, or to at least try. Brook took a deep breath and snatched up the medicine pouch. It didn't move, it didn't issue any unusual smoke, nothing leaped out at him. So he eased back the flap and looked inside.

"What? There's nothing in here! Nothing that can help me!" He emptied the contents onto the ground. Out fell a few rolled-up bundles of sage and Sweetgrass, a small shaman's rattle, pieces of cedar bark wrapped together, a length of devil's club stem, a sprig of fresh-cut newborn cedar and a couple of other handmade items he knew the old man employed during some of his ceremonies.

He threw the empty pouch between him and Raven. He'd been duped. He had found the strength to go on, to prove to himself, but it had all been a ploy.

Brook jerked his head up. It was a trick and he knew who'd set him up. He wanted more than anything to crush Raven's throat between his fingers and shake the feathered creature until its last breath escaped its lungs.

Throat … the immortal stone.

Raven crowed. "You are a brave man. Or a stupid one. To think you could beat me with bundles of Sweetgrass."

As he spoke, blue smoke curled from the pouch and from the pieces of cedar bark littering the ground. It billowed in thick clouds and covered both of them. Brook tried to move but his body refused to obey his commands. His head whirled as his consciousness slipped away.

* * *

The instant Charlie closed his eyes he felt himself fall, tumbling down through the darkness. Something was wrong, terribly wrong. Disoriented, he tried to open his eyes, but couldn't. It was a trap; damn. More of Raven's work, he realized as he went hurtling through unlit caverns, and slammed into something solid. Breath left his lungs.

Where was he? As he regained consciousness, Charlie heard the thousands of voices locked in eternal screams. What was this place? He had to get back, or Brook was doomed. The white man could never hope to defeat Raven single-handedly.

"The dead zones. You are in one of the many and ever-increasing number of dead zones." A gentle voice entered his head. Darkness spread aside for as a dimly glowing figure walked

towards him. A young Haida male, but instead of hair, his head was covered with tree needles and his skin was rough and knotty, like a thin layer of bark. Prince Kiidkayaas? Charlie was astounded. How could this be?

"Yes. I am Prince Kiidkayaas. *Dida Cwaa Nang Qaaruns* has trapped me and keeps me under surveillance, except for here in this terrible place." He pointed to the thousands of roots dangling overhead.

The screams ... he should have known where he was. "So this is what our logging does. Small wonder my ancestors gave offerings and prayed to the trees before they were to be cut down."

The prince's expression clouded. "If this continues, the entire earth will cry in agony."

"Nice company you keep. Explains why I couldn't find you when I was searching for you earlier. You see, I don't hang out in bars like this one. But I'm honored to finally meet you. I'd love to know how you went from being trapped in a tree to looking like a teenage werewolf with a bad case of acne."

"I am puzzled by the expressions you use. In any case, the time to explain is not now. We must act with urgency, or all will be lost. *Skaga*, know this, Raven has indeed tricked you, and if I am to help you and the former native-born, you must turn *Dida Cwaa Nang Qaaruns'* attention away from me."

"How? How can I do what you ask of me?"

"I have a plan —"

Charlie screamed as searing pain tore into him. White light exploded from his chest.

"It is too late," the prince declared as Charlie fell to his knees.

The shaman's heart, the connection to his mortal body, ripped free. The phantom image of a raven's beak impaling his chest faded. He moaned, unable to stem the white energy spewing onto the earth. He fell face first into the radiance of his soul's light.

* * *

Reeling, Brook felt a tug, as if something were extracting his mind from his body. The bundles of Sweetgrass smoldered, filling the area with thick, aromatic smoke, and everything disappeared into the blue haze.

From a distance, he watched himself and Raven both slump over and vanish behind the hazy veil. Displaced, the smoke from the sweet grass lifted and swirled.

Then everything went absolutely black. He was engulfed in nothingness.

"No!"

He heard Raven crow, lost somewhere with him in the darkness. Heard and felt the thump of his own body as it struck the ground. Another thud reverberated nearby ... Raven?

Brook looked down at himself from above, his body still and empty. He was disconnected from his physical shell, his mind drifting free.

From the void, cackles of enchantment pealed through the emptiness. The crack of rocks splitting and drums pounding with the ancestral heartbeat of earth sounded through the air, accompanied by the slow steady breathing of the ancient trees. An owl hooted. Something swam by, undulating through the darkness.

Somehow, Brook knew where he was. What had Chelen said about everything having spirit, everything being connected? He must be inside the earth. Yet he had no substance. He was just a ball of energy, of conscious thought. Was this his soul? Was this what it was like to die?

Invisible winds raced by, shrieking like eagles. Something latched onto Brook's essence and pulled him along.

"Come."

They sped through the ebony canyons, tumbling down the exhilarating cliffs, like hurtling along on a roller coaster without light. Finally, the energy guiding him stopped and a warm brown glow split the perpetual night, giving him a focus. He looked up into splayed tentacles ... no, tree roots. He wanted to run from that face of aged soils and decayed leaves, those dark, dark, orbs that held him in thrall. The vision from his nightmare, only this time there was no opening his eyes to escape. Staring into the mass of writhing maggots and rancid earth, Brook fought down the fear that threatened to unman him.

"Human, I mean you no harm." The voice echoed in his head.

Brook recognized the same spirit that had tried to speak to him beside the Golden Spruce that day with Chelen. The spirit that led him to Chelen. His guardian spirit, she'd called it, and if it had led him to her, it couldn't be all bad.

"I have brought him," the voice of whatever had been escorting him reported.

A long silence followed, and then a root reached out and touched a part of Brook's energy. Caressing him, calming him.

"Yes, that is the one," said the voice that was so hauntingly familiar, a voice he'd heard years ago, when he was a child bent on rescuing a dying tree. A voice that had spoken inside his head and had been there ever since.

"Thank you for saving me," it said, and then it was gone, sucked back into the morass of unending, disorienting darkness. Brook bit back his frustration. There was so much he'd wanted to ask his guardian spirit, but that would have to wait for now.

"Who are you?" he thought to his escort, realizing that if the tree could speak, then whatever was in control of him could also.

"I was Prince Kiidkayaas. What I am now, I'm not sure. I spent what seemed like eternity trapped in the Golden Spruce with Raven."

Kiidkayaas? He was actually in the presence of the prince in the story he'd first heard at

Ninstints, told to him by Tom the Watchman? The same prince carved on the totem that had mesmerized him, depicting the human and the Raven locked in combat.

So it was true. *"You're real, then?"* he blurted out. How did one address a mythological prince, one that wasn't even a prince anymore?

"Of course. Isn't all mythology rooted in reality?"

Ask a silly question, Brook thought. Raven was alive, apparently, so why shouldn't the prince be as well? But here was his ultimate opportunity to prove that fact, if only to himself. His chance to test the truth of Raven's claims, of the legend Marten Crow relayed at the café.

"How ... how did Raven get trapped inside the tree with you?"

"So you know what really happened. I had reached down his throat and grabbed his immortal stone. Later, to get it back, he tried to trick me and turned me into a spruce tree. But I in turn, tricked Raven, by fooling him with a fake stone. And when he realized I still had his true immortal stone, he had to fly into the tree with me, or else he would surely die. We awoke when the Golden Spruce was cut down, and Raven ripped my heart out and flung it against a cedar tree. Somehow, I don't understand how exactly, my essence was drawn inside the cedar and I've been evolving ever since. I thought I was transforming into a cedar tree, but I'm turning into something much different. Perhaps I'll eventually become one of *Dida Cwaa Nang Qaaruns'* spirit essences."

"Dida ... who?"

"A multifaceted being, also named *Sins Sraanaarwaay*, the Power of the Shining Heavens. We have no singular god, as you do. This is an elder god that exists in higher dimensions, at levels neither you nor I can comprehend. It is the spirit of the forests, and especially the essence of the cedars. In one of my travels I encountered that cedar tree I just presented you to. It claimed a human had saved its life, and I suspected, by studying *Dida Cwaa Nang Qaaruns'* thoughts, that you were that human. I was curious to confirm this."

"So that cedar I saved all those years ago ... it's part of this Dida being?"

"I can only explain so much, but you need to know that it was *Dida Cwaa Nang Qaaruns* that urged you to save that cedar tree in your youth. And those remembrances you are experiencing now are indeed past-life regressions sent by *Dida Cwaa Nang Qaaruns*. I haven't determined yet why it is doing this. Maybe it knew that eventually Raven would awaken and that someone would have to be there to stop him. Perhaps not; I truly don't know. Why, for instance, am I not dead or reborn as another human, as I should be? The intentions of such powerful beings can be unfathomable."

"But ... why me? Before I came here, I knew very little about native beliefs. Don't even go to church, although after this, that might change."

"In this lifetime you know little, maybe. But you were once one of us, and this is most likely why *Dida Cwaa Nang Qaaruns* has selected you to be drawn to our land and our beliefs. Has called you to one of our daughters, and now, to aid us against Raven. To do that, and succeed, you need to know more. I can manage the curtain of time for only so long, but come with me."

In the span of seconds, or hours — Brook had no way of determining time in the timeless darkness — Kiidkayaas shared many things. Of his ability to travel between all the cedar trees and communicate with them. How the other tree species could communicate among themselves, and yet retain some semblance of understanding of each other's existence, because of their connection by the earth. He confirmed that everything was connected and that existence was based on certain unchangeable laws of the universe. Most importantly that everything was in a state of flux, and time could not move backwards. The universe was always evolving, creating new beings.

"Great, then if I'm to be part of that evolution, as you suspect, how am I to defeat Raven?" Brook asked. His head was spinning ... all these revelations were way too much to

accept. All he cared about after this was done —
if he lived, and hopefully was not reborn as a
slug or some other life form — was to get
Chelen back. She was all that mattered.

"The cedar sapling you saw in the forest.
Coerce Raven near it. That is the only way I can
help, without breaking one of the laws of the
universe."

"Law? What law?"

"I have no time to explain. But you must do
it. If my plan works, Raven will be under my
control for eternity."

Chapter Fourteen

Charlie opened his eyes and looked around. He was where he hoped he'd be and walked up to the shores of the foul waters marking the border to the land of the dead ones. Raven had ripped his heart out, beaten him once again. Last time Charlie was in this place, he'd made the mistake of underestimating Raven's ability to sense his presence. This time it was Raven who'd made the mistake of underestimating him. He grinned. Like they say in baseball, you get three strikes before you're out. For even from here, as a shaman, he knew how to send his soul traveling. He might not be able to return to the living world to help Brook directly, but there were other ways, other realms from where he could perhaps be useful. The first thing he had to figure out was how to get Dida's attention.

He couldn't deal with Dida alone. That would be like a flea stinging an elephant. Across the waters, the canoe with the monstrous *sisiutl* in the prow was coming for him. But this time, the occupants were clutching the sides of the craft, for the surface of the eternally calm river was roiling. Sulfur fumes were thick in the air, stirred up from the depths of the wretched waterway. Raven's meddling was obviously upsetting the balance of even the peaceful place that awaited on the far side of the river. As the canoe grated onto the rocks, nearly spilling out its passengers, he recognized *Gaada Xhuuya* White Raven, *Hiilinga* Thunderbird, *Xuuadjii* Grizzly Bear, *Guut* Eagle, *Jiijaat* Hawk, *Kkung* Killer Whale and *Ghuudj*, the blue-eyed gray wolf, his totem spirit.

"Another of Raven's mistakes," the shaman muttered. A plan formed instantly.

He stood before the canoe while the shadowy beings within shuffled around, unused to the heaving waters, many leaning over the sides and spilling their guts into the seething current.

"This is Raven's fault." Charlie addressed White Raven. "He tricked you into dying for him, and now look at what he's doing." He spread his hands to encompass the waves towering in the background. "He's tricked you, and all of us, and see what's happening to everything we know."

He pointed to the mute form of White Raven, and then stared hard into the ice-blue eyes of Gray Wolf. The most loyal of his totem spirits … would it still obey him?

"Come join me in setting everything right again, before it is too late for us all."

Charlie closed his eyes and visualized the head of Foam Woman's valley, and the one creature he couldn't trust, hoping it wasn't too late. He prayed that Brook had opened his medicine pouch and bought him some time. Hoping Wolf and the others would follow his trail.

* * *

A coughing spasm shook him. Acrid smoke filled his lungs. Brook sat up … he was back in his body.

Fire raged all around. The smoldering Sweetgrass had ignited into a dozen blazes, and screams shattered the air. Shrill screams of death.

The ancient ones were on fire! From his conversation with Kiidkayaas, Brook knew that even if the trees had the power to help themselves, they would do nothing. They were, after all, trees, and would let themselves die, eventually to be reborn, so the cycle would begin again. He rushed over to them anyway, pulled off his shirt and beat at the flames licking at the base of the trees. He choked as the smoke filled the glade.

"It's too late for them. Too late for yourself, Brook, and the other pale-skinned ones."

A figure emerged from the haze. Raven, in the form of Marten Crow, was holding a lighter. "Imagine fire contained in such tiny things. Some modern inventions are quite handy, I think."

The cedar sapling. Brook had to find the sapling. But the smoke licked at his eyes and stung his nostrils. He gagged again.

"Why are you doing this?" he demanded of Raven.

"Everything will return to the way it was. The way it always was. The Haida will return, in all their strength and glory."

"A noble aim, I suppose. But the world isn't the same any more. You can't go back to the past. It's done and gone. Only the future can be altered." He struggled for breath. Under Raven's hypnotic stare his strength drained away, leaving him weak, just like when he was trying to rescue Chelen from the *kushtakas*. Only this time, Raven was stronger.

"I have to do this." Raven glared at him, seemingly unaffected by the smoke, his stare sucking any remaining will from Brook. He had to think of something or he was finished. Chelen, Charlie, life as he knew it ... all would be lost, wiped out as effectively as a white-man disease had all but eradicated the Haida. Well, revenge might taste sweet to the crazy bird deity, but in Brook Grant's book two wrongs sure as hell didn't make a right.

The heat of the flames lifted the smoke for a second and just behind Raven, he saw the cedar sapling. "Oh, don't think you'll fool me and make me fall against the sapling. I know what you're trying to do. I know everything about what happened to Kiidkayaas since he and I were released from the Golden Spruce. I was there in the darkness, and I heard it all. Heard you both plotting to defeat me. But it won't work. That foolish prince has tried to trick me one too many times. Kiidkayaas will be the next one I deal with." Marten Crow laughed. Or was it Raven? His image kept wavering, back and forth.

Brook thought fast. The bird was too damn smart, too damn cocky. How could he use that against the demi-god? He had to find a way to throw Raven off guard, work on his weakness.

Maybe appeal to his sense of pride, or play the guilt card, perhaps.

"You know what? You can't handle the truth. The truth about what happened to your people. All the technological changes, all the deaths, all their torture. Being put into residential schools and being made to think like the white man. Robbing them of their spirituality, of their culture, of who they were. It was all your fault."

As the words left Brook's lips, Marten Crow's image shimmered and Raven's body shifted back into focus, eyes narrowed in anger.

"You should be ashamed of yourself," Brook went on, warming to his task. "You're supposed to be some mythological creator, yet all you want to do is destroy everything that's come into existence since your arrogance and bungling trickery got you trapped inside that spruce tree with the prince. In the end, what good will bringing back the past accomplish? Creation might not be always good, but undoing it isn't the answer. Leadership is what the Haida have missed most all these years. Your leadership."

Fire blazed all around them, originating in the depths of Raven's eyes. Brook swallowed in fear. Perhaps he'd pushed him too far. The conflagration grew hotter. As the bird's anger took hold, the strength of his hypnotic gaze dissipated.

"You can't handle the guilt of leaving your people. The guilt of what happened to them. You can't handle the guilty knowledge trapped inside you. You left them to die."

Raven's eyes turned black with fury. "No!" he screeched. Then he lifted his head and flung his rage at the heavens. Flames towered above the ancient trees.

In that moment Brook's will returned. He dove and rammed his fist into Raven's open beak and down his throat. Brook's frantically grasping fingers latched onto the lapis lazuli stone. But before he could pull his hand back,

Raven closed his beak, clamping his fist in a vise-like grip. Brook struggled to pull free and Raven overbalanced and tumbled backwards, towards the sapling. Brook fell with him, the razor-sharp bill crunching down on his wrist. The sticky trickle of his blood running down his arm registered in his mind, but there was no pain. His fingers were numb. He couldn't feel the immortal stone anymore. Please, God, don't let it have slipped away. More blood flowed, hot and cold at the same time, as the bird's beak crushed even harder. The sharp copper scent stung his eyes.

The cedar sapling was only a few meters away. Brook threw himself towards it. Man and Raven twisting over top of each other until Brook feared he would succumb to the pain and smoke.

Where was the damn sapling? He'd lost it in the haze that blurred his vision.

A hideous snapping sound followed by a burst of agony brought tears to his eyes. Blood flowed. He couldn't tell if it was all his or if Raven was wounded too. Another crack brought the sound of final defeat to his ears. The slender cedar sapling flashed by his face as they rolled over it, breaking it in two.

Brook lay motionless for a long moment, his hand still down Raven's throat.

"It's over." Raven released him.

Brook's arm hung limp and useless, barely attached. He screamed in frustration and defeat. Chelen, he'd never see Chelen again.

Gloating in his triumph, Raven rose and stepped on the stump of the sapling, squashing it. Then he reached down to pluck Brook's heart out, as he'd ripped out Charlie's.

* * *

Charlie's spirit returned to the entrance of Foam Woman's valley. The buhkwuss still stood where he and Brook had left it on guard, shuffling from foot to foot.

"Restless, are ya? Follow me, we've got some serious god-stomping to do," he told it as he sped down the trail into the lush forest. He wasn't about to give Buhkwuss any time to react or think about what he asked. He only hoped Wolf and the other spirit beings were bringing up the rear, as they said in the movies. At least he knew the Wild Man of the Woods was still shambling along behind him, if only because he could smell its stench. "Thank the Creator I've got at least one ally on my side," he muttered.

Soon his spirit floated into the glade, hovering near where his physical body lay slumped over, and settled before the mightiest cedar in Foam Woman's valley. The amount of energy emanating from the tree was so blinding that he had no doubt it was connected to the great being he sought.

"*Dida Cwaa Nang Qaaruns*, come on out and fight like a tree."

No response. It was as he'd feared. He was too insignificant to matter to such a powerful being. Behind him the buhkwuss kept shuffling, alert, and like himself, nervous. How do you mess with one of the elder gods?

He turned to the overgrown, smelly relative of an orangutan. "Tag, you're it. Do your best."

The Wild Man of the Woods stared at him, resisting the shaman's control.

"If you don't do this, we all will cease to exist. Even you will die."

The buhkwuss moved forward and filled its chest with air, then let out a cry that forced the shaman to cover his spirit ears. It pounded the base of the cedar until the forest floor shook. Charlie had never been directly exposed to the rage of a buhkwuss and his spirit quailed. If it turned on him he wouldn't have the strength to battle it. He'd been very lucky to capture it in the first place.

Still no response from the mighty cedar.

At the pad of paws behind him he turned, relief flooding him at the sight of Gray Wolf, along with his mate, his children, and the others from his pack.

"Hang on, Brook." What was that famous line from those cornball westerns? "Oh yeah, I brought the cavalry with me."

More movement parted the forest and the passengers from the canoe — White Raven, Thunderbird, Grizzly Bear, Eagle, Hawk — entered the clearing. Even the many-toothed Orca swam in the air behind them. Thunderbird raised his wings, causing lightning to crackle through the air and thunder to shake the ground so hard it sent Charlie tumbling backwards.

WHO DARES!

The voice boomed up through the earth, making it tremble knocking the shaman back on his butt, and some of the others senseless.

Ah, the great spirit had finally reacted to his summons. He had Dida's attention.

"Raven has to be stopped," Charlie huffed out. "He's trying to set time backwards and he's upsetting the balance of everything."

The assemblage cawed, growled, and screeched in agreement.

I CANNOT HELP YOU. INTERFERENCE IS NOT MY WAY. THE WAY OF THE UNIVERSE, THE NATURAL LAWS, MUST BE UPHELD. BEGONE.

"But — "

BEGONE!

Well, he'd tried. It was the best he could do, given the situation. Now he could only hope that

300

would be enough to enable Prince Kiidkayaas to step up to the plate and hit it out of the park.

Charlie stepped back and closed his eyes. He had one more destination on his agenda. Somewhere he couldn't return to if he, Brook, and the cavalry won and defeated Raven. But should they lose then he couldn't think of a better place to be.

Sometime later, with haste, the shaman disembarked from the abandoned canoe he'd appropriated. The spirit that formed its *sisiutl* had been uncooperative, and it hadn't been easy guiding it over the turbulent waters by his power alone. The nausea subsided as he stepped onto the fine sandy beach. The sun was shining, the sky a brilliant blue. Birds sang in the trees and the air was sweet with the perfume of the wild flowers. Beauty, nothing but beauty lay all around. Thanks to Raven having divested Charlie of his heart, he'd finally been able to reach the realm on the other side. No wonder some called it heaven.

Several souls milled about, and he recognized relatives he hadn't seen in a long time. They glanced his way and called him over, happy to see him.

Then the crowd parted and Lucy stepped toward him.

* * *

Brook closed his eyes, trying to shut out the searing pain flooding his senses from his partially severed arm. Raven's beak, stained with Charlie's blood, and Brook's, was aimed at his heart. "I'm sorry, Chelen. I failed you."

He would never see his soulmate again. Not in this lifetime, anyway. She would become a *kushtaka*, trapped for eternity in their village beneath the ocean. The real world would keep on turning, but civilization would regress, not advance. He had done his utmost, and it was not enough.

"Good for nothing." His dad's voice echoed in his head.

"Go away." Brook gritted his teeth.

"Always will be."

Okay, maybe Dad was right. But so what? In the end Brook would matter to no one but himself. That was the important thing, wasn't it? He mattered to himself. Maybe that was what this *Dida Cwaa Nang Qaaruns* was trying to show him. That he was good enough. He could do this. From writer to warrior ... evolution. Dida, the prince, everything was evolving. Wasn't that what Charlie, and the prince himself, had said?

And what was it Chelen told him? *"When you wake up in the morning you're different from the man who went to sleep."* Was he really different today? Could he put his childhood, and his father's scorn, behind him? Had he been carrying it around all these years unnecessarily? If he was good enough for himself, then that was all that counted. Which meant he was good enough for Chelen.

Chelen! She was part of him, had always been a part of him. A part he could no longer deny.

Energy, blinding white and hot seared through him. *"Never, never again,"* he vowed, finding the voice he'd never let speak before. He filled with the courage and determination to stand up for himself. Now he understood that only he could determine his own self-worth.

The immediate need for action spurred him into motion as his gaze followed Raven's beak descending in slow motion. He lunged aside, and rose in the same movement. Raven's beak buried itself in the forest mulch.

"Never again will I be put down, humiliated."

Raven's eyes widened as Brook hurled himself at him and flung the two of them backwards, twisting Raven around to land on his stomach. Brook fell on the feathered back and wrapped his one good arm round the bird's neck. Rising, and carrying Brook with him, Raven staggered backward, slamming Brook against a tree. Raven paused to gasp for breath.

Brook tried to gulp in air, stars spinning around as Raven battered him against the tree. His useless, bleeding arm slammed against the rough bark. Shards of agony ripped through him as blood splattered around him. Raven was only toying with him, punishing him. Why didn't he just finish him off?

"Give up, stubborn white man. You can never defeat me. You were never good enough to beat me."

Never good enough. His dad's litany was still there, only it didn't have the power over his emotions it once held. Blackness swam in dizzying waves across his vision.

"Oh, yes I am. I am good enough, bird."

If he was meant to die here, he would go down fighting like the native warrior he knew existed inside. With a supreme effort Brook turned his head and glanced around him. The cedar sapling, trampled though it was, lay only a couple of meters away. His grip on Raven's throat was slipping, and the nub of his other arm throbbed like hell. If only he had the use of all his appendages. Right now he needed more strength than he could muster.

Closing his eyes, he focused and concentrated. Connections … now was the time for connections. Everything was connected: hadn't he sent energy by thought to Charlie once before? Then again, Charlie was a shaman who knew how to receive and send energy. Could he, a white man unskilled in such things, make this wild scheme work?

He had to. He hadn't the reserves to hang on much longer. Once he let go of Raven's neck it was all over.

The roots ... a thought ricocheted through his mind ... Kiidkayaas used those to travel along, and to communicate. Brook visualized himself reaching out along that network, seeking and connecting to Charlie, Chelen, and the prince. Envisioned each of them as he'd last seen them. Imagined the tough, slender roots of the cedar tree reaching down into the earth. Brook melded with his guardian spirit, the multifaceted being that was *Dida Cwaa Nang Qaaruns*, and he called them all to his aid.

"They can't help you, Brook. No one can help you. It's just you and me, and you can't beat a god." Raven was regaining his breath. Shaking his great head in an attempt to free himself.

Brook's grasp on him loosened further. Closing his ears to the crowing tone, he pictured the root systems of all the forests, the bedrock of the islands and the ocean ... the entire planet, the universe, linked as if by the silvered threads of a spider's web. That holography stuff Chelen had talked about, getting in phase with a signal. Like the quantum crystals, everything connected. He believed.

And then it came to his call, funneling up through the trunk he was pinned against. The intense surge of energy, from the earthy essence of the cedars and the forests, from Charlie and his protective animal spirits, and most of all the energy of Chelen's love for him. It converged with the evolved spirit of Prince Kiidkayaas and streamed into the tree at his back. He became part of the universe, part of all that is. *Sins Sraanaarwaay*, the Power of the Shining Heavens.

"I *am* good enough to beat you." He redoubled the strength of his grip around Raven's throat, squeezing it with a force that felt superhuman and at last, the bird's gullet collapsed. "I am and I will."

Raven coughed and out spat his immortal stone. "No!"

The two reeled forward, Raven faltering, Brook energized by the knowledge that he was winning. It was a heady feeling, knowing he could actually defeat a god. As they tumbled again, Raven's foot brushed the cedar sapling. With a mammoth effort, Raven flung him aside and fell, still choking, trying to gasp in air before lunging at his fallen prey. The ebony feathers were already turning gray.

Gray! The immortal stone! Brook glanced frantically and spotted the shiny lapis lazuli nestled amongst the leaves on the forest floor. He rolled, grabbed the stone and shoved it in his mouth.

"Noo-o!" Raven croaked again as Brook picked himself up once more. Through the sweat and blood smearing his vision he saw the great bird kneeling right beside the crushed sapling.

"Push ... push ... the sapling." The prince's faint command reached Brook's inner ear.

Finding a reserve of strength he didn't know he possessed, Brook hurled himself headfirst towards the sable-feathered form. His momentum carried them both to the ground one more time, over the broken stump of the young cedar.

"My claw! It's stuck."

Brook jerked his head around in time to see another sapling sprout, springing up next to the trampled remains. He threw himself free of Raven as the tiny tree increased rapidly in size, expanding and engulfing Raven.

"No! Not again." Raven's eyes bulged, the last thing visible before the red-gold bark obliterated his features completely.

Before Brook's eyes, the needles of the tree turned golden.

He hovered on the edge of consciousness, trying to keep his senses from slipping away. The excruciating pain in his arm brought more tears that he blinked away. The vision that lingered was Raven glaring, or smirking, as the pith closed around the bird-deity, trapping him inside the newborn Golden Spruce.

* * *

A tap on his shoulder roused Brook.

"What happened?" Charlie leaned down and peered into his face. "Where's Raven? The last thing I remember was telling you to look in my pouch."

Brook opened his eyes and shook the fuzziness out of his head. He was leaning against one of the trees in the glade. Reaching up, he touched the elder's chest. There was no gaping hole over his heart.

"Oh, thank goodness, you're alive." Relief swept over him.

He had done it, hadn't given up. Victory was his reward. Would there be a legend now about the prince, the shaman, and the journalist? He almost cackled at that thought. Maybe looking in Charlie's pouch had driven him mad after all. Well, it would be worth it. Raven was defeated. Brook laughed.

Charlie looked at him like he was high on good drugs. "Don't tell me. You did nose into that pouch of mine, and now you're crazy as a loon chewing on a full moon."

Brook was too engrossed in examining his arm. Remarkably, it seemed to be intact. "My arm, it's okay. You're okay. Thank the heavens."

He stood up, laughing some more. There was no sign of fire or any smoke damage in the forest surrounding the scene of his epic battle with Raven. The ancient ones were safe, as was the present-day world.

"I did it. We did it," he cried, hugging the old man.

Charlie shrugged. "Now I know you've been smoking some of my peyote. But hold on here, I do vaguely remember some sort of dream." He stared hard at him. "That damn bird stabbed me with his beak and relieved me of my heart, didn't he?"

"You got it. I looked into your pouch, and to make a long story short, ran into the authentic version of you wouldn't believe who ..."

"Prince Kiidkayaas."

They chuckled in unison.

"Don't rightly remember much after that," Charlie continued. "Just something about gathering an Indian cavalry to distract our friend *Dida Cwaa Nang Qaaruns*."

"And you thought I was smoking something funny and was out back talking to little animals." As he spoke, a glint of gold caught his eye and Brook noticed the tree he'd been slumped against. A tall golden spruce. Nowhere near as lofty as the other behemoths in the cathedral-like glade, but larger than a normal tree, just the same. Certainly more than big enough to hold Raven. An all too familiar blue stone lay at its base. He must have spat it out before he finally passed out. At least he hadn't swallowed it or choked on it. Although eternal youth could have proved an interesting experience.

Charlie reached for the lapis lazuli and peered up at the glinting needles. "Well, well, whaddya know. Raven's gone and lost his immortal stone again, and our Prince Kiidkayaas has trapped him inside another tree. Inside a new Golden Spruce." He opened his pouch. "I think this'll be the safest place to keep the immortal stone, what do you think?"

Brook nodded his agreement, and Charlie dropped the stone inside. "That's how it seems, and if you're to be believed, everything has returned back to the way it was."

"Not everything."

The soft tones of a woman's voice interrupted their conversation. The two of them turned, Brook expecting to see Chelen. Where was she? She should be here. He'd saved her from the *kushtaka* village ... hadn't he? His heart leaped in anticipation, but it wasn't Chelen. Instead, another beautiful native woman, this one in green and blue flowing robes that shimmered like ocean waves, approached.

"Foam Woman," was all Charlie could manage to squeak out.

She was older than Brook expected, but her face still glowed with a radiant serenity. "You did defeat Raven, and had you not, the universe would surely have suffered. After he woke me, I told him that what he wanted to do was not possible. The fool would not listen to me.

Nonetheless, I explained too much has changed. Magic has changed, weakened; it is not like it once was. Raven could not make things the way they were but he was determined to try. Once he had possession of his immortal stone his efforts to cure what he thought was wrong would have created chaos."

Her sea-flecked gaze fell on Brook. "You are right, Brook. The past is past, and it can never be recreated. But the future ... well now, that is another story. I insisted to Raven the only way he could help his people would be to guide them into what lay ahead. He could not accept that."

"Foam Woman, what about Chelen? Is she safe? Is she coming back?"

"That depends on you, Brook." Foam Woman searched his eyes. Surely she could see the spirit threads connecting their souls? "By defeating Raven, you have enabled her return. If you choose to stay on the islands and be with her, she will come to you."

Foam Woman waved her hands and the crash of surf dissipated as she vanished in a spray of ocean mist.

"Wait!" Brook cried. "I love her! I'll stay forever, if she'll let me."

A bank of mist rolled through the forest and wrapped itself around them. Charlie yawned, as did Brook. His sight blurred as he collapsed on the forest floor.

* * *

311

When awareness returned Brook was lying on a beach. Thick mists were burning away in the morning sun, faint tendrils of evaporating dew rising into the sharp blue of the sky.

Averting his eyes from the bright sunlight, he glanced around. "Hot Spring Island."

Nearby, Charlie grunted and sat up. "Oh man, I had such a bad dream. That's the last time I eat ice cream before bed. Hate being lactose intolerant. Cramps me up and gives me wicked gas."

Over the shaman's shoulder Brook saw three kayaks lined up on the beach above the high tide mark. Beside them a prone figure with raven-colored hair sprawled on the sand.

He couldn't seem to find his voice. "Chelen!" he managed to choke. He scrambled to his feet and ran to her. She lay so still, drenched in moisture. Panic seized him as he searched for a pulse in her neck. Brook picked the cold wet body up in his arms. Chelen looked like she had been flung up by the ocean like driftwood.

Her eyelids fluttered and opened.

"What? What happened?" She coughed, spewing ocean water.

He held her, stroking the silky softness of her hair. "Thank the Creator, you're back. I've missed you and ..." Her slight smile stole his breath away. "Everything you told me about the universe and connection is true."

"True? What are you talking about?" She regarded him as if he were more than a little crazy. "How'd I get on the beach? I had the weirdest dream, of being underwater and hairy."

"That was no dream. When I woke up, you were gone." He explained everything that happened since the morning after they'd made love. Even Chelen looked skeptical, and that rattled him. Did he himself truly believe what had happened? Had it just been some kind of absurd nightmare after all?

"Is she okay?" shouted Charlie as he hurried toward them.

She peered behind Brook. "Charlie!"

Surely, now she'd seen Charlie, she'd realize Brook must be speaking the truth?

"Charlie? What are you doing here? What's going on?"

The elder sunk his orca-headed cane into the sand and leaned against it. "I can vouch for him. He hasn't gone loco. Everything he said really happened."

She looked up at Brook. "I don't remember anything other than being in some kind of daze and paddling away from here. I remember you, trying to get to me. Everything going black, and then me being happy living with my grandmother and all of my other ancestors." Realization shone in her eyes. "That wasn't Rosemary, was it? I was in the *kushtaka* village. Hey, wait a minute, you were there too, Charlie.

You gave me this." She felt for Land Otter's tongue on the thong around her neck.

She searched Brook's face. He and Charlie nodded in confirmation.

"Oh, boy. You mean you really did defeat Raven, and rescue me? Maybe Amanda was right. You white guys aren't all the same, are you?"

Brook feared he might choke on the happiness that tightened his chest. Chelen was back where she belonged. His real-life Haida princess. His father was wrong. After all the years of remembering his terrifying imperialistic voice in his head, it finally faded into the background and became just another dim echo in his memory.

Charlie cleared his throat. "I think I'll go do something important, like put the coffee on. You know what they say: two's company and three just gives the government tax auditors headaches." He grinned and started to wander away, muttering, "Ya gotta like happy endings. Too bad I couldn't find myself a female shaman in the deal."

"Hey, hold on. You don't look too upset about being dead for a while there, Charlie," Chelen said. Brook detected a new lightness in his bearing.

The shaman halted and rested on the handle of his orca cane. Then he turned back to face them, beaming. "Let's just say while I was

314

supposedly dead, I managed to visit an old friend."

"Lucy?" Chelen whispered, her tone misty with unshed tears.

With a chuckle, Charlie strolled on down the beach. "It's good to know the equipment still works." He threw the enigmatic comment over his shoulder as he disappeared into the tall grasses lining the shore.

Epilogue

We do not inherit this land from our ancestors;
We borrow it from our children.
Haida Saying

"Too bad you never got any evidence of Raven's antics for your hot news scoop," Charlie mused, breaking the silence in the truck. The three of them were driving to Tlell, to meet with Bob Burns to discuss the sale of the *Northern Islander Report*. Brook had cashed in a few investments and figured he could work a deal for the paper.

"Oh, but I did. Take a look at this picture I had developed this morning. Took it while Chelen and I were at Skedans. Didn't realize that our black feathered friend was there as well." He passed around the photo of Raven sitting wide-eyed in a tree behind the totems. His feathers were gray at the ends and he had one kinked wing.

"Looks to me like a bad taxidermist job," Charlie spluttered. "It's hard to judge the size of him in that picture, but that sure is one large bird. I guess you got your evidence."

"Yeah. Not that anyone would believe it. If I sent this story to Stan, he'd have me locked up for insanity."

"He'd have to find you first. Seeing as how you're staying." The elder glanced sideways at Brook, whose arm rested around Chelen's shoulders. "Always figured you would. Did you know there's an old native saying that goes, 'Any man that would rescue a native princess from the *kushtakas* is a man worth marrying'?"

"Yeah, right. More likely that St Mary's spring water mixed with a whole lot of vodka." Brook glanced out the window as they all laughed. Every once in a while the highway weaved its way out of the forest and he'd catch a view of the coastline and the ocean. Rugged wilderness, towering trees overloaded with blankets of green moss. Beaches littered with seashells and pools of water brimming with life.

Brook sighed. He finally understood the feeling he'd had when he came back to Haida Gwaii this time. Now he knew why its people would spend winters potlatching and connecting to the spirits, knew what had called him to be here. With Chelen, the feeling of being anchored to this part of the earth was strong. He was proud to call Haida Gwaii home. Yesterday, he'd sent Stan a travel article about Haida Gwaii from the cyber café in Queen Charlotte City, along with an email reporting that he hadn't found anything newsworthy regarding the felling of the Golden Spruce. That and his resignation.

When he'd told Chelen what he'd done, she'd simply squeezed his hand and smiled. He knew in his heart he belonged on Haida Gwaii with Chelen who, as some country song said, "rocked his socks". He'd already begun to depend on her company, savor the way she explained things from a perspective that, until days ago, he hadn't even known existed. So much had changed, he thought, as the truck's tires hummed through the cab, the recent events parading through his thoughts.

"This land grows on you in odd ways," he muttered as he took Chelen's hand. When they'd kayaked back to Sandspit, she and Charlie shared the history of the ancient villages, the people, their ways. A beautiful land, no longer silent. Brook no longer felt like a stranger. He was home.

Cherishing that thought, he turned to Chelen, who was raising a hand to shield her eyes.

"Man, are those rays ever bright, and I never brought any sunglasses."

"It's not the sun that's blinding you." Brook squinted into the distance. "Just look at that reflection off the mountainside."

"Why is it so gold?" she wondered. "Aren't we in the middle of a clear-cut?"

He looked out the side window. Everywhere, for kilometers, the hills were ablaze with yellow-gold. "Charlie, pull over and take that turnoff, just ahead."

"What's up?"

"Not sure. But something's not right here."

After a couple of minutes of bouncing along an old logging road, they stopped amid the remnants of a clear-cut, strewn trees and tossed branches lying everywhere. Brook stepped out of the truck, walked down an embankment and climbed through a barbed-wire fence.

"Crazy white man. Where are you going?" Charlie hollered after him.

"Hey, Brook, we're going to be late for our appointment with Bob," Chelen yelled.

A little way into the clear-cut, he bent over and scrutinized what was causing the golden glow. What was going on? Either this was one helluva fluke of nature, or ...

He waved to Chelen and Charlie to join him, facing them as they approached and spreading his arms wide. "How do you explain this?"

They stooped to study the saplings, the young needles glinting in the sun.

"They're all Golden Spruce, just like the one Chatwick cut down. There's one growing beside every single stump, every tree that's been logged." Brook ran to the top of the small hill. "And it goes on forever," he called back to them.

"But that's not possible. The Golden Spruce was a genetic anomaly. It was supposedly one of a kind," Chelen said when she and Charlie caught up to him.

"Well, I think Bob just got his ground-breaking world exclusive news report, and I just got more evidence to prove it was all real. How else can you explain this?" Brook raised his camera.

"Come on, I'm serious ... how can this be?" she insisted.

"You look stumped, my dear," Charlie observed.

"Hah, hah, very funny. No, I mean look at these plants. They're a foot high. It takes a tree ages to grow that much, not the few days since we last drove to Tlell along this road. And these trees weren't here then, were they?"

"Well, my best guess would be that our Prince Kiidkayaas has just found a way to help his people," Brook said. "By producing a billion sources of lumber."

She rolled her eyes and laughed. "You Westerners will never change, will you? All you think of is money."

Charlie lifted his scruffy Toronto Blue Jays ball cap and scratched his head. "Just a minute here. Didn't you say, Brook, that Kiidkayaas was sucked into a cedar tree after the Golden Spruce was cut down? And we know that while I was supposedly killed by Raven, Raven became trapped inside another Golden Spruce."

"That's right. But, hang on." Brook pondered. "The prince told me I had to make Raven fall against a certain cedar sapling. When we were battling in the grove of the ancients we fell on the sapling and broke it. A Golden Spruce sapling is what sprang up and swallowed Raven, but the prince had no control over spruce trees."

"Exactly," said Charlie. "So where did that new Golden Spruce spring from?"

Brook shrugged. "You tell me. Maybe that Dida forest spirit sent it? To stop Raven breaking one of the laws of the universe by moving time backwards?"

Charlie put his hands on his hips. "Could be, I suppose. Except that when I told *Dida Cwaa Nang Qaaruns* what Raven was up to, it said it couldn't interfere with the natural laws of the universe. But since time being reversed isn't natural, maybe it had second thoughts. Or else … well, knowing Raven, let's see. Once Foam Woman had refused to help him by changing things back to how they were, maybe he decided to beat the prince at his own game, to become like Kiidkayaas? I mean, become a tree spirit. Raven did spend over a hundred years inside the Golden Spruce, and don't forget, he's a shape-shifter."

Brook thought for another moment. "I guess so. When I was sucked into the … ah … earth, or wherever I went, so was Raven. Or so he said. Claimed he'd heard everything the prince told me. He knew Kiidkayaas evolved into a cedar tree spirit, and that the trees could communicate amongst their own kind. Knew too that once he was inside the cedar sapling, he'd be finished. Powerless against the prince for eternity."

Charlie chuckled. "Looks to me like Raven did heed Foam Woman after all, when she told him the only way he could help the Haida was to guide them into the future."

Chelen's eyes were shining. "There wouldn't be any better way for Raven to help his people than to use his new powers as a Golden Spruce spirit to turn all this desolation into fertile land again."

Brook stared at the baby Golden Spruce trees. "You know, I could have sworn Raven had a funny look on his face when that Golden Spruce closed around him, but it was so hard to tell in the smoke. Almost like he was smiling."

They stood there in silence, gazing out over the miraculous golden hills, the summer afternoon sun beating down. A raven's harsh cry rang out, carried on the breeze that suddenly stirred. Charlie and Chelen breathed deep.

Brook cocked his head, listening. The same lilting voices he'd heard in Foam Woman's valley were adrift on the wind, singing. Mother Earth calling her children home, just as she'd called him.

"It's coming, isn't it?" He draped an arm around Chelen.

"Yes." She smiled and held him tighter. "It's early this year. The Haida's windsong, the *sghaay haw* are returning."

Charlie smirked as they began to walk back towards his truck. "Well, your scientists are going to have a hell of a time trying to work their way out of this one. I think Raven just pulled his best stunt ever. I think he's tricked us all."

So let us, in walking gently on the earth,
Leave behind a simple legacy-
That we loved the earth and were
New warriors, mystic warriors,
Who had the courage to try to save it.

Ed McGaa

Eagle Man (1990)

About the Author

Frank Talaber was born in Beaverlodge, Alberta, where the claim to fame is a fox with flashing eyes in the only pub. Yeah, big place, that's why his family left when he was knee high to a grasshopper and moved to Edmonton, Alberta. Eventually he got tired of ten months of winter and two of bad slush and moved to Chilliwack, BC. Great place. Cedar trees, can cut the grass nine months of the year and, oh, it does snow here once or twice. Just enough to have to find out what happened to the bloody snow shovel and have to use it. GRRR.

He's spent most of his life either fixing cars or managing automotive shops, and at fifty-six is blessed with two children (okay, he had them earlier and they've grown up and begun living on their own), two loopy cats and a bonkers-mad English wife. His insatiable zest for life, the environment, and the little muses that keep twigging on his pencil won't let his writing pad stay blank.

http://www.bookswelove.net/authors/talaber-frank/

Author's Notes

The preceding novel is purely a work of fiction. All characters and events in this novel are fictitious, and any resemblance to actual persons living, dead or in other realities is purely coincidental.

The Haida were the unquestioned fiercest warriors and cultural leaders on the West Coast. This novel is centered around some of the Haida oral legends of the Golden Spruce and the being they believe resides trapped within it, Prince Kiidkayaas. The Greek and Roman mythologists were much copied and emulated by historians and, as writers sometimes do, I have altered events to suit the novel.

Any mistakes in the telling or spelling of the Haida language, culture, or places are mine and I hope they do not detract from the story. When using Raven's voice I tried to use old Haida language taken from John R. Swanton's, The Haida Indian Language, and Robert Bringhurst's A Story As Sharp As A Knife, by Douglas & McIntyre. As such, many of the names used are also derived from older texts such as The Queen Charlotte Islands Vol. One and Two by Kathleen E. Dalzell, by Cove Press Books. Also valuable research was derived from During my

Time, Florence Edenshaw Davidson, A Haida Woman, by Margaret B. Blackman, published by Douglas & McIntyre books.

The Haida language was originally an oral guttural language before being translated into English and for those who would like to properly pronounce it refer to Nine Visits to the Mythworld, Robert Bringhurst, published by Douglas & McIntyre.

It is historical fact that on January 22nd, 1997 Grant Hadwin chopped down the Golden Spruce, a rare genetic anomaly according to scientists, in protest of the logging industry. Arrested, he disappeared before his court date and his blood-stained kayak was later discovered on Mary Island, Alaska, 110 kilometers Northwest of Prince Rupert, BC.

Grant Hadwin was never found to this day.

In November of 1997 another rare genetic anomaly, a white raven, was spotted around Port Clements, just south of the Golden Spruce tree.

"After being stranded twenty kilometers from the nearest road at the tip of Rose Spit, Haida Gwaii, and having to push Frank's spanking new SUV a few kilometers along the beach before the tide came in and we ran out of booze, my first reaction on being asked to write a back cover blurb was, "over my dead body." Some people will do anything to get an endorsement."

Susan Musgrave